PRAISE FOR KAREN KATCHUR

COLD WOODS

"Intricately interweaving the past and present, Karen Katchur ramps up the tension and hits every mark with *Cold Woods*, the second installment in her compelling Northampton County series. Once again, Katchur has crafted an intense psychological thriller that pounds with heart-thrumming suspense and unexpected twists. With its intriguing characters and clever plot, *Cold Woods* will keep readers frantically flipping pages late into the night."

—Heather Gudenkauf, *New York Times* bestselling author of *The Weight of Silence* and *Not a Sound*

"Karen Katchur nails it with *Cold Woods*, the second in the Northampton County series and a perfect follow-up to her bestselling hit, *River Bodies*. Katchur starts *Cold Woods* with a bang, then builds the action steadily, a gradual unfolding of truths and small-town secrets among three former best friends. Dark and chilling, creepy and emotionally complex—and enthralling all the way to the shocking end."

—Kimberly Belle, bestselling author of *The Marriage Lie* and *Three Days Missing*

"*Cold Woods* kept me in its chilling grip from its eerie opening lines to its unexpected finish. I'm entranced by Karen Katchur's direct, well-crafted prose, artful plotting, and characters that leap from the page. She perfectly captures the strange insularity of a small town, and unravels its secrets with an expert hand. Not to be missed!"

—Marissa Stapley, bestselling author of *Things to Do When It's Raining*

RIVER BODIES

"Karen Katchur's *River Bodies* has it all: a horrific murder, mysteries resurrected from the past, a story line packed with tension, and vivid characters to bring it all to life. A riveting thriller that suspense readers will love."

—Mary Kubica, *New York Times* bestselling author of *The Good Girl*

"With a striking sense of place and a foreboding feeling of unease throughout, I was glued to the story. With relationships so complicated and layered that they feel like your own and plot twists that will leave you gasping, *River Bodies* is an unforgettable read."

—Kate Moretti, *New York Times* bestselling author

"Karen Katchur is a master at writing into the dark spaces of our intimate family relationships, and *River Bodies* is her most stunning work to date."

—Mindy Mejia, author of *Everything You Want Me to Be*

"*River Bodies* weaves an engrossing mystery with richly developed characters for an enjoyable, fast-paced read."

—Laura McHugh, award-winning author of *The Weight of Blood*

"Dark secrets of the past flow into the present in this emotionally resonant, deeply insightful tale of family bonds, betrayal, violence, and redemption. Part engrossing love story, part riveting murder mystery, *River Bodies* is a must read."

—A. J. Banner, *USA Today* bestselling author of *The Twilight Wife*

COLD
WOODS

OTHER TITLES BY KAREN KATCHUR

COLD WOODS

A NORTHAMPTON COUNTY NOVEL

KAREN KATCHUR

THOMAS & MERCER

Published by Thomas & Mercer, Seattle
www.apub.com

Amazon, the Amazon logo, and Thomas & Mercer are trademarks of Amazon.com, Inc., or its affiliates.

ISBN-13: 9781542093033 (hardcover)
ISBN-10: 1542093031 (hardcover)
ISBN-13: 9781542093040 (paperback)
ISBN-10: 154209304X (paperback)

Cover design by Shasti O'Leary Soudant

Printed in the United States of America

First edition

*For my childhood friends Tracey and Mindy
and for my mother, Johanna, for teaching me the
importance of friendship*

PART ONE
THE BODY

CHAPTER ONE

DECEMBER 1986

She smelled him before she saw him.

Two weeks in the cold may have slowed the decomposing process, but in the last three days the temperature had risen to an unseasonable fifty degrees. The sun had melted most of the existing snow. The warm air had baked his corpse.

She covered her mouth and nose with her scarf. "We're close."

The moon was high in the sky, illuminating the surrounding woods. Shadows from the trees distorted their view of the ground. They stopped twice, thinking they had spotted his body, only to have discovered large rocks instead.

Ten more minutes passed as they circled the area where the stench was the strongest. She found him not far off the trail. "Here he is."

He was lying on his side. His red Phillies baseball cap had slid to the back of his head. The gash above his brow where the blood had oozed was black.

She swallowed the warm saliva collecting in her mouth. Her partner lit a cigarette and stared off into the trees.

"Put that butt in your pocket when you're done. We're not leaving any evidence behind."

"Yeah, okay," her partner said.

She lifted her shovel, tapped the ground. "It's hard, but once we dig a few inches, the soil should soften up." The walkie-talkie strapped to her belt crackled. "Go ahead," she said.

"Find anything?" their lookout asked.

"We found him. All clear on your end?"

"All clear," their lookout said.

Her partner put the cigarette out and stuffed the butt in her coat pocket. Then she wiped tears from her eyes.

"He had it coming."

Her partner nodded.

"Let's do this."

They started digging. The work was as hard as the ground. After thirty minutes, they had barely managed to clear the surface.

"Move back," she said. She swung the pickax with all her strength. Over and over she struck the ground, chipping away at the frozen, rocky terrain. Sweat stained her shirt inside the winter parka. She peeled off her coat, tossed it to the side.

She returned to her work. With each swing, the muscles in her shoulders and back ached. She hit a stone, and a painful vibration shot up her arms. She cried out. Her partner swooped in and dug the stone out. The process was slow. The woods were silent except for the sound of the pickax striking the ground.

She was breathing heavily, and after a large gulp of rancid air, she turned and threw up. When she finished and her stomach was empty, she swiped her mouth with the back of her hand. "We'll have to bury that too," she said and returned to digging. Her partner sobbed.

An hour passed, and they'd managed to clear a few inches of ground.

"There must be more than twelve inches of frost." She wiped the perspiration from her brow, peered over her shoulder.

"Keep digging," her partner said and returned to shoveling.

After that they didn't talk. There was nothing to say.

The walkie-talkie crackled again. "Go ahead," she said.

"Almost done?" their lookout asked.

"Almost," she said. "All clear?"

"All clear, but I'm cold."

She shook her head in exasperation. She turned to her partner. "We need to pick up the pace."

After another hour of nonstop labor, she leaned on the pickax. The hole had to be at least four feet deep: two feet less than the typical grave. "Deep enough."

"I'm not touching him," her partner said.

"We'll push him in with the shovels."

They stood alongside his body. She edged the metal blade under his shoulder. Her partner did the same under his hip. They lifted. His body ripped and peeled from the cold ground as though he were stuck with Velcro. The sound tore through the quiet woods.

Her partner wailed.

"Don't stop," she said, and with one last heave, his body rolled into the hole.

She didn't waste time and began throwing dirt on top of him. Faster and faster she pushed her sore muscles. Her partner continued to cry, but she kept working.

Side by side, they tossed more and more dirt on him. When they were close to finishing, their fear kicked into high gear. They had come this far; they couldn't get caught now. They looked over their shoulders, not once but continuously.

The smell of rotting flesh slowly dissipated.

She breathed a little easier as she packed the soil with the shovel. She tossed sticks and stones onto the mound in an attempt to blend the area with the surrounding landscape. When she was satisfied the mound melded with the rest of the woods, she covered her vomit with the little dirt that was left. Her partner sat on a large rock under a big oak tree not far from the grave and smoked another cigarette.

Snow started to fall.

She plucked the walkie-talkie from her belt. "All clear?" she asked.

"All clear," their lookout said.

"We're coming down."

PART TWO
THE BONES

CHAPTER TWO

Detective Parker Reed leaned against a hundred-year-old oak tree. An old carving next to his shoulder read *Kilroy was here*. Someone had taken a pocketknife to the trunk, scarring the tree for life. The phrase, a folktale really, had been popular long before Parker had been born, turning up in places all over Europe and the United States since World War II. It had become somewhat of a fascination for soldiers at the time, a kind of meme. Whether it had anything to do with the case was anyone's guess. But it gave the area they were searching an eeriness Parker would've preferred to do without.

"That's the datum." Cheryl Leer pointed to the tree Parker rested on. She was the forensic anthropologist Lieutenant Sayres had called when they'd gotten word a human skull had been found deep in the Blue Mountains not far off the Appalachian Trail.

"What's a datum?" he asked and moved out of her way, careful where he stepped. There were enough rocks around to twist an ankle.

"It's the marker we're going to use if we need to locate the scene later," she said. "The subdatum is the stake we're going to place close to the remains, using the tree with the carving as our guide. Joe," she called to one of the guys on her team. "Come here. Watch where you step. Record the distance for me." Her team began moving, laying down a kind of map with stakes, chaining pins, and string.

"We're going to make a grid over the site," she continued to explain, brushing the dirt from her hands, and then she rubbed them together to keep them warm in the frigid December air. "It will serve as a reference when we start excavation and collection." White clouds whirled from her lips. "Is this your first dig?" she asked.

"Yeah," he said. On the few cases he'd worked since becoming a homicide investigator, the bodies had been fresh, or at least fresher. Although for the last two months, he'd been sitting at his desk pushing paper around, ever since Lieutenant Sayres had learned Parker had been involved with Becca, the key witness in his last case. Sayres had been punishing Parker for not removing himself from the investigation. It wasn't until this morning that Parker had gotten the call to head up the mountain and that he was finally getting the partner he'd been promised. Geena Brassard was expected to join him. Where was she, anyway? She should've been here an hour ago.

He pulled the collar of his jacket up in an attempt to fight off the cold. He didn't much like the cold, didn't like the way it left his fingers and toes numb, his ears raw, his skin dry and itchy. He often wondered why, after living in the area his entire life, he didn't move away. He then had to remind himself it was only the winter months, three months out of the year, that he found miserable. The rest of the year offered up mostly beautiful weather if you loved the change of seasons, which he did.

The temperature was expected to drop overnight, with windchills in the single digits. The frozen ground made it that much harder to dig. They had to get as much done today as possible. In another few hours dusk would roll in, and sometime thereafter, the woods would become so dark that you wouldn't be able to see what was in front of your nose. He'd heard mention of spotlights being brought in on the back of ATVs. He might as well forget about any plans tonight, not that he'd had any. He was looking at either a long night on the mountain or another night alone in his cabin by the river.

Cheryl's team worked on the grid. He stood around feeling useless and in the way. There wasn't anything he could think to do but wait. He couldn't walk around, not wanting to contaminate the scene. Instead, he flipped through his notes. He'd talked to the kid, Jeremy, who had found the bones initially. Jeremy was a freelance photographer, young, early twenties. He worked for the local newspaper, which meant word of the discovery would make the evening news. Jeremy had been on the trail with his dog, Lincoln, taking photographs for some new mountain resort, when the dog had started digging, unearthing the skull. The kid had been shaken, but he'd been smart enough to know to stop the dog from digging further. He'd marked the spot in his memory by using the *Kilroy was here* carving as a landmark. And once Jeremy had come down off the mountain—because you couldn't always get a signal while you were on it—he'd called 911.

"Excuse me," one of the techs said and squeezed around Parker. She was young, fresh faced. She smiled at him, brushed up against him, and not for the first time.

He nodded in a friendly way, but not too friendly. It wasn't that the tech wasn't pretty; nor was she the first female to flirt with him on the job. According to Sharmaine, who worked the front desk back at the station, Parker was a *real looker*. She'd pointed out on more than one occasion that women must love the scruff on his chin, the same scruff that was frowned upon by his superiors. It wasn't his intention to piss off command; nor was it his goal to attract the ladies. Most days he just plain forgot to shave. He'd been so focused on his job the last few years that it didn't leave him much time for anything or anyone else.

Except for Becca, of course: the only girl for him, whether she knew it or not.

He moved away from the pretty tech, putting his back against the large oak that was quickly becoming known to the team as the "Kilroy tree." Karla, their forensic photographer, moved around the site snapping photos of the grid as it was constructed. The pictures would help other experts and potential jurors understand the scene if necessary.

When the grid was completed, Cheryl's team gathered around and discussed the best method to handle the excavation due to the hard ground. They talked about soil collection. Rakes, trowels, wire-mesh screens, and buckets lay on the ground at their feet. The team looked like a bunch of prospectors panning for gold.

"How did you get so lucky to land this one?" Karla asked, holding her camera off to the side. She was close to his age, early thirties, and four months pregnant. Her jacket was pulled tight across her growing stomach. When he'd asked if she'd needed help climbing up the mountain, worried about her falling, she'd shrugged him off. So much for being chivalrous.

"Good question," Parker said, not really answering her, although he had an idea. It could've been as simple as being next in line as cases turned up, but he suspected he'd been given this one regardless of protocol. According to Lieutenant Sayres, Parker could "sit his ass on the freezing-cold mountain and think about his mistake."

If Parker had any regrets about his last case, which he did, it was that he hadn't solved it fast enough. If he had, maybe he could've stopped the motorcycle-gang member from putting a gun to his own head. Sometimes Parker woke in the middle of the night shaking and sweating, the scent of blood in his nose, the iron taste on his tongue, the image of brains splattered among the trees and autumn leaves. He'd let it get to him, but that wasn't something he was willing to share, and now wasn't the time to indulge in personal matters. If Sayres had an inkling Parker was struggling to move on, he'd put him back on desk duty—the last place any detective wanted to be.

Karla shooed him away from the tree. "I want to get a couple more shots of that carving."

"And just when I got comfortable," he said teasingly and pushed off the trunk.

"Some of us have to work around here." She winked.

Cheryl waved him over. She squatted inside a square in the grid. "What we're looking at is the skull of a male. In simple terms, you can tell he's male by the U-shape, or square, jaw, and the square orbits. Also, if you feel the top of the orbit here, it's smooth. In a female it's sharp. And this hole here is for the ear. The zygomatic arch stops in a female before it reaches the hole. If it extends past the hole like it does here, it's male." She paused. "I'd say, based on the coronal suture, he's somewhere between forty and fifty years old." She pointed to an area near the temple. She had since slipped on rubber gloves that looked nowhere near warm enough for the kind of cold they were experiencing in the high elevation.

Parker pulled his knit hat down over his ears. It made him look much younger than he was, and he'd taken some ribbing from the team about his punk beanie, but he didn't care. All he wanted was to be warm.

"Do you see this area by the left temple, how the bone is depressed?"

Parker nodded.

"This was caused by blunt-force trauma," she said. "It's perimortem. That means it happened around the time of death." She looked closer. "I'll know a lot more once I get it back to the lab."

"So we're looking at homicide?"

"That's for the coroner to decide. But this didn't occur naturally, that's for sure."

Parker's phone went off, an unusual signal breaking through the mountain barrier. "Excuse me," he said to Cheryl and stepped away, checking a text message from G. Brassard. Heading up the mountain now. Geena was the only female homicide investigator in his troop. He'd met her on a few occasions but only in passing. What he remembered most was that she was not only tall but also attractive. The other guys in his unit didn't want to partner with her because she was good looking. They didn't want the headache at home.

Maybe that was why he hadn't told Becca about her, yet.

Parker texted Geena back. Blunt force trauma left temple. He'd have to let Sayres know, too, but first he wanted as much information as possible before contacting him.

He returned to Cheryl and the skull. "Anything else you can tell me?" he asked.

She stood and pointed to the area inside the grid, not far from where they were standing. "Do you see how the ground is raised?"

He nodded.

"My guess is that someone moved quite a bit of dirt around, and it wasn't easy. The rocks in this area make for some tough digging. Of course, I'll know more once we get a better look at the stratum."

"Meaning someone went through a whole lot of trouble to cover him up."

"Exactly."

Most bodies were found closer to the roads, a few hundred feet into the woods. Other times bodies, or body parts, were tossed out of vehicles in garbage bags and found along the mountain highways, as if the killer couldn't be bothered with the effort of hiding his crime. Or maybe the killer assumed, like countless other motorists, that the bags would be thought of as nothing more than trash thrown out a car window by a litterbug.

Until someone noticed the smell.

Parker looked down the trail. They were a good way up the mountain. The climb had been steep. Tree roots and rocks jutted from the ground, making it that much harder to navigate. "It's not likely someone carried his body this far up the mountain and dumped it here."

"Not likely," Cheryl said. "If you ask me, we're looking at the original crime scene."

CHAPTER THREE

Trisha Haines stared at the house from the back seat of the taxicab. She hadn't moved since they'd double-parked more than twenty minutes ago. The driver didn't ask why she wasn't getting out of the car. Instead, he sat patiently, listening to news radio at a low volume. The hundred she'd tossed him earlier had kept him quiet.

She continued watching the house, where she had a near-perfect view of the comings and goings. The siding was old and faded and covered in years of grit, harsh winters, hot summers. The slate roof looked as though it had been patched recently and the downspout reattached. Otherwise, not much about the house had changed.

A few more minutes passed. An older couple emerged, slowly making their way down the porch steps, where the concrete crumbled on one side and the rusted metal railing leaned. They were followed by other guests wearing heavy winter coats, their faces somber.

The house Trisha watched sat directly across the street from where she'd grown up, and sure enough, one of the stragglers in the back of the crowd was her mother. She'd know her anywhere, although it had been three decades since she'd last seen her. Her mother lit a cigarette, made her way across Second Street. There was a noticeable limp in her stride as she lumbered onto her porch and disappeared inside.

Trisha waited a few more minutes. When it was clear most of the mourners had gone, she got out of the car. The cold December air pricked her face.

"Do you want me to wait?" the driver asked.

"Yes, thank you," she said, not sure how it would go once they saw her. She tossed him another hundred. It was Sid's money, and she didn't care about throwing it away.

She stood in the doorway of Dannie's mother's home. There were still some guests hanging around, possibly family members of Dannie's whom Trisha had never met. The stench of flowers and food, along with the lingering odor of numerous bodies packed into a small room, filled her nose, coated the back of her tongue. Her underarms were sticky. Her entire body was a little sweaty, but no one would be able to tell in her sleek black pants and sweater. She'd dressed carefully, considering her nervousness, and then there was the alcohol she had to contend with that regularly seeped from her pores.

She stepped into the living room gingerly, her arm protecting her sore ribs, apologizing for elbowing an elderly woman. The woman averted her eyes from Trisha and quickly moved away. It was probably one of Dannie's mother's churchgoing friends. She must've smelled the evil incarnate on Trisha's skin.

Trisha picked her way through the room, slipped a breath mint into her mouth. It had been several hours since she'd had her last cocktail at the airport bar. The shakes would start soon.

She stopped next to an end table that was littered with discarded plates and half-eaten food. It was as good a place as any to wait it out. She scanned the few remaining faces in the crowd, none familiar, except one. Carlyn. She leaned against the far wall. She was holding a plate of finger sandwiches, dabbing at the corner of her lip with a napkin. There was no mistaking her strong jawline, the lean runner's body underneath the gray cotton dress. Carlyn had aged. They all had aged, turning into older versions of their younger selves. She willed Carlyn to look her way, to recognize her—if only she would be happy to see her.

It was a lot to ask.

"Trisha?"

Trisha turned and found herself face-to-face with Linda Walsh, Carlyn's mother.

"Hello, Mrs. Walsh," she said somewhat sheepishly. Mrs. Walsh had never been a fan of Trisha's back when Trisha, Carlyn, and Dannie had been in high school. She'd looked at Trisha as though she were trouble, someone who would lead her daughter down the wrong path. She had seen Trisha for exactly who she was.

"It's good of you to come," Mrs. Walsh said. "Have you seen Dannie?"

Trisha shook her head. "How's she holding up?"

"She's strong. She has her faith to get her through."

Trisha stopped herself from rolling her eyes. She couldn't stand Dannie's constant praying back when they were kids, Dannie's unwavering faith, her firm belief in right and wrong. Trisha didn't share Dannie's views. The lines between good and evil had remained forever blurred in Trisha's mind. Besides, no amount of praying had ever stopped bad things from happening. All the crying, begging, pleading had been nothing but a waste of time.

And yet she couldn't discount the fact that at least Dannie had something—her church, her God—where Trisha had nothing.

Mrs. Walsh touched Trisha's arm. Trisha recoiled. It had been so long since anyone had touched her in a kind way. She'd forgotten what it had felt like, how good it could be. Mrs. Walsh eyed her and then stepped away without saying anything more.

Trisha kept her distance from the other guests after that. She'd lost sight of Carlyn. It was just as well. She ducked into the bathroom, peed, checked her makeup. Already the dark circles under her eyes had bled through her foundation. The hollows in her cheeks were deep, hole-like. Her face was emaciated. What she wouldn't give for a drink.

Another thirty minutes passed, and finally the last of the mourners headed out, dabbing at watery eyes, a sea of black dresses and dark suits piling out the door.

Trisha licked her dry lips, moved from the corner of the living room, where she'd been standing, hiding, next to an artificial plant. She entered the kitchen. Carlyn sat at the table across from Dannie. Dannie's round cheeks were flushed and wet with tears. Her blonde hair had thinned through the years: so much so that Trisha could see clear through to Dannie's scalp.

Carlyn was patting Dannie's hand and stopped when Trisha approached. If Carlyn was surprised to see her, it didn't register on her face. Dannie, however, looked up, a small smile on her lips.

It took everything Trisha had not to scratch her arms, pick at her skin. "I'm sorry about your mom," she said. "I came as soon as I heard."

Dannie stood, a little reluctantly, Trisha thought. She reached out to give Trisha one of her big, warm, enveloping hugs.

Trisha stepped back, out of reach. She hadn't meant to, but it was a reflexive reaction, to pull away, to not allow herself to be touched if she could help it. And then there were her bruised ribs to consider.

Dannie dropped her arms, folded them, covered the rolls on her belly, her eyes cast down. "It's been a long time," she said. "Too long for old friends."

"Yes." Trisha wanted nothing more than to collapse in Dannie's embrace, to cry, to not let go. *Hold me,* she longed to say. *For old times' sake.* But she was here to offer her condolences, not break down.

"Hey, Danielle." A man stepped into the kitchen. He was short, thin, with dark hair that was graying at his temples.

Dannie went to him. "Where are the girls?" she asked.

"They left with my parents a little while ago."

So Dannie had kids. Wasn't that nice.

"I'm sorry; where are my manners? Vinnie, I'd like you to meet Trisha, an old friend from high school. And you remember Carlyn."

"Sure," he said of Carlyn. "Nice to meet you." He held out his hand to Trisha.

She offered hers, limply, a dead fish, and quickly pulled it away.

"It's nice of you to come. I know Danielle really appreciates it." He wrapped his arm around Dannie. She rested her head on his shoulder. The stress of the day was on her face, in her eyes.

"You ready to go?" he asked.

"Yes," Dannie said. "I'll come back tomorrow to clean up. I just don't have the energy to do it tonight."

"We're right behind you," Carlyn said, finally acknowledging Trisha, giving her a look that asked her to stay behind.

"Good to see you," Dannie said to Trisha and then looked to Carlyn. "Lock up for me," she said before leaving.

Once they were alone, Carlyn handed Trisha the newspaper that had been sitting on the table. "Dannie's mom was found holding this when she had the heart attack."

Trisha read the headline: Human Bones Discovered near Appalachian Trail. "I see," she said and put the paper down. If Carlyn was expecting a reaction from her, she wasn't going to get one. Trisha had become a master at hiding her feelings, wiping any emotion off her face. "I gather you and Dannie keep in touch?"

"We see each other on occasion."

Trisha nodded, hurt by those two little words, *on occasion*. They'd never reached out to her, come looking for her, kept in touch with her. She felt cheated.

Carlyn stared at her, and Trisha could feel her disapproval, her *disappointment*, as though they were still teenagers and no time had passed at all. "Do you have something you want to say to me?" she asked.

"Why are you here?"

"You haven't seen me in years, and that's the first thing you want to know?"

"Look, it's not that I'm not happy to see you," Carlyn said. "It's not that at all."

"Like hell it isn't," Trisha said.

"Then what are you really doing here, Trisha?"

"I'm here to make sure you two keep your mouths shut."

CHAPTER FOUR

JULY 1979

Trisha was ten years old when her family moved to Bangor, a small town in rural Pennsylvania.

They rented a truck; packed the few pieces of furniture, dishes, and odds and ends into boxes; and drove from Illinois straight to the small semiattached house on Second Street. They pulled the clunky truck into the parking space in front of their side of the home and unpacked. In an hour boxes and garbage bags full of clothes littered the curb.

Trisha's mother was convinced the move was a good thing: a fresh start for both mother and daughter.

Now her mother sat on the worn plaid couch in the patch of yard smoking a cigarette, the red polish on her fingernails cracked and chipped. Sometimes Trisha thought of her mother as a woman down on her luck, trying to find her place in the world. Not today. Today was one of those days she believed her mother was nothing more than white trash. Compounding this low-life image, Trisha's stepfather, Lester, downed a beer, belched, and tossed the can into the back of the truck.

Trisha turned away, stared at the dirt under her toenails. She knew what her family looked like to the outside world. She knew what she looked like—poor white trash sitting on the stoop outside a row home in another stinking small town. No one had ever said this to her; it was something she understood, having seen a glimpse of a better life, or at least a richer one.

She'd been on a school trip back home to the Art Institute of Chicago. A black limousine had been parked alongside the curb, and four young girls, maybe in their twenties, had slipped out of the doors with their long legs, platform shoes, maxi dresses. They'd clutched little handbags, giggling, tossing salon-styled hair over their shoulders.

Trisha had watched them walk into a fancy restaurant, the taste of envy on her tongue. Staring out the dirty window of the school bus, she'd made a promise to herself that one day she would buy designer clothes and ride in limousines. One day she would escape her shitty, white-trash life.

She picked at the threads fraying on her jean shorts, taking a break from carrying books, eight-tracks, and posters into her new bedroom. She'd already hung her favorite poster of Tom Petty on the dingy white wall. A mattress lay on the floor in the corner covered in yellowing sheets and a purple comforter. She always slept on the floor. They'd never had enough money to buy her a bed frame.

One day, she thought as she ripped a string from the fray, somehow, someway, she'd get herself some money and buy herself the biggest, fanciest bed she could find.

She looked up and down Second Street. All the homes, or half homes slashed down the center to make two, were carbon copies of white siding, slate roofs, cement porches. Dust hung in the air, kicked up from the slate mines and settled at the bottom of Bangor's hill. The gray film coated the windows of the houses and cars, dulling any color that may have otherwise brightened the small town. She licked her teeth and felt the grit in her mouth.

Still, it was a nice-looking street: much nicer than the one she'd lived on in her old home.

Sensing Lester's eyes on her, she quickly covered her bare legs with her arms, making herself as small as possible. She kept her head down and pretended to be engrossed in watching an ant move the body of a dead worm. It wasn't until the weight of Lester's stare lifted that she raised her head again.

He'd turned his attention to the beer in his hand, poured it down his throat. He'd polished off a six-pack. It wasn't even noon.

Three houses down, two girls played hopscotch while holding on to beach towels wrapped around their heads, the long material cascading down their backs.

Across the street, a woman waved at Trisha's mother. "Hello," she said, making her way over. She was dumpy, shuffling on her feet. Her face was bright and cheery. She shook Trisha's mother's hand. "I'm Evelyn. Welcome to Second Street." They exchanged a few pleasantries. "Is this your daughter?" she asked and walked toward Trisha, welcoming her with the same huge smile on her big moon face. She pointed to the two girls playing hopscotch. "That's my daughter, Danielle, and her friend Carlyn. Why don't you go say hi?"

Lester stepped onto the porch, a fresh beer in his hand. His fingers brushed Trisha's shoulder as he reached out to shake Evelyn's hand. "Nice to meet you," he said.

"You too," Evelyn said. "I saw the Illinois tags. What brings you all this way?" she asked, making friendly conversation.

"New job at a carpet store."

"Are you a salesman?" she asked.

"No," he said and didn't elaborate. He'd gotten the job in the warehouse two weeks after the backyard wedding to Trisha's mother. He'd complained the entire drive to Pennsylvania that he didn't want to work in the warehouse. He wanted to be on the floor selling. "You'll work your way up," her mother had said.

"Well." Evelyn wiped her hand on her thigh. She turned to Trisha's mother. "I'm heading to the grocery store. I'd be happy to pick up a few things for you while I'm out. Do you need milk or bread or anything?"

"That's so nice of you," Trisha's mother said. Trisha thought it was really nice of Evelyn to ask too. She didn't recall any of their old neighbors being so neighborly.

Her mother fished around in her pocket for cash. "We could use some—"

Lester cut her off. "Thanks anyway," he said. "We're all set."

"Oh, okay, sure," Evelyn said. She looked to Trisha's mother when she said, "I'll be back in a few hours. Don't hesitate to knock if you need anything." Then she turned to Trisha. "Go on—say hi to the girls."

Trisha pulled herself up from the porch step. The sun scorched the top of her shoulders, and the heat from the sidewalk burned her bare feet as she walked toward the other kids. She was nervous, a little self-conscious, as she approached.

"Try again," the tall wiry girl said, balancing on her long leg.

The shorter, chubbier girl picked up her foot and lost her balance. "I'm no good at this."

Trisha stopped next to the chalked hopscotch. She lifted her chin and stuck out her barely budding chest with the faded decal of Tom Petty and the Heartbreakers stamped on the front of her T-shirt. The two girls stopped talking, looked her over.

"I'm Trisha. Just moved in a few houses down," she said.

"I'm Carlyn," the wiry girl with the long legs said. "And this is Dannie."

The chubby girl, Dannie, gave Trisha a timid smile. "How old are you?"

"Ten." She shifted her weight onto her right hip. "You?"

"The same." Carlyn pointed to Lester as he stumbled off the curb and into the street. "Is he okay?"

"He's had a couple of beers," she said.

Dannie stared at him, eyes wide.

"Does he always drink like that?" Carlyn asked.

Trisha shrugged, trying to make it seem like it wasn't a big deal. "He's not my real dad. My real dad lives in Chicago." She'd write a letter to her dad tonight, tell him where she was. They'd become something close to pen pals in the last year since his latest incarceration. "Why do you have towels on your heads?" she asked.

"It's our hair." Dannie touched the streaming terry cloth. "See how long it is?"

"That's cool," she said.

Dannie smiled.

"Do you have a towel for your head?" Carlyn asked.

"We're still unpacking." She had a bath towel but not a beach towel. She hadn't done much swimming back home. Mostly, she'd run under the fountain in the neighborhood park.

"Come on. I'll get you one inside, but we have to be quiet. My mom sleeps in the day. She works the night shift at the hospital. She's a nurse," Carlyn said.

They walked up the front steps and crept inside.

"You two wait here while I go upstairs and find another towel," Carlyn whispered.

"Make sure it's a long one," Dannie whispered back and pulled Trisha toward the kitchen.

The inside of Carlyn's house unfolded in much the same way as Trisha's. They followed a worn beige carpet through the family room and dining room. The walls had the same dingy white paint. The staircase to the second floor separated the dining room from the kitchen at the back of the house.

Dannie opened the gold refrigerator door. "You want something to drink? She's got Kool-Aid."

They sat at a collapsible card table and drank fruit punch. Pink stains ran up the sides of Dannie's mouth.

"Are you from Chicago like your dad?" Dannie asked.

"Just outside of Chicago." She wiped her lips with the back of her hand, wondering if she had a juice mustache too. "Some shitty little town you probably never heard of."

Dannie's eyes widened again. "You always cuss like that?"

"Don't you?"

"My mom would stick a bar of soap in my mouth if I ever talked that way." She drank from her cup, keeping her eyes on Trisha's face.

"If your mom heard the stuff that comes out of my mouth, she'd want to shove a bar of soap so far down my throat it would come out my ass."

Juice sprayed from Dannie's lips. They stared at each other and then burst out laughing.

Carlyn walked into the kitchen with a beach towel. She handed it to Trisha. "What's so funny?" she asked.

"She is," Dannie said, pointing at Trisha.

Trisha tied the towel around her head.

From the bottom step, Carlyn's mother poked her head inside the kitchen. Her brown hair was tangled and messy.

Trisha watched, waited, expected to be introduced as the new girl, but Carlyn's mother ignored her.

"Get outside and give me some peace and quiet," Carlyn's mother said.

Carlyn made no attempt to get up. Instead, she sat back in the chair and crossed her arms. Dannie kept her head down and fiddled with her cup. Trisha leaned back in the chair and crossed her arms like Carlyn to show her solidarity.

Carlyn's mother glared at them. "Go on. Get. I need to get some sleep before my shift. I'm not asking you again." She turned and stomped up the steps.

"Come on—let's go," Carlyn said under her breath.

Trisha and Dannie trailed her outside.

Carlyn sat on the stoop and rested her elbow on top of her thigh, her chin in her hand.

"Do you want to play hopscotch?" Dannie asked.

"I don't feel like it anymore," Carlyn said.

Down the street on the porch of Trisha's new house, her mother and Lester shouted, arguing over something, or quite possibly nothing.

"I have an idea." She sat next to Carlyn. "Let's make a club."

"Like a secret club or something?" Dannie asked.

"Sure," Trisha said.

"Okay," Carlyn said. "We should make it official, with a name and ceremony."

Trisha hadn't had friends in Chicago—not close friends anyway. Most girls her age were mean, catty, and she didn't have time for that kind of drama, not with everything else wrong in her life. But she was here in a new town with a whole new batch of girls. Maybe things could be different for her, like her mother had said: a fresh start.

"Let's make it a friendship club," she said at the same time Lester called for her. She pretended not to hear him.

"Let's grab our bathing suits. Do you have a bike?" Carlyn asked and pulled the towel off her head, her brown hair falling to the tops of her shoulders. Trisha and Dannie yanked their towels off too.

"Yeah, I got a bike," Trisha said. Her mother had picked it up for her at a yard sale last summer. The blue paint was chipped and the handlebars were rusty, but the tires were in good shape.

Lester called for Trisha again, spotting her on Carlyn's porch. Out of the corner of her eye, she saw him walking down the sidewalk toward them. She braced herself.

"There you are," Lester said and turned his gaze on the other two girls. "Aren't you going to introduce me?"

CHAPTER FIVE

Trisha was the last to leave Dannie's mother's place after arguing with Carlyn about Trisha's return to Second Street. Carlyn had walked out on her, leaving her to lock up the house.

Trisha turned off the lights, carried a bag of trash outside, stuffed it into an overflowing garbage can at the curb. Then she crossed the street and paid the taxi driver.

"You never saw me," she said. "I never got in your cab. You never drove me here."

He nodded, took the stack of bills from her hand.

After sending him away, Trisha stood on her mother's front porch next to her suitcase. She knocked once. Her mother opened the door, stood on the other side of the glass, looking out at her. For a panicked second, Trisha thought her mother wasn't going to let her in. She hadn't planned on being turned away when she'd told the taxi driver to leave. She hadn't made other arrangements. When she'd fled the penthouse suite, leaving Sid and Vegas behind, she hadn't thought any further ahead than hopping on a plane and flying home. Although she hadn't thought about this place as home in many years, she supposed it had never left her. Nothing ever did. She'd learned that lesson a long time ago: that no matter how far she'd run, how much time had passed, she couldn't escape where she'd come from, the things she'd done.

Her mother finally opened the storm door. "Linda said she saw you. I wasn't sure whether you'd stop by."

Ah, yes, Linda and her mother had become best friends. Linda probably couldn't wait to tell her that Trisha had returned home.

"I'm hoping to do more than just stop by." Trisha hated admitting it, but there it was. She was asking if she could stay here, in her mother's house, for an undetermined length of time. Oh, she had enough money that she could've gone anywhere, stayed anywhere. She'd squirreled away Sid's money through the years, the amounts so small that he'd never noticed. So going anywhere had been possible but not practical. He'd come looking for her eventually. But he'd never think to find her here. She'd only ever mentioned to him once who her father was, that she was born in Illinois, but she'd never mentioned she'd grown up in Pennsylvania. And everything she'd purchased on her trip here—the plane ticket, taxicab, the drinks at the airport bar—she'd paid with cash.

Paying with actual paper money had come with a price. Everything came with a price. Something else she'd learned early on. Apparently, buying a one-way ticket to New York with a stack of dough instead of a credit card set off all kinds of alarms. She'd been manhandled by airport security and then later locked in a small room, where she'd undergone what had felt an awful lot like an interrogation. Uniformed men had questioned her up and down and sideways until she'd finally convinced them she wasn't some kind of terrorist. They'd rummaged through her suitcase, pulling out her toiletries, lace bras, fingering her underwear, not once but twice. It hadn't been until they saw the fresh fingerprints on her biceps, the black-and-purple bruise spreading across her rib cage, that the pieces had come together. And still they'd gone through with a full strip search, leaving nothing untouched. If they'd thought they were putting her through one last humiliation before she'd make her escape, they were wrong. She'd endured years of degradation: so much so that she could brush off one more hour of abuse as though it were nothing more than crumbs in her lap.

"Well, get in here and let me look at you," her mother said.

Trisha lugged her suitcase in, pretended the pain in her ribs didn't exist, set the case down next to the couch. The foam stuffing oozed from one of the cushions. The beige carpet was stained, and the place smelled like smoke and stale beer. She hid her disgust. No point in provoking her mother by the mere look on her face.

"Vegas, huh?" Her mother tapped the airline's tag still stuck to the handle of Trisha's luggage. "Is that cashmere?" She touched the sleeve of Trisha's sweater.

"Yes," Trisha said and pulled her arm away.

Her mother looked her up and down. "What are you, like that Sharon Stone character or something from that movie? What was it called? *Casino*?" Her mother ran a hand through her short hair, which was no longer bleached blonde and teased but now gray and spiky like a porcupine.

"Sort of, but her character was classier."

It took her mother a moment to understand; then she laughed out loud. "You want a drink?"

Trisha followed her to the kitchen, noticed the limp again. Her mother pulled open the refrigerator door, grabbed two cans of beer, handed her one. She couldn't remember the last time she'd drunk from a can. She'd grown accustomed to top-shelf liquor, expensive champagne, priceless wine, crystal glasses. She took a sip. The beer was awful, but it was alcohol, and it would do the trick. It would stop the shakes that had started a few minutes ago.

"I can't believe Evelyn's gone," her mother said of Dannie's mom. "We were friends for so long. For nearly forty years she was right across the street, and now she's dead. I can't wrap my head around it, you know?"

Trisha nodded. But she didn't know. What did she know of friendship, let alone the lifelong kind? Her two best friends had ditched her their senior year of high school, each going their separate ways, or so she thought. It really grated on her that Carlyn and Dannie had kept in touch *on occasion*, as Carlyn had said.

Her mother continued. "I don't know why I'm so surprised. The heart can't take that kind of fat."

Trisha paused from taking another sip of beer, arched an eyebrow.

"Don't look at me like that," her mother said. "She got so much bigger than what you must remember. She always struggled with her weight, you know. But this was more than just being heavy. She was downright obese. I kept telling her it was going to be the end of her one day. Linda—being a nurse, if you remember—she was always on her, trying to get her to diet and exercise. But Evelyn . . . well, she just didn't have it in her." Her mother looked away.

Trisha wasn't sure what she was supposed to say to this. She settled for "I'm sorry."

"Dannie was good to her, though. She was a great daughter, taking care of her the way she did. At least Evelyn had that."

"Yes," she said, wondering if it was meant to be a dig directed at her for leaving town, for not even bothering to phone.

Her mother plopped onto one of the kitchen chairs.

Trisha hadn't expected to see her so defeated. She remembered a much stronger version of the woman in front of her, one who knew how to take a hit and pull herself back up. But this woman was old and broken, weakened during the years they'd been separated.

She finished her beer in two long swallows. "It's been a long day. If you don't mind, I'd like to head up and get some sleep." She tossed the empty can in the trash under the sink. She plucked another can from the refrigerator: something to drink while she unpacked.

"You can have your old room," her mother said.

Trisha left her mother sitting at the small round table from Trisha's childhood. She grabbed her suitcase from the family room and carried it up the narrow stairs, forced herself not to wince from the pain the lifting caused in her ribs.

Her old bedroom was exactly as she'd left it. The mattress she'd slept on her entire adolescence was still on the floor in the corner with the same faded purple comforter. The bedspread and sheets were crumpled as though she'd just slipped out from under them and the last three decades had never taken place. Her dingy robe hung from the hook on the door. Old posters of Duran Duran and Madonna were tacked to the wall, the edges curled and yellowed with age.

Her mother hadn't changed a single thing, as though she'd been waiting all this time for Trisha to come home.

She popped the tab on the can of beer and took a sip. Dust bunnies scattered when she strode through the room to the closet. She slid the door open. The clothes inside were the ones she'd left behind all those years ago. She lifted the sleeve of a hot-pink sweatshirt, bringing the cotton material to her nose, smelling the hair spray she wore as a teenager. She took a deep breath, but the scent was lost, replaced by a musty odor. She slid the closet door closed. On the small dresser, she touched a bottle of dried-up nail polish, a deck of playing cards, and an empty can of the hair spray she'd smelled a moment ago. Everything was the same and yet completely different.

She poked around the room some more, drinking, pulling open drawers, lifting the lid off an old shoebox, finding it empty.

The wear of the day settled into what were now sore muscles. She downed the rest of the beer, reached for her suitcase, wanting to shed her clothes and the smell of traveling in them all day. She didn't know if she could make it through the rest of the night without a drink. For the first time in years, she wanted to try.

She turned, startled to find her mother standing in the doorway, covered her racing heart. "I didn't hear you come up."

"You shouldn't have come back here," her mother said.

CHAPTER SIX

Parker stood under the hundred-year-old Kilroy tree near the site where the bones had been recovered. It was day four and what he hoped was their last day on the mountain. The cold wind whipped through the bare branches of trees. Every now and again it picked up speed and made an awful howling sound.

Geena sat on a large rock on Parker's right. Her hands were shoved deep inside her winter parka. She wore hiking boots, fur lined with deep tread.

Parker shivered. "I hate the cold," he said.

"I don't mind it if I'm doing something fun like skiing or snowmobiling," Geena said. "It's in my Nordic roots."

"Brassard is Nordic?"

"Nope. I got the Nordic part from my mom. My dad is French. *Was* French."

Parker waited for her to explain, but she didn't say anything more about it. He wasn't surprised. They were just getting to know each other. He said the only thing he could: "I'm sorry."

She nodded, turned her gaze back to the site. Parker had noticed the way she'd watched Cheryl and the team's every movement the last few days, as though she were taking mental snapshots of not only the site but also the collection of evidence. Her intensity, the sharp clear blue of her eyes, made him a little uncomfortable. Not that he'd admit that to anyone, and never to her.

The word around headquarters was that Lieutenant Sayres had taken her off her last case when her previous partner, Albert Eugenis, had announced his retirement. She'd been working what was the second rape and murder of another young woman in the last thirty-six months. Parker was under the impression that neither the removal from the case nor the transfer to the field station had been Geena's idea.

He moved away from the Kilroy tree to stretch his legs, keep the blood flowing in his cold limbs. Technically, neither of them needed to be on the mountain at this point. Much of the evidence had been bagged and sent to the lab. Although the victim hadn't been identified officially, based on the age of the bones and missing persons data, they had a good idea of who he might be.

But Parker wanted to be here. The best way for him to understand the victim and what had happened was to spend time in the space where they'd taken their last breath and left their final clues. Photographs couldn't capture the same gut feelings he'd come to expect from his presence at the scene, but he wasn't going to tell Karla that.

Geena must have had her own reasons for climbing the mountain, none of which she'd shared with him. Whatever. They'd get to know each other soon enough. It was the nature of the job.

"Hey, I got something," the pretty tech said. "A last-minute find," she added and held a small object in her gloved hand.

Geena was on her feet. She had to be close to six feet tall, standing almost shoulder to shoulder with Parker.

The tech continued. "It's a lighter, plastic—nothing special. Looks like the original color might've been pink."

Cheryl made her way over, peered at the object. "Bag it. They can run some tests, see if it means anything."

Geena sat back down on the rock. Parker leaned against the Kilroy tree.

And so the process went.

Outside of recovering the bones, forensics had collected and bagged a broken whiskey bottle, pieces of rubber that could've come from sneakers or boots, and a shred of threadbare fabric found near the skull. They would have to run tests, but there was a good chance the victim had been wearing a hat. Who knew—maybe they'd get lucky and find hair tangled in the material. They could learn a lot from hair, like whether it belonged to the victim or someone else. The soil had preserved the bones all these years, so anything was possible. It had something to do with pH components: the particular acidity or lack thereof found in the earth in this particular oversize dirt mound. Then add in the frigid temperature of the soil if the body had been buried deep enough, which appeared to have been the case. It was clear whoever had done this hadn't wanted him found. But they hadn't counted on erosion bringing the bones closer to the surface, or the black lab, Lincoln, coming along and digging them out.

Another thirty minutes passed before the team started the process of disassembling the grid. A couple of techs packed up their gear.

Something about the grid, the search area, nagged Parker. He stepped away from the tree, stood over the site where the last of the bones had been removed on that first day. He turned over everything he knew up to this point about the case, which wasn't much at all, when he really thought about it. If the victim had been struck in the head and dropped to the ground in this spot, or close to this spot, what would the person who'd struck him do next? Were they carrying a shovel with them, or did they leave and come back? Or maybe they'd hit him with a shovel and then used it to bury him with afterward? Parker made a swinging motion with his arms and then turned, staring at a spot on the other side of the grid, closer to the trail.

"What is it?" Geena asked.

"I think we need to extend the search a little farther out."

Some of the techs groaned. No one wanted to spend any more time on the mountain than was absolutely necessary.

"Why? What are you hoping to find?" Cheryl asked.

"I'm not sure, but whoever did this would've eventually headed back in the direction of the trail. Maybe they dropped something along the way."

"Joe," Cheryl called. "Do me a favor and drag a rake over here."

Joe did as he was told. He was followed by two more techs.

Karla appeared with her camera out and ready.

Another two hours passed as the team processed the new search area. Parker shook off the sideways glances he got from some of the techs. They were all cold and tired. He bet they hoped their next assignment would be someplace warmer.

"Cheryl," Joe said. "You're going to want to see this."

Cheryl moved to where Joe squatted on the ground. She bent down, gently brushed a thin layer of debris away with her gloved hand.

Parker maneuvered his way around the perimeter of the site. "What is it?" he asked. Geena followed him.

Cheryl straightened. Her cheeks were pink from the frigid air. "Well, I know what it is, but the question is whether or not it's relevant." She bent over it again, cleared more debris. She continued. "It looks like it's been here a good long time." She talked more to herself than to anyone else when she said, "It could definitely crack a skull."

Parker and Geena came to stand next to Cheryl. They stared at what was a partially buried aluminum baseball bat in the ground at their feet.

CHAPTER SEVEN

JULY 1979

An hour after meeting the new girl, Trisha, Dannie jumped on her bike, excited about their plans for a friendship club. There was something worldly about Trisha, exotic even, with her sleek dark hair and porcelain skin. They didn't get many families from outside the state moving to their small town. Most people couldn't find it on a map. But Trisha's family had found it, bringing with them a change to the neighborhood.

Dannie pedaled across the street to Trisha's house. They were going to meet at Carlyn's with their bikes and bathing suits. She stopped pedaling when Trisha's stepfather stepped from behind the moving truck and into her path.

"That is one fine-looking bike you have there," he said, resting his hand on the back of the banana seat where she was sitting.

"My dad bought it for me," she said. It was a pink Huffy, complete with a basket and streamers dangling from the handlebars. Her father had bought her the bike three weeks ago, right before he'd moved out. She loved the bike and took special care of it, and not because it was the nicest bike on Second Street but because it was the last gift she knew she'd ever get from him.

"Well, you must be a special girl for him to give you such a special bike."

"I guess," she said and gave him a weak smile.

Trisha came around the side of the house with her bicycle.

"Come on, Dannie—let's go." She pulled on Dannie's arm harder than she should, turning the handlebars on Dannie's Huffy, almost knocking her over.

"Careful now," Lester said.

"Let's go," Trisha said, urging Dannie to follow her. Carlyn was waiting for them in front of her house. Dannie pedaled down the sidewalk after Trisha.

They rode their bikes to the path that led to the slate quarry. Dannie breathed a little heavier than the other two girls, feeling out of shape. Her chubby legs struggled to keep up. When they reached the path, they stopped and climbed off their bikes. She checked to see if the bag with the snacks she'd packed was still in the front basket. Next to the snacks was a cheap transistor radio that she'd purchased at the five and dime at the start of summer.

Trisha leaned over and peeked inside Dannie's basket. Then she smiled at Dannie, and something inside of Dannie seemed to shift.

"This way," Carlyn said, pulling at her T-shirt with the rainbow iron-on.

They walked their bikes onto the path. Dannie trailed a step behind. The sun burned the top of her head through her thin blonde hair. Brush and weeds crunched under her feet. They hadn't had rain in over two weeks.

"Did everyone bring something?" Carlyn asked, stashing her bike next to a small dogwood tree.

Trisha dropped her bike next to Carlyn's. Dannie reached in her basket and grabbed the brown paper bag and radio before carefully laying the Huffy on the ground with the others.

"Where should we do this?" Trisha stepped toward the edge of the quarry.

Carlyn joined Trisha at the rim. Dannie stood on the other side of Carlyn. Flat gray rocks surrounded them. Some of the edges looked sharp, dangerous. Others peeled in layers, exposing lighter, breakable slivers of rock.

Dannie had been afraid of the quarry after hearing a boy had drowned last summer. He'd jumped off a rock pile, hit his head on a chunk of slate hidden beneath the water. Rumors circulated about others drowning, about kids not jumping out far enough, striking the sides of the slate before sinking to their deaths. She didn't know if the stories were true, but she never jumped. Instead, she would slide on her bottom into the cold, metallic-tasting liquid.

She stepped back from the ledge. "We should have the friendship ceremony before we swim." Underneath her terry-cloth shorts, she picked at the elastic band of her bathing suit that had been wedged between her cheeks ever since she'd gotten off her bike.

"This is where you swim?" Trisha asked.

"There's a park pool at the top of the hill, but this is kind of our spot," Carlyn said. "Come on—there's a flat rock over here we can sit on." She walked up a small path, crawled onto a slab of slate overlooking the water, tucked her long legs underneath her.

"Where does that go?" Trisha pointed to another path farther up the hill.

"That takes you to the Appalachian Trail," Dannie said and sat next to Carlyn.

"Get out!" Trisha said. "I read about that in school. Isn't it some kind of old Indian trail?"

"It goes from Georgia to Maine," Carlyn said. "Two thousand one hundred and sixty miles. It follows the oldest mountain range in the United States . . ." Her voice trailed off.

Dannie jumped in. "Carlyn knows all kinds of facts about stuff. She's smart like that, reading all the time." She wanted Trisha to know how smart Carlyn was. She wanted Trisha to like her, to think they both were worth hanging out with.

They sat in a circle with their paper bags in front of them. Dannie fiddled with the transistor radio. Through the static, the Knack crooned about a girl named Sharona. The sun beat down on the slate rock, making it hot to touch. A red-tailed hawk soared high in the sky.

"I'll start. Friends forever." Carlyn stuck her hand in the center of their circle. Dannie and Trisha followed, covering each other's hands, their arms outstretched like the spokes of a wheel.

"Friends forever," they said before dropping their arms.

Trisha dumped a cigarette and a pack of matches onto the slate tabletop. "We take a drag of the cigarette, hold our breath until we've all inhaled, and then exhale together. Like we're one spirit breathing out the same drag."

"I've never smoked before." Dannie stared at the cigarette. She was afraid she wouldn't like the taste or she'd cough before the others were ready to exhale. "I better go last in case I can't hold the smoke in."

"You ever smoke a cigarette?" Trisha asked Carlyn.

"I've tried it once."

"I steal them from my mom all the time." Trisha put the cigarette between her lips, lit it with a match. She inhaled and then passed it to Carlyn.

Carlyn took it between her pointer and middle finger, inhaled, passed it to Dannie.

Dannie held the cigarette like Carlyn had, between her pointer and middle finger, but it felt awkward. She dropped it.

Keeping her lips pressed together, Trisha urged from her throat, "Come on."

Dannie picked up the cigarette. This time she put it between her lips and inhaled. The smoke filled her mouth, burned her throat. She willed herself not to cough.

Trisha held up her hand and counted with her fingers, one, two, three. They exhaled. Dannie coughed. She covered her throat with her hand, feeling as though she had swallowed a fistful of fire ants. Carlyn patted her on the back.

"First time's rough." Trisha took the cigarette from Dannie and continued smoking. "What did you bring?" she asked her.

Dannie swallowed, tried to soothe the sting with spit. "Tastykakes. I couldn't think of anything else." She handed Carlyn and Trisha the cupcake packs. "I did think of a name for our club." She looked around at the mountains of slate. "Slate Sisters, no question," she said and took a big bite of her cream-filled chocolate cupcake.

"It's perfect," Carlyn said.

Trisha motioned to the path near their bikes. "Who's that?" she asked.

Carlyn and Dannie turned as two boys from their class approached. Dannie quickly ducked behind Carlyn, said a silent prayer, *Please, God, make them go away.*

The girls grabbed their cupcake wrappers and stood. The radio had gotten knocked over in their haste; static crackled from the tiny speaker. Carlyn scooped it up and turned it off.

"What's this?" Jeff, the meaner of the two, grabbed the paper bag Dannie had brought the cupcakes in. He blew air into it before smacking it between his hands, popping it. He stepped toward Dannie. Her heart leaped to her throat. Wearing a big toothy grin, he grabbed her boob and twisted. "Titty twister."

She threw her arms over her chest. "Stop it!" Tears filled her eyes almost instantly from the pain of her stinging nipple.

Trisha jumped in front of Dannie and pushed Jeff hard enough for him to stumble backward. "Leave her alone."

"What?" Jeff laughed and charged at Dannie again.

Trisha shoved him harder, sending him flying backward into a pile of slate.

He pulled himself up, brushed the grit from his shorts. "Come on—we all know she likes it."

"Don't ever touch her again," Trisha said and went to hit Jeff, but Scott, who had done nothing but watch up to this point, stepped into the scuffle, putting his arm out to separate them. "You new around here?" he asked Trisha.

"That's for me to know and you to find out," Trisha said.

Dannie hid behind Carlyn. Trisha and Scott continued to stare each other down. The lines were drawn. They were at a standoff. Dannie's armpits began to sweat, and she worried Jeff would see her pit stains, giving him another reason to pick on her.

Finally, Scott said to Jeff, "Leave her alone."

"Wuss," Jeff said under his breath, but he took a step backward, retreating.

Dannie stepped out from behind Carlyn. She stared at Trisha, in awe of this rough new girl taking on two boys by herself. But the longer she stared, the more she began to see something else in Trisha, a kind of vulnerability hidden beneath her tough exterior, something she carried deep inside that, unless a person looked closely, they wouldn't see.

Jeff pulled off his T-shirt and tossed it to the ground. "Later, losers." He got a running start before jumping and yelling, "Cannonball," hitting the water with a *thwump*.

Scott lifted his shirt over his head. His chest was golden brown. He already had the makings of bulging biceps, a washboard stomach. He stared at Trisha.

"What are you looking at?" Trisha asked.

"You." He turned and dove headfirst into the quarry. Dannie held her breath until he surfaced.

The boys splashed around under the hot sun. The water looked inviting. Trisha twisted the hem of her shirt, possibly contemplating taking it off and jumping in. Dannie shrunk behind Carlyn again. No way she'd ever take her shirt off now.

Jeff floated on his back, pointed at Dannie, made like he was holding two melons.

"Come on." Carlyn tugged Dannie's arm. "Let's go."

They walked down the path to their bikes. Dannie kept her eyes straight ahead, embarrassed by her chubby body, the small mounds protruding underneath her bathing suit. The other girls were thin and didn't have breasts yet.

Her body had changed over the last few months. Blondish hair had sprouted under her arms and between her legs. But it was her breasts the boys noticed, and because of this she stuck out, becoming a favorite target for creeps like Jeff. She wiped her eyes as she pedaled toward home, hating Jeff, but most of all, hating the way she felt in her body.

Once they were a safe distance from the quarry, Carlyn and Trisha stopped and got off their bikes. Dannie, the least athletic of the three now, caught up and hopped off her bike too. They pushed their bicycles on the sidewalk as they walked.

"Are you hurt?" Carlyn asked her.

"No." She whimpered a little, but she stopped herself from crying. She didn't want to sound like a baby. "Thanks for sticking up for me back there," she said.

Trisha nodded and wiped the sweat from her brow, tucked her black hair behind her ear. "Where is that park pool you were talking about?"

"At the top of Bangor's hill. Let's drop our bikes off first," Carlyn said. "Who has money?"

"How much does it cost?" Trisha asked.

Carlyn stopped pushing her bike. Trisha and Dannie stopped too. After a moment, realizing none of them had money for the public pool, they continued pushing their bikes another three blocks, walking in silence.

Dannie dragged her feet, wishing Jeff and Scott hadn't shown up and spoiled their plans. Although swimming in the quarry made her nervous, at least they'd had someplace to go. Now it felt like the entire day had been ruined.

They reached Trisha's house first. The moving truck was empty. Lester was leaning on the bumper drinking a beer.

"There you are," he said. "Your mom's been looking for you. She needs help unpacking."

"Okay." Trisha laid her bike in the yard. "I'll catch you guys later," she said.

Dannie watched Trisha walk into the house with him. There was a closeness between them in the way he put his hand on the small of Trisha's back. The sight of them together created an ache inside of Dannie, a longing for her own father.

CHAPTER EIGHT

Trisha opened her eyes. She didn't recognize the water stain in the corner of the ceiling. She panicked and scrambled from the twisted sheets, put her back against the wall. She covered her hammering heart. Her pajamas were damp with perspiration. Slowly it came back to her: how she'd gotten on a plane, flown home for Evelyn's funeral, how she'd come to be lying on the mattress in her old bedroom in her mother's house.

Downstairs she heard knocking. It must've been what had woken her up, what had scared her. Too many times Sid had locked her in their closet overnight. Sometimes when he'd been kind, he'd left her a magnum bottle of Grey Goose vodka on one of the shelves, next to a pair of $400 shoes. "Nothing but the best for my girl," he'd say. The next morning the bottle would be empty, and Trisha would be passed out on the floor. She'd rouse to the sound of rapping on the door, the clicking of the lock having been opened, Sid standing over her.

The knocking grew louder. What time was it, anyway? The dim light from the gray sky leaked through the cracked blinds. She must've slept the day away. She looked for her phone, then remembered she no longer had it. She'd tossed it in the trash can on her way out the door of the penthouse suite. She was certain Sid had been tracking her on it.

"I'm coming, I'm coming," her mother said from somewhere downstairs.

Trisha threw on the dingy robe from her teen years. She crept down the stairs, sat on the bottom step, out of sight, and listened.

"Sharon Haines," a man said. "I'm Detective Reed, and this is my partner, Detective Brassard."

Silence.

Trisha peeked around the corner. Her mother was just standing there in front of the cracked storm door. She wasn't saying anything.

"May we come in?" the detective asked.

Her mother hesitated; then she stepped aside, let them in.

The detective was tall, broad shouldered. Trisha couldn't get a good look at his face, just his profile, but she could tell he was young. She'd spent a lot of time around older men: their wrinkly necks, their thin blue veins, their sagging skin. She might be middle aged, her body a little weathered, but Sid was twenty years her senior, and so were most of his so-called friends. There weren't any lines by the detective's eyes, the skin smooth, firm. A baby by comparison. The other detective was a woman, but from where Trisha was sitting, she couldn't see her clearly. All she saw was the back of the woman's head, her blonde ponytail.

"Reed, you say?" Trisha's mother asked, coming around. "You wouldn't be related to a Dr. Reed in Portland, would you?"

"Yes, ma'am. I'm his son."

"I know the doc. I was in a bar up your way—Sweeney's I think it was. A lot of them biker guys you see around town hang out there. You probably know that, though, don't you? Anyways, one of them was hitting on me. I know it might be hard to believe, but back then, I was a looker. Some gal didn't like it and hit me upside the head. See this scar." She leaned toward the detective, pointed to the side of her forehead. "Your dad stitched me up good. Hardly noticeable unless you're up close."

Trisha had never heard this story before. She'd never known how her mother had gotten the crescent-shaped scar. She'd always assumed it had come from Lester.

"That's a real interesting story," Detective Reed said. Trisha got the distinct impression he was just being polite. He turned his head in the direction of the dining room and staircase. She ducked behind the wall.

He continued. "You might've heard by now about the remains that were found in the woods a few days ago." He paused. "We have reason to believe they could belong to your husband."

"Lester?" Trisha's mother sat on the torn couch cushion, her hand at her throat. "How can that be? It's been thirty years he's been gone. Missing."

"Yes, ma'am, but I believe we may have found him."

Trisha craned her head forward, strained to see, hear. Her body began to shake, tiny tremors that reached as far as her toes.

Her mother's voice was raspy from cigarettes, thick with emotion. "I told a couple of your guys back then that he didn't run out on me. They didn't believe me. They thought he left me."

"They must've believed you, ma'am, because your husband's name has been in the missing persons system all this time," Detective Reed said. "I'm sorry to be the one who has to tell you this, but I wanted you to hear it from us first. Of course, nothing is official—not yet anyway. I want you to know that we're doing everything we can to make a positive identification as quickly as possible, and we'd like your cooperation." His partner stood quietly beside him.

"My cooperation? What do you need from me?"

"I'll need you to release your husband's dental records to my office. It's the fastest way we can confirm an ID." He handed her a card.

Her mother took it. "Okay, sure, I can do that." She paused. "Did a bear get him?"

"Excuse me?" Detective Reed said.

"A bear. Did a bear get him?"

"No, ma'am. I don't think so."

She continued as though he hadn't spoken. "You couldn't get me near them woods. I'm a city girl at heart. Bet you didn't know that, did you? Born and raised near Chicago. Moved here with him. I won't ever step foot on that mountain. Not with all that wildlife running around."

Trisha wished her mother would just shut up for once in her life. *Shut up. Shut up. Shut up.* Babbling made it worse, made everything worse. Didn't she know that? Trisha turned then, had every intention of crawling back under the covers and hiding in her room, only to stop halfway up the staircase when she heard the female detective's voice.

"Is someone else home?" the female detective asked.

Trisha closed her eyes, cursed the old house and its creaky wooden floors.

"My daughter flew in from Vegas yesterday. A good friend of ours passed. She came home for the funeral."

"I'm sorry," the female detective said. "Would you like me to speak with your daughter?"

Trisha scrambled up the rest of the stairs.

"If you don't mind," her mother said, "I'd like to be the one to tell her."

"Okay, sure," the female detective said.

It seemed to Trisha as though the two detectives were leaving. Then she heard Detective Reed say, "One more thing. Was your husband a hunter by any chance?"

"What? No."

"Did he like to hike the trails or walk around the quarry? I know a lot of people in town like to do that sort of thing—hiking and camping on the mountain."

"No, he didn't do anything like that. He wasn't much of an outdoorsman, if that's what you're asking."

"Okay." He hesitated. "Do you have any idea why he might've been in the woods?"

"No, none that I can think of. Why? What are you saying? What do you think happened?" her mother asked.

"That's what we're trying to figure out," Detective Reed said.

More words were exchanged, but Trisha couldn't hear over the buzzing in her head. When the front door opened and closed, she rushed to her mother's bedroom, paused near the foot of the bed. She peeked out the window as the detectives got in their cruiser and pulled from their parking spot.

Across the street Dannie was standing on Evelyn's porch, watching the detectives drive away.

CHAPTER NINE

Trisha was waiting in her house for Dannie and Carlyn to show up. She was now thirteen years old, soon to be fourteen, and it seemed like, ever since they'd become best friends four years ago, she was forever waiting for them to knock on her door. Tonight was no different as she sat on the couch, peered out the window at Dannie's front porch. They said they'd come and get her as soon as they'd finished eating dinner. Where were they? *Hurry up.*

Her mother walked into the room. She was dressed in her work clothes: a tight black skirt that barely covered her bottom, a tank top so small her chest spilled out the top and sides. It wasn't a flattering look by any means, but ever since her mother had started bartending nights at a place called Foxy's, she'd gotten more tips showing some skin—her mother's words.

"Who are you looking for?" her mother asked, tugging at the hem of her skirt.

"My friends," Trisha said.

Her mother wouldn't meet Trisha's eyes, not since the cops had been to their house earlier that morning. Their neighbor, old Mrs. Sherwood, had called when the shouting penetrated the walls they shared. Trisha's mother's cheek had been red, swollen. "Walked into a door," she'd told the officer. Mrs. Sherwood had shaken her head and had gone back inside her house. Trisha's mother had held a frozen bag of peas to her face. Now, the makeup she'd smeared on her skin wasn't doing much to hide the bruise.

Trisha cleared her throat, tried to get her mother to look at her. *See me*, she wanted to say, but her mother was preoccupied fussing with her skirt, then touched her sore cheek.

"Don't go in to work tonight," Trisha said. "Stay home."

"I can't. You know I can't," her mother said. "What do you think all that yelling was about, anyway? He didn't show up for work again. But at least I got him to go in today."

Outside a car door slammed.

"That must be him," her mother said. "Don't stay out too late. You have school tomorrow." She pulled the door open and stepped outside.

Trisha peered out the living room window again, watched her mother pass Lester on the porch. She took the car keys from his hand without saying a word. Then she turned her head away from Trisha and the house and made her way to their only car.

Lester caught Trisha peeking out the window. She quickly dropped the curtain and curled onto the far corner of the couch. Her friends should've been here by now. He stepped inside and sat on the cushion next to her. She pressed her hip against the side of the armrest, putting as much space between them as possible. He scratched his head. He'd let his hair grow long in the last few years. It had gotten so long that he'd ended up tying it back in a ponytail most days.

"Well," he said. "I guess you're mad at me too."

She shook her head, too afraid to tell him the truth.

"That's my girl." He patted her leg. "Why don't you go fetch me a beer?"

She got up from the couch and went into the kitchen, got him a beer from the refrigerator. "Here." She handed it to him and turned to go, hoping he wouldn't want anything else from her.

"Where are you going? Come join me. I've had a long day, and I could use the company." He set the beer aside when she reluctantly sat back down, pressing her hip against the armrest again. He talked about his day, how his back was sore from lifting and moving carpets. He hadn't worked his way into a sales position like her mother had said he would. A person had to show up for work in order to move up.

He rubbed his neck, continued rambling about his job. Trisha nodded in the appropriate places, but she wasn't really listening. This was how it started: he'd talk about his day, his aches and pains, the kinds of things he should share with Trisha's mother, not Trisha. But he talked to her as though she were an adult, conversations she was certain other daughters didn't have with their fathers or, in her case, stepfather.

He grew quiet, and she wondered if she'd missed something while she was off in her own thoughts. He picked up his beer and guzzled it down. She counted the seconds until her friends would get here and she could leave. He remained silent. She thought about getting up, waiting for her friends on the porch.

Then he leaned back against the couch, inching his way closer to her. Her breathing quickened.

Deep inside her bones in a place she wasn't always aware of and yet she was, she understood the reason behind these little talks and what they led to. And for this she blamed herself, for not knowing how to stop it. Now, he brushed her hair away from her shoulder. Her muscles constricted, her spine rigid.

He tickled her side. "Give me a smile," he said, edging closer still.

She closed her eyes, tried to pretend to be somewhere else, anywhere else.

There was a knock at the door.

Her friends called her name. Was she dreaming? Were they finally here?

She heard her name again.

"Coming!" she called and sprang from the couch. She raced for the door and flung it open. Dannie and Carlyn were standing on the porch. They looked startled. She ran outside, pushed them toward the steps. "Go, go, go," she yelled. The three of them ran down the sidewalk.

Lester hollered something she couldn't make out.

They continued running until they reached the end of the block. The sun lingered over the mountaintop. They'd have an hour, maybe more, of sunlight left.

"We need to keep moving," Trisha said, looking over her shoulder, catching him coming off their porch. "This way," she said, slipping between two houses.

"What are we doing?" Carlyn asked.

"Just follow me," Trisha said, leading the way, Carlyn behind her, and Dannie trailing them both, huffing and puffing and calling, "Wait up."

When they reached the quarry, they stopped. Dannie bent over and held her stomach, trying to catch her breath.

Trisha paced up and down the gravel path, pausing every few seconds to check that he hadn't followed them. Anger welled up inside her along with shame, the two tumbling and turning below the surface of her skin. She couldn't remember a time when she hadn't felt this way. Maybe when she was a child and living with her real father in Chicago.

"The quarry's not safe," she said. "Too open." It would be easy for Lester to find them there. And she didn't want to chance bumping into Scott. Ever since that day she'd first met him, the way he'd looked at her had made her feel warm and funny inside. But she couldn't think about that now. She couldn't handle anything else.

"Safe from what?" Dannie asked.

"I know where we can go," Carlyn said.

They took the path away from the quarry, veered left onto a smaller path that led to the AT, stomped through the brush, stopped when Dannie got snagged on a branch.

Once on the trail, they started up the side of the mountain. They kicked up dust and stones, ducked under low-lying branches. New leaves sprouted from trees, and ferns fanned out on both sides of the dirt path. It should've been a beautiful spring evening for a walk in the woods, and maybe it was to anybody else. But to Trisha, it felt like a slap in the face, a sharp contrast to the ugliness tearing through her.

"How much farther?" Dannie asked.

Carlyn stopped, looked around. "This should be far enough." She checked with Trisha.

Trisha nodded and sat on a rock underneath a large oak tree.

"Why'd we run?" Carlyn asked. "What was he doing?"

Trisha shook her head. "Just don't be late again," she said. "Just promise me you won't be late again."

CHAPTER TEN

After the detectives' car disappeared down Second Street, Trisha scurried from her mother's bedroom to the bathroom. She filled the tub with hot water and climbed in, careful of her bruised ribs. She was hoping to avoid her mother at least for a little while and to put off the conversation they were sure to have about Trisha's stepfather.

She scrubbed her skin until it was pink and raw, tried to wash off decades of unwanted hands touching her, groping her, violating her in ways she'd never dreamed possible. But no amount of soap or water could ever stop her flesh from crawling with the memories.

When she couldn't stand it any longer and the itch for a drink became unbearable, she stepped out of the old claw-foot tub and dressed in designer jeans. They were the closest thing she had that resembled anything casual. The silk blouse she slipped on was ridiculously overpriced—each pearl button hand sewn, custom made specifically for her.

She found her mother in the kitchen in front of a can of beer and an ashtray full of cigarette butts. Trisha helped herself to her own can of beer, the bitter taste like candy on her tongue. She hadn't made it through the night like she'd planned, finding the harder stuff, a half bottle of Jack Daniel's, in a cabinet by the stove. She'd polished it off, filled it back up with water: a trick she'd learned as a kid so her mother wouldn't notice it was empty. It bought Trisha some time to replace the bottle.

"We had visitors," her mother said. "A couple of detectives. They came to talk to me about those bones they found in the woods." She pulled on the cigarette, exhaled. "They think they're Lester's."

"What makes them think that?"

"They didn't say. They asked me to get them Lester's dental records. They said it's the fastest way to make an ID."

"Are you going to do it?"

"What kind of question is that?"

Trisha didn't know. She didn't know what to say next. Of course her mother would help to identify him. Why wouldn't she?

Her mother rubbed her brow. "I don't even know if the dentist would've kept his records after all this time." She paused. "Do you think they'd still have them?"

Trisha met her mother's gaze, saw worry in her eyes. What did she want from her? What did she expect her to say? She couldn't bring herself to say she was sorry. She would never apologize for Lester. She hated him. Although many years had come and gone since she'd last seen him, her anger was as fresh and rough as it had ever been.

No, Trisha wasn't sorry. The only thing she was sorry for was that they'd ever found him in the first place.

⁂

Trisha left her mother sitting in the kitchen with her beer and cigarettes. She knocked on the front door of Evelyn's house, or what used to be Evelyn's home. She supposed Dannie owned it now.

The cold December air cut through the flimsy silk blouse. She knocked again. When she didn't get an answer the second time, she tried the door. It was unlocked. She opened it and stepped into the living room. The place had been straightened up since the funeral. The discarded plates with half-eaten food had been cleared away. The worn carpet had been vacuumed, from the looks of the fresh tracks. Warm air blew from the electric baseboard heater.

Trisha followed the sound of voices to the back of the house, paused outside the entranceway of the kitchen, where she found Dannie at the table in front of a large piece of pie. Carlyn sat across from her. They didn't hear her come in, and, instead of announcing herself, she slipped inside a shadow and out of sight, taking up her usual position for spying. Eavesdropping on conversations was the only way she'd ever learned anything, because no one had bothered to talk with her directly. She'd lurked on the fringes of parties, lingered on the outskirts of black-jack tables and poker games. She'd tucked herself into the corners of the suite during Sid's soirees. The less she'd been seen or heard, the better chance she'd had of staying out of the way of his wrath.

"Do you want some pie?" Dannie asked Carlyn.

"No, thanks," Carlyn said.

"I didn't want it either," Dannie said and licked the fork before pushing the plate away.

"How are you holding up?" Carlyn asked.

"I don't know. It's hard to explain. Nothing feels right. *I* don't feel right. I don't feel like myself."

"I think that's understandable."

"Is it? Is it normal that I don't know how to live in a world without my mother?" Tears rolled down her cheeks. She swiped them away. "I've been taking care of her for so long. It's like I don't know what to do with myself now. I don't know how to feel, how I'm supposed to act, without the constant worrying about her weighing on my mind."

Carlyn nodded like she understood, although Trisha didn't see how she could. Carlyn had a terrible relationship with her own mother. They'd barely talked when Carlyn had been a teenager, and when they had, it had usually ended in a heated argument. Trisha wondered if that had changed through the years—if they'd become close during Trisha's absence in their lives.

"Have you decided what you're going to do about the house?" Carlyn asked.

"I'm going to put it up for sale," Dannie said. "Vinnie and I and the girls love our house. We love being close to Vinnie's parents. It doesn't make sense for us to move." She looked around the kitchen. "And this place needs a lot of fixing up. I suppose a thorough cleaning would be a good place to start."

"I can help you," Carlyn said.

Neither of them moved.

Dannie played with a napkin, folding and unfolding the corners. Trisha stayed hidden, waiting, sensing a shift in the air. There was more they had to say.

"The police were at Trisha's mom's this morning," Dannie said.

"Okay," Carlyn said.

Dannie continued. "There were two of them, but they weren't in the typical cop uniforms. They were wearing plain clothes. Could've been detectives, I guess. They were there for about fifteen minutes or so before I saw them drive away."

"It has to be about the bones they found on the trail."

"Yes." Dannie wiped her eyes, sniffed. "That's what I thought too."

They were quiet for a while. Carlyn was the first to break the silence. "What do you make of Trisha showing up here yesterday?"

Before Dannie could answer, Trisha stepped into the kitchen. She thought she'd want to hear what they had to say about her behind her back but found she couldn't bear it.

Dannie looked surprised.

"I knocked, but I guess you didn't hear me. I hope you don't mind that I let myself in."

"No, it's fine. Of course you're welcome to come in anytime," Dannie said, twisting the napkin in her hands.

Carlyn and Trisha stared at each other.

Dannie looked back and forth between them. "What did I miss?" she asked.

"It's nothing," Trisha said, looked away. She hadn't talked with Carlyn since they'd exchanged words after the funeral.

"Well." Dannie cleared her throat. "Carlyn and I were just about to clean up the rest of these dishes." She stood.

"Let me help you." Trisha picked up a dish towel.

"Oh, you don't have to do that," Dannie said.

"I want to."

"Oh, well, okay, but not in that shirt, you're not," Dannie said. "Come with me. I have something you can slip over it."

Carlyn hadn't said a word as Trisha followed Dannie upstairs to one of the bedrooms. The layout of the house was the same as Trisha's mother's, the same as Carlyn's old house: not exactly row homes but darn close. There were three bedrooms: the master at the front of the house overlooking the street, the bathroom at the opposite end, and two small bedrooms in between, separated by the staircase. Dannie's old bedroom was a replica of Trisha's, but Dannie's bed had a frame, her dresser had a mirror, and the walls had been painted recently.

"Here." Dannie handed her a sweatshirt.

It looked too big, but she said, "Thanks" and took it anyway.

"I'll let you change, then," Dannie said and walked out.

Trisha lifted her arms over her head to slip on the sweatshirt. Her blouse rode up, exposing her stomach. Pain shot down her side. It was at that moment that Dannie peeked into the room, as though she'd forgotten something. Trisha covered her torso as fast as she could, but by the look on Dannie's face, she hadn't been fast enough. She'd seen the bruise that covered a large portion of Trisha's rib cage.

"What?" Trisha snapped.

"I was . . . forget it," Dannie said, taking a step closer. "What happened to you?"

"It doesn't matter."

"Yes, it does," Dannie said. "It matters to me. *You* matter to me."

Trisha had a strong urge to flee, to escape the concern in Dannie's eyes. When was the last time someone had been worried about her? The meanness of people was what she understood, what she could take. But not this, this *kindness*.

Dannie took another step toward her, made the sign of the cross.

"Don't pray for me," she said and pushed past her.

"Why not?" Dannie called.

"Just don't," she said.

CHAPTER ELEVEN

OCTOBER 1986

Dannie got off the bus with Carlyn and Trisha and the rest of their classmates. They were pushing and shoving, bumping into each other in a hustle for freedom. Dannie lagged behind, half listening to their chatter. She lifted her face to the cool breeze and fading sun. She loved this time of day in autumn and what she thought of as jeans weather. She liked wearing bigger, warmer clothes to hide her ever-growing body.

"Come on, Dans," Carlyn said, and both she and Trisha stopped to wait for Dannie to catch up.

Dannie reached her friends at the same time a car raced up Broadway's hill. She recognized Trisha's mother behind the wheel. Trisha saw her, too, and for a second, Dannie could've sworn Trisha's face had fallen.

They turned then and walked down the sidewalk together shoulder to shoulder, Carlyn in the middle, the hub. They'd walked in the same formation ever since Trisha had moved to Second Street seven years ago.

Trisha lit a cigarette.

Scott jogged up behind them and pulled Trisha across the street. Carlyn and Dannie followed.

"Do you want the bus driver to see you?" Scott asked Trisha. "You couldn't wait to cross the street to light up? Do you want to get in trouble or something?"

"I'm not afraid of getting into trouble," Trisha said.

"I didn't say you were."

They continued walking toward home with Scott at Trisha's side.

Dannie hugged her notebooks, hiding her chest behind them. She'd never gotten over the day at the quarry when Jeff the Meanie twisted her boob. She had been self-conscious of her size ever since. She'd started twelfth grade with her friends two months ago, and the boys in their class talked to her chest rather than to her face, rarely looking her in the eyes.

They stopped walking when they reached Second Street. Some of their classmates milled around, kicking rocks, goofing off. A napkin blew in the gutter. The breeze turned the pages of a discarded magazine. Trisha and Scott stood close to each other, looking like a couple. Trisha wouldn't admit it, but Scott had become more or less her boyfriend in the last few weeks.

Carlyn shifted her books onto her right hip. She pulled a sheet of paper from her notebook and began reading whatever was written on it. Dannie noticed Carlyn had been spending more and more time studying, hanging out at the public library, intent on making honor roll again.

Dannie looked away. She didn't have time to indulge in her studies. She had bigger concerns than homework assignments. Her house was a few steps away. She spied pieces of slate from the roof lying on the ground near a broken downspout. One more thing they didn't have the money to fix.

"Do you guys want to hang out on the trail?" Trisha asked and crushed the cigarette onto the pavement with her sneaker. She was always asking to hang out on the trail. Dannie knew it was because she never wanted to go home.

Trisha looked first at Carlyn, who shrugged a shoulder, and then at Dannie, who shook her head.

"I have to check on my mom," Dannie said and slipped around the corner. She ran up the porch steps to her house, opened the front door that her mother never locked.

She wondered if maybe her mother wanted someone to walk in, steal the few possessions they had—a TV, toaster oven, a radio. Or possibly, her mother didn't care who walked in, a murderer even, someone to end her misery since Dannie's father had left.

In those first few weeks after he'd walked out on them, her mother had pretended nothing had changed. She'd fooled herself into thinking the other woman was nothing more than a fling, and he'd be back. But then the months had turned into years, and he still hadn't returned. And her mother had never recovered.

But Dannie didn't really believe her mother wished to be murdered. In reality, her mother refused to stand up and answer the door if someone knocked. She'd rather shout, "Door's open" and never move an atrophied muscle. Depression did this, and Dannie feared she would find her mother dead from gluttony more than anything else.

When she walked through the door today, she almost dropped her notebooks on the floor, surprised to find Lester standing in the middle of her living room. Her mother was on the couch, where she spent most of her days in her nightgown.

"Hello, Danielle," he said.

She looked to her mother for an explanation as to why he was here in their house.

"Sharon sent him over to help us with the roof," her mother said.

"Why don't you show me this downspout your mother's been telling me about?"

"Okay." She put her notebooks on the coffee table, glanced at her mother.

"We could use the help," her mother reassured her.

Dannie stepped back outside. Lester was close behind her. She felt his breath on the back of her neck. Trisha never talked about Lester, about what was happening inside her home, but Dannie knew something wasn't right. More than not right. And she no longer envied Trisha's relationship with him as she'd done when Trisha had first moved here.

She rushed down the porch steps to put distance between them, looked up and down the sidewalk. Her friends weren't anywhere to be found. Maybe they had already gone to the trail. The street was deserted.

"It's right there," she said and pointed to the broken downspout.

He walked to the corner of the house. She felt like she had no choice but to follow him. He was doing them a favor. Or was he?

He crouched over the downspout and broken pieces of slate that had fallen from the roof.

"We can't pay you," she said.

He looked up at her, then stood, putting his hand on her shoulder. He stood so close that she smelled beer on his breath. "This one's on me," he said and slid his hand down her arm, his fingers brushing her breast.

"Dannie!" Trisha called from across the street.

Dannie turned to the sound of Trisha's voice. Her mouth opened, but nothing came out. The next thing Dannie knew, Trisha was standing beside her, pulling on her arm, leading Dannie down the sidewalk and away from the house.

CHAPTER TWELVE

Parker was waiting for confirmation on whether or not the baseball bat was the murder weapon.

Apparently, aluminum bats were fairly resistant to extreme weather conditions and for long periods of time. Aluminum didn't rust. If it had been a wooden bat, it would've rotted, turned to mulch, become a part of the soil they'd swept away.

But sometimes in a case you got lucky.

And Parker was feeling lucky for no other reason than the fish were biting. He wasn't superstitious, but he took it as a good sign, a great start to what was going to be another long day. The six inches of snow they'd gotten overnight, the cold winter air that he loathed, couldn't keep him from dropping a line into the icy river. He'd caught and tossed back a half dozen smallmouth bass in the last hour. Too bad Becca wasn't here to witness it. She wouldn't believe him otherwise. She'd accuse him of telling tall fish tales, which of course he never did. Well, maybe he did sometimes, adding an inch to the length when he was bragging: *It was this big.* But hey, he was a guy. It was what guys did to impress girls, or rather in his case, a certain girl.

Ever since she'd returned to their hometown to take care of her ailing father, who had since passed, she'd sometimes joined Parker in the early-morning hours on his dock. Their childhood friendship had turned into something more since she'd come home.

But she hadn't shown up again this morning.

Other than the occasional text messages, it had been almost two months since he'd last seen her. He tried to ignore his disappointment, turning over an old expression in his mind: *These things take time.* But how much more time did she need? Her father had passed in October. Parker had thought she would've come around by now, but her grieving had kept her away.

He laid his fishing pole down, picked up a mug. The coffee had gone cold in the frigid air. His mind jumped to work—a built-in defense mechanism he relied on whenever he rubbed up against the void in his heart that only Becca could fill.

Sharon Haines had been denied access to her husband's dental records. The darn HIPAA law made it that much harder to do his job. And Sharon hadn't thought to file a court order to have Lester's dental and medical records placed in the missing persons and unidentified victims database in the years since he'd been missing.

Parker made a mental note of her lapse in judgment and considered maybe she hadn't been that broken up about her husband's disappearance after all. Maybe she hadn't wanted him found. Otherwise, the records would've been filed; measures would've been taken by family and friends to keep the case active.

And yet, she'd given Parker permission to file a court order to have the dental records released, which the judge had approved finally. He'd sent the records straight to Hannah, the forensic odontologist. He'd submitted his request as a priority and expected to hear anytime now. The last he'd spoken with Hannah, she'd been certain she'd have the information for him today.

His phone went off. He recognized the number lighting up the screen. It was really turning out to be a good day.

"Detective Reed," he said and listened, then promised to take Hannah out to lunch the next time he was in Lewistown, where her dental practice was located, a three-hour drive west of Portland.

He hung up the phone and gathered his fishing gear, took his time climbing the snowy steps up to his cabin. Once inside, he passed the boxes full of Christmas decorations he'd stacked in the living room. He kept forgetting to pick up a tree—or rather he'd been putting it off, hoping Becca would show up and offer to help. She'd picked out Christmas trees with him when they were kids, riding along with his mom and dad to the Christmas tree farm. They'd spend hours walking up and down the rows of blue spruces and Douglas firs, searching for the fattest tree. His parents would head off in another direction to cut down a smaller tree to display in the waiting room of his dad's medical practice. Parker's fingers and toes would go numb as he lay on the frozen terrain, sawing the trunk while Becca held it steady so it wouldn't fall on top of him. Then they'd drag it out of the field, laughing, singing Christmas songs like something in a Hallmark movie you'd see on television. He'd fallen in love with her then: the girl next door.

After a quick shower, he was feeling better, focused. He'd do what he did best and immerse himself in work. He pulled the original missing person file on Lester Haines. There was one photo of Lester wearing a red Phillies baseball hat. He sent a quick text to the trace-evidence team, where they were working on the fibers they'd collected at the scene. **Photo of vic wearing red Phillies baseball hat.** They would know what he was asking, whether the fabric was consistent with that of the hat. Also, he was waiting to hear whether they'd found any hair in the fabric. Even though his case was listed as a priority, he felt as though much of the lab work was taking forever.

Next, he made a list of all the witnesses who had been interviewed back in 1986. Then there was the fact that Lester had been in the system on unrelated charges. He'd had two summary offenses for public drunkenness and several disorderly conduct complaints filed against him dating back as far as 1979. A couple of the neighbors on Second Street had called them in. He'd been suspected of domestic violence. Sharon had defended Lester, denied he'd hit her, refused to press charges. This wasn't all that uncommon in these types of cases, where the woman was more scared of what would happen to her once her husband came home after she'd had him thrown in jail.

He checked his phone. One of the techs from the lab texted about the hat: I'm on it.

He texted Geena, updated her with the information he had received from Hannah, asked her to meet him at Sharon Haines's house.

He grabbed his car keys. It was time they let Sharon know it was official. The dental records confirmed the remains belonged to Lester.

⁂

The people closest to the victim were the first people you looked at when dealing with a missing person case, and especially one that ended in homicide. The first time Parker had met Sharon Haines, she'd seemed genuinely upset upon hearing the news about her husband. She'd appeared shocked, a little weepy, and then very confused. But there had been something about her face, the expression she'd made, that didn't sit right with him. And then he'd found out how little information there had been in the missing person file, raising more questions than answers.

He wanted to see what her reaction would be today. He'd need to speak with her daughter as well. The daughter had been in the original file as someone they'd questioned along with three other teenagers, two girls and a boy, presumably the daughter's friends. There was also a list of neighbors who had been interviewed. He wondered if any of them would still be around.

He parked on Second Street in front of Sharon's house. Geena was already there. She joined him in front of his car, smearing ChapStick on her lips. Her blonde hair was pulled back into a ponytail.

"Do you want to take the lead this time?" he asked.

"I think you should take it. She seemed comfortable with you. Let's not switch it up just yet."

"All right," he said.

Sharon greeted them at the door as though she'd been expecting them. She motioned for them to take a seat. She sat on the torn plaid couch. Her daughter, Trisha, sat next to her. Geena sat on the edge of a recliner. Parker pulled a folding chair from the corner of the room, sat next to Geena. He'd taken a small notepad from his jacket pocket, ready to write down whatever information Sharon and Trisha were willing to give them.

"Well, is it him?" Sharon asked.

"Yes, ma'am," Parker said. "It was confirmed this morning. We came over as soon as we got the news."

Sharon slouched against the back of the couch, her shoulders collapsing. Her daughter, Trisha, hadn't moved. Her hands were folded in her lap, her face expressionless.

Parker waited. The next question the family usually asked was how their loved one had died. Another minute passed. They continued to wait. Geena leaned back in the chair, crossed her legs, a signal she wasn't going anywhere anytime soon.

"How?" Sharon asked finally.

"He died from blunt-force trauma to the head." Parker watched them closely. Sharon covered her face. Distressed? Hard to say. As for her daughter? Her face remained blank. She was well into her forties, but there was something about her. She was petite, sharp. Her features had a rough edge to them, and yet the way she held herself, her posture, showed a level of sophistication she hadn't acquired from living around here. Her clothes fit her small frame to the point of exactness—not that

Parker knew or cared about fashion, but he could tell she wasn't shopping at the local department store. He stole a glance at her left hand. No wedding ring.

"I'm not sure I understand," Sharon said. "What does that mean exactly?"

"It means somebody hit him in the head hard enough to kill him," Geena said.

Sharon made a small noise from the back of her throat.

Parker gave her a minute to collect herself and then said, "We'd like to ask both of you a few questions about the time he went missing."

"Why?" Trisha asked.

It was the first time she'd spoken since the detectives had entered the house. Her voice was deep, raspy, probably from smoking.

"Your stepfather was murdered," he said bluntly, wanting to get some kind of reaction from her.

She showed no emotion one way or the other.

He continued. "It's our job to find out who's responsible."

Sharon made a hiccuping, sobbing sound.

Geena stirred next to him.

"Your mother said you flew in from Vegas?" he asked Trisha.

"That's right," she said.

"How long have you lived there?"

"Thirty years."

"Long time."

"Yes."

"And you're staying here?" He motioned to Sharon. "With your mother?"

"I am."

"How long are you planning to be in town?"

Sharon wiped her eyes, nose, looked at her daughter.

"I'm staying for as long as she needs me to." Trisha didn't break eye contact with him.

He was the first to look away, immediately wondering if she was testing him in some small way and whether he'd just failed by turning his attention to Sharon.

"What do you remember about that day?" he asked, checked his notes for the exact date Lester had last been seen. "December fourth, 1986."

Sharon rubbed the wrinkled skin on her neck. "I don't know. It was so long ago. He was drinking a lot around that time," she said.

"How much is a lot? Every day? Weekends?" Geena asked.

"Every day."

"Did he have a certain kind of drink he preferred? Beer? Whiskey?" Parker asked. They'd found a broken whiskey bottle near the bones.

"He drank both. But he preferred his whiskey. I guess if I had to pick one, I'd say Wild Turkey was his favorite."

Parker wrote it down.

"What else can you remember about that time?" he asked.

"He wasn't showing up for work. His boss called and told me he'd missed too many days, and he shouldn't bother coming in anymore."

"Where was he working at the time?"

"Cal's Carpet and Flooring. They sold wall-to-wall carpet, area rugs, some laminate wood-type stuff." She continued, "I didn't think anything of it when he wasn't showing up for work. He'd pulled that kind of thing before. But after a few days when he wasn't coming home either . . ." She wiped her eyes. "I began to think something might be wrong." Her shoulders shook. "I mean, something *was* wrong, obviously, if what you're telling us is true."

Parked noticed how Trisha made no attempt to console her mother. She didn't put an arm around her, rub her back, pat her knee. Nothing. "And this boss's name?" he asked.

"Cal."

"Right. Of course. And his last name?"

"Rawlins."

"How long was Lester missing before you notified the police?" Geena asked.

"A week? Maybe two? I don't remember exactly, but like I said, it wasn't unusual for him to be gone for a while. He'd usually turn up sooner or later."

Parker checked his notes: a timeline he'd jotted down from the day Lester went missing to when Sharon filed the report. It wasn't much, pretty thin actually. He hadn't shown up for work. No one had seen him around. No witnesses had come forward. There wasn't any video to review, since cameras hadn't been installed at traffic lights or gas stations or other storefronts back in 1986, at least not in their small towns. People had come and gone, went about their daily business without anyone knowing, no cameras or cell phones or GPS tracking devices in their pockets.

"From what I understand," he said, "you waited two weeks before you decided to look for him. Does that sound about right?"

"Yeah, that could be right. It was a long time ago. I guess I just kept hoping he'd walk through the door, you know? I just kept hoping."

"Where did your husband like to hang out?" Geena asked. "Did he have a favorite bar? Restaurant?"

"He liked to drink at a place called Red's. He'd sleep it off there in one of the back rooms. Other times he'd drink at the hotel bar on the corner here in town. I'd find receipts that he'd rented a room."

"Where is this Red's? I'm not familiar with it," Parker said.

"That's because it closed several years ago. I think it's a Chinese restaurant now."

That made their job harder. But Parker knew Cal's Carpets and Flooring was still in business, and so was the hotel. It was a long shot, but it was a place to start. "Okay, so when Lester didn't come home after a few nights, did you go looking for him?"

"No."

"You didn't call anyone or talk to anyone about where he might've gone? Friends? Family?"

"Lester didn't have friends. Most of his family was dead by then. Besides, people around here were saying he skipped out on me. I ignored it for a while. I didn't want to believe it. But eventually, I went to the police."

"What made you finally go to the police?" Geena asked.

"I wanted the gossip to stop. I was embarrassed, okay? I wanted him home so I could prove to everybody that he didn't run out on me." Sharon glanced at Trisha. "I know how that sounds, but it's the truth."

"But why wait a full two weeks to report him missing?" Parker asked. "Seems like an awful long time to wait when someone you love is missing."

"Like I said, it wasn't that unusual for him to be gone on a bender."

He turned to Trisha. "What about you? When was the last time you saw your stepfather?"

"I gave my statement back then. Don't you have a copy?"

"We do," he said. "But now that some time has passed, maybe you remember something you hadn't thought of before."

"If I think of anything, I'll let you know," she said.

"Okay," he said and addressed his next question to Sharon. "We know there were a couple incidents where the local police were called, but you refused to press charges. Would you tell us about what happened?"

"There's nothing to tell," Sharon said.

"Why did you refuse to press charges?" Geena asked in a kind way.

"Because I didn't see what good it would've done," Sharon said.

Trisha turned away from them then, the most movement she'd made since they'd gotten here.

"Did he ever have an altercation with one of the neighbors?" Parker asked. "Perhaps with the ones who had called the police?"

"Not that I knew of," Sharon said.

"Can you think of anyone who would've wanted to hurt him?" Geena asked.

Parker noticed Geena made a point to look at Trisha.

"I can't think of anyone," Trisha said. "What about you, Mom?"

"No," Sharon said. "No one." She blew her nose.

"Okay," Parker said and stood. Geena stood with him.

"If you think of anything else, no matter how insignificant you think it might be, call me. Let me be the one to decide if it's important or not." He handed Sharon another business card in case she'd lost the last one. He passed a card to Trisha. "We'll be in touch."

When they were at the door, Geena slightly ahead of him, Parker turned back, smiled. "I'm curious," he said. "Are either one of you baseball fans?"

CHAPTER THIRTEEN

OCTOBER 1986

Carlyn stomped up the Appalachian Trail. Autumn leaves crackled underneath her feet. Now and again a breeze blew, sending more of the brightly colored leaves raining down on her. Dannie and Trisha were somewhere behind her. Neither one would tell her what had happened with Lester on the side of Dannie's house.

The incline was getting steeper. She pumped her arms to keep her pace. It was late in the day, and the sun was waning. Soon it would be dark. They shouldn't be on the mountain at night.

She stopped walking when she reached what had become their rock ever since that day three years ago when Trisha had pushed them off the porch, running from her stepfather. She turned, crossed her arms, waited for her friends to catch up.

It took a couple of minutes, but they finally made it. Dannie was out of breath. She sat on the rock, wiped her eyes. Trisha wouldn't look at Carlyn.

"Someone tell me what happened," Carlyn said.

Dannie pulled her knees to her chest, buried her head in her arms.

Carlyn looked to Trisha to answer, but she turned away as Scott walked up the trail carrying a six-pack of beer.

"What's he doing here?" Carlyn asked. Why was it whenever the three of them got together, Scott always turned up? She was never alone with her friends anymore, not without him. She hadn't been alone with Trisha in weeks.

"Trisha told me to meet you guys here," Scott said. "Remember, you were there when we talked about it."

Yeah, she remembered all right. But something had changed, something neither of her friends was willing to share with her.

He put the beer on the ground at the base of the oak tree with the *Kilroy was here* carving, then moved to stand next to Trisha. Carlyn knew he'd wanted Trisha ever since that first day he'd seen her at the quarry when they were ten years old. And now he'd finally convinced her to go out with him.

Carlyn reached for a beer, circled the rock where Dannie was sitting. She couldn't be still, not while Scott was pulling Trisha closer to him. A kind of possessiveness tightened Carlyn's chest. She couldn't say why exactly. It wasn't that she didn't like Scott. He was okay for a boy. But Trisha didn't belong to him. She belonged to her. Maybe she belonged to Dannie too. But it was Carlyn who had to fight the urge to drag Trisha away from his wandering hands, his strong forearms that seemed Popeye-like from years of playing on the school's baseball team.

She sipped the beer. No one said anything for what seemed like a long time. Finally, Dannie said, "I don't feel like partying."

"Me either," Carlyn said and tossed the can into the woods, spraying beer onto her arm.

"What did you do that for?" Scott asked.

But Carlyn wasn't paying attention to him. All she knew was that she couldn't stand here and watch the two of them touching each other. It hurt too much. The next thing she knew she was off and running as though a starting gun had gone off inside her head.

"Wait," Dannie called after her.

But her urge to run couldn't wait. Ever since she'd joined the cross-country team at the start of school, she hadn't been able to stop running. She'd first joined thinking it would be a way to fill her time, since Trisha had become preoccupied with Scott, and Dannie had been busy taking care of her mother. Carlyn had thought her own mother would be proud to watch her compete, feel joy in seeing her daughter good at something. But her mother never came to a meet, her shift at the hospital beginning at the same time Carlyn would walk up to the starting line. After a while cross-country was no longer about her friends or her mother.

Carlyn found she'd needed an escape, and running was the one thing that truly freed her from her life at the bottom of the hill. It was while she was running that her thoughts took her to places outside herself, places where doors opened, where dreams flourished, where anything was possible. Running was a place where she could think and sort through problems or simply leave them behind.

Tonight, she wanted nothing more than to run away from her confusing feelings about Trisha, her friends' recent silence.

Her eyes filled with tears. She pushed harder, running faster, stretching her long legs as far as they would go. The crisp air pierced her lungs. She raced down the mountain, the last of the sun's rays shining through the branches of trees, giving off just enough light to see the narrow trail. Somewhere far behind her, she could hear Dannie chasing after her.

She reached her house and dropped onto her porch steps. The muscles in her thighs trembled from the exertion. In another few minutes, Dannie collapsed next to her.

"Why'd you run?" Dannie asked, breathless.

Carlyn wiped her eyes.

Dannie sat up. "What's wrong?"

"Nothing. It doesn't matter," she said. Crying was for babies. Crying was a sign of weakness, but the tears kept coming. "Tell me what happened."

"I'm not sure," Dannie said. "It happened so fast."

"Did Lester do something to you?"

Dannie nodded. "He touched me," she whispered.

Carlyn clutched Dannie's arm. "You have to tell someone."

"No," Dannie said. "No way. Promise you won't say anything," she pleaded. "Maybe I'm wrong. Maybe I just think he did."

"Dannie."

"No, you don't understand," Dannie said. "Please don't say anything."

Whatever was going on inside of Carlyn—her confusion about who she was, how she was feeling—was nothing compared to what was happening to her friends.

"We have to do something," she said.

"No. No, we don't. Promise me," Dannie said. "I'm scared."

She was scared too. She put her arm around Dannie. If Carlyn had learned anything from Trisha, it was that fear was a powerful silencer and that some things were so terrible a person couldn't say them out loud.

Carlyn looked down the street at Trisha's house. The evil was no longer contained inside its walls. It was spreading, its legs crossing over Second Street.

CHAPTER FOURTEEN

Trisha found Dannie on her knees at the side of the bed, her hands in prayer. Boxes were scattered across the floor. Most were empty. The dresser drawers were open, stuffed full of clothes. Dannie had barely made a dent in packing up her things in her old room in her mother's house.

Trisha slipped a mint into her mouth to cover the smell of beer on her breath. "What are you doing?" she asked.

"Praying," Dannie said, keeping her head bowed.

"Right." Like she didn't know that. "Where do you want me to start?"

The clanking of pots and pans traveled up the stairs. Trisha's and Carlyn's mothers were busy emptying the cabinets in the kitchen. Carlyn was out searching for more boxes. She hadn't said more than two words to Trisha since the other day when they'd cleaned the dirty dishes and tidied up before the real packing began. Trisha had no way of knowing if Dannie had told Carlyn about having seen Trisha's bruised ribs.

Dannie hoisted herself up from the floor. She'd gotten rounder over the years, her full cheeks smoothing out the wrinkles by her eyes: the one positive of being middle aged and overweight.

"Did you hit the lottery or something?" Dannie motioned to Trisha's cashmere sweater, this one powder blue.

"No," she said.

If Dannie were waiting for some kind of explanation, she wasn't going to get one. What could Trisha have said? Sure, at first she'd loved the glamorous clothes Sid had bought her, some custom made, the slinky silk dresses, fur for around her neck on chilly desert nights, $400 red-bottomed shoes. But it didn't take long until she loathed it, loathed *him*, his hands like snakes slithering up and down her body, the silk burning like fire on her skin, her toes broken and bloody, crushed in the points of three-inch heels.

"Okay," Dannie said. "Then throw this on." She tossed a flannel shirt to her. "Everything in this house is old and dusty. I don't want you to ruin something so pretty."

Trisha tugged the flannel on over the sweater. She didn't care whether her shirt got dirty, but it seemed important to Dannie, since this was the second time she'd asked her to cover up.

"Look at this," Dannie said and passed a small notebook to her. It was a "slam book," where you'd write your name at the top of the page, and your classmates would write one word about you underneath. "What possessed us to expose ourselves to such cruelty?"

Trisha shrugged, stopped on the page with Jeff's name, the boy who had given Dannie a titty twister at the quarry. *Creep. A-hole. Dickwad.* She continued flipping through the notebook looking for Scott's name. Sometimes when she was sober long enough to remember who she was, where she came from, she'd think of him, his dark hair glistening under the bright sun, the sweat clinging to his tanned chest. She hadn't forgotten the way he'd looked at her, the innocence and longing in his eyes. He'd believed she'd been worthy of love. No man had ever looked at her that way again. But what Scott hadn't known was that she'd already been damaged by then. She'd already been broken beyond repair before she'd ever hit puberty.

Dannie pulled clothes out of the dresser drawers and shoved them in garbage bags, not bothering to sort them. Trisha was about to close the slam book, never finding Scott's page, but stopped when she found her own name. *Whore. Bitch. Tramp. Perfect.* She recognized the handwriting in the last comment. Carlyn's voice carried up the stairs. She was back with more boxes.

Trisha closed the slam book and tossed it in the trash.

For the next hour, they filled garbage bags with clothes, old notebooks, and knickknacks. Items Dannie had decided to keep—a Magic 8 Ball and Rubik's Cube for her girls, her high school diploma, a crucifix hanging on the wall by her bed—were put in a separate box and set aside.

Once everything in Dannie's old room was packed away, the piles organized into donations, keepsakes, trash, they headed to Evelyn's bedroom. Trisha walked in first, familiar with the layout of the house, the master bedroom an exact replica of her own mother's room except that Evelyn's dresser was pushed into the far corner rather than up against the center of the wall. The smell of greasy hair and oily skin—what Trisha thought of as Evelyn's smell—permeated the air. She resisted the urge to open a window. It was cold outside. They'd gotten six inches of snow overnight. Trisha hadn't seen that much snow since she'd left Pennsylvania. They'd get the occasional dusting in Vegas, only to have it turn into a "rain event." Since when was weather considered an event? But late last night when the sky rained white, she'd rushed into the street, head tilted, arms spread wide. She reveled in the taste and feel of snowflakes on her lips and eyelashes, in her hair, soaking her bare feet. She'd been drunk. Her mother had watched her from the opened door in silence.

She pulled the curtains aside to look at the snow-covered trees: one more thing she'd taken for granted when she'd lived here. Trees, *real* trees in her mind, were ones that had bare branches in winter and brightly colored leaves in autumn, unlike the palm trees on the Strip, which stayed the same year-round. "I missed the snow, the changing seasons," she said and turned to find Dannie standing in the doorway, crying in her hands.

Trisha let the curtain fall.

"I miss her," Dannie said.

Trisha nodded.

"It just hurts so much," Dannie said.

Dannie had a way of bringing out Trisha's softer side. Even now, her tears penetrated Trisha's hardened heart.

"I didn't expect it to hurt so much," Dannie said.

Trisha didn't know that kind of love and loss, but she found herself reaching for Dannie. "Come here." She pulled her onto the bed, lay down next to her. Evelyn's scent on the sheets lingered between them. She forced herself not to move her arm out from under Dannie's elbow. She had to tell herself Dannie wouldn't lash out, strike her. It was okay to be close to another person, to lie next to them and not be afraid. "I suck at this kind of stuff, you know," she said.

Dannie smiled. "I know," she said. "I remember."

"Do you? Do you remember how we used to be?"

"I remember how you loved me once and stood up for me at a time in my life when I was most vulnerable," Dannie said.

Trisha opened her mouth to agree but then closed it. Her chest filled with anger, a certain rage. *Then why did you stop being my friend? Why did you stop loving me?*

She wanted to scream, to accuse Dannie of leaving her when she'd needed her the most. But it wasn't the time or place to unleash what was inside of her. It didn't serve her bigger purpose, her reason for being here in the first place. Her voice was steady, calm, when she said, "It's going to take some time to get through this." She waved her hand around the room. "And it's going to take some time to get through this too." She pointed to her chest, her heart.

Dannie's tears dribbled down the side of her face and onto the pillow.

"Close your eyes," Trisha instructed. "Close your eyes and leave this place for a while. Take a break from the pain. I'll be here when you're ready to come back."

Dannie nodded, closed her eyes. "You don't suck at this at all," she said.

⁊

Trisha lay on the bed next to Dannie, listened to the slow breathing of her sleep. She picked at her skin on her wrist, her flesh crawling with the longing for a drink. She'd lost track of time. The chatter from downstairs had been intermittent, the buzz of busyness and nothing more.

Sometime later Dannie rubbed her eyes, yawned. "I must've dozed off," she said, turned to look at Trisha.

"You did."

"For how long?"

"I don't know. Does it matter?"

"I wanted to be home when the girls got home from school." Dannie pulled her phone from her pocket.

Checking the time? Text messages from her kids? Her husband? Trisha could only guess. "How old are they?" she asked.

Dannie shoved the phone back in her pocket. "Marie is fifteen, and Jenny is seventeen. Jenny wants to go to college in Virginia next fall. I can't believe she'll be leaving. It's going to be so weird not having her home. They're my whole world, you know? I stayed home with them since they were babies. I loved every minute of it. Well, not *every* minute. But I'm happy being at home. I wanted to give them a better life than what our mothers were able to give us."

"And did you?"

"Give them a better life? I think so. I mean, yeah, I did."

"That's great, Dannie. It is," she said and found she meant it. "Let me ask you something. Would you do anything for your girls? Anything at all?"

"Of course. You know I would," Dannie said.

"I'm happy to hear you say that."

"Why? What are you getting at?"

"I'm not getting at anything."

"Yes, you are."

"No, really, I'm not," she said. "It just makes me glad you're a good mom. I always thought you would be."

"There you are," Carlyn said and entered the room.

Dannie sat up, smoothed her shirt, swung her legs off the bed, put her back to Trisha.

"The kitchen's finished. We left some dishes on the counter for you to go through. There might be a few things you want to keep," Carlyn said.

"Sure. Okay." Dannie got up.

Trisha pulled herself up, too, straightened the front of the flannel shirt that hung to her knees.

"I better get to it," Dannie said and looked over her shoulder at Trisha before walking out of the room.

"What's going on?" Carlyn crossed her arms. "What were you two doing?"

"Why?" Trisha leaned in close, breathed in Carlyn's familiar scent. "Jealous?"

CHAPTER FIFTEEN

OCTOBER 1986

Trisha watched Carlyn run down the trail through the woods. Dannie took off after her, slow and clumsy in Dannie's way of running, which wasn't really running at all but something more like a labored jog.

Scott moved behind her, slipped his arms around her waist, rested his chin on the top of her shoulder. "Do you want to go after your friends?" he asked.

He was giving her an out if she wanted one. She'd convinced herself the last few weeks that he wasn't her boyfriend. She'd insisted on not calling him that. She didn't want a boyfriend, never wanted a boyfriend. But he was good to her. And now, he was being so considerate of her feelings. A part of her loved him for it and hated him for it too.

"No, it's fine," she said. Her friends were going to talk. Dannie was going to tell Carlyn what had happened with Lester. And Trisha didn't want to be there. They'd have questions Trisha was too afraid to answer. And what if they blamed her? Was it her fault for allowing him to get close to her friend?

Scott grabbed a beer from the six-pack and took Trisha's hand. She let him lead her to an area away from the rock where the ground was flat and covered in a blanket of leaves. They sat, and the dampness of the earth bled through her jeans onto her bottom and the back of her legs. He didn't say anything. He didn't need to. She knew what he wanted from her, what all boys wanted from her.

Was this all she was worth?

They both kept their eyes straight ahead, stared into the woods, the shadows eating the light from the ground as the sun set. The cool air sent goose bumps up and down her arms.

"You know I like you, right?" he asked.

"Yeah, I know." She turned to look at him.

He turned to look at her, too, and before she thought about what she was doing, she let him kiss her. His lips were soft and moist, his tongue laced with beer. She didn't care for the bitterness of it, but her own mouth tasted the same.

They continued kissing, lying back on the leaves, the earth now cool on her back as well as her legs. Scott rolled on top of her, his hands fumbling under her shirt, pushing her bra aside. She came alive under his touch, rising up to meet his palm. She shouldn't like it as much as she did. It wasn't right. Dirty. *She* was dirty. A "flirty, dirty girl," Lester had called her.

Scott pressed his hips against her.

"Stop," she said.

"What?" He continued kissing her, his hands roaming her body.

"I said stop!" she yelled and pushed him away.

He sprang off her, his hands raised as though she were holding him at gunpoint. "I'm sorry. I didn't mean to push you. I didn't mean to do anything you didn't want to do." He kept babbling, apologizing over and over again. "I didn't mean it. I'm sorry."

"Shut up," she said and yanked her shirt down. "Just shut up, Scott!" She crossed her arms, covered her chest; her twisted bra cut into her armpit. She wasn't mad at Scott. He didn't do anything wrong. She wanted to kiss him. She wanted him to touch her. But she couldn't let him. What was wrong with her?

He knelt in front of her, rested his hand on her forearm. "I didn't mean to hurt you."

She wiped her nose. "You didn't hurt me, okay? It's not you."

"Then what is it?" he asked.

"It's just . . . I'm not . . . I'm not . . ." How could she explain it? She was ruined, damaged goods. "Just forget it."

"I don't want to forget it. Tell me, Trisha. You can tell me anything. I won't judge you."

"You don't get it, do you?" She rocked, pressed her knees tightly to her chest. "You just don't get it."

"Get what?" he asked, sounding hurt. "What don't I get? Talk to me."

She didn't answer.

"What is it?" He put his hand on her shoulder, coming closer; he slid his arm around her.

"I can't, okay. I can't do it with you."

"It's okay. I understand. We don't have to do anything."

She shook her head. He didn't get it. He didn't get it at all. "Stop being so nice to me," she said.

He stared at her, the concern on his face clear in the waning light. "What did he do to you?" he asked. When she wouldn't answer him, he pulled her close, and in a soft voice he whispered, "I swear I'll kill him if he ever puts his hands on you again."

CHAPTER SIXTEEN

Sharon Haines smoked. Parker had smelled cigarettes on her breath, in the air, on the furniture's upholstery. It was embedded in the walls, the floors, the nuts and bolts of her house. He'd bet she'd been a smoker most of her life. She hadn't smoked in front of him, but she'd carried a pack of cigarettes in the breast pocket of her flannel shirt. The ashtray had been hidden in another room, possibly the kitchen. He had no idea what brand of cigarettes she smoked or what kind of lighter she used. It was the lighter he was particularly interested in. She could carry a personalized lighter, a Zippo maybe, or she could use the disposable kind, like a Bic.

Sharon was still on his mind when he pulled into the parking lot of the field station. The brick building squatted in the middle of a wide-open grass-covered lot. Anyone could see the comings and goings of the officers and visitors. It left Parker with an uneasy feeling of being exposed, a walking target without cover. He parked next to the building. What they needed were a few large trees to offer some protection, provide some shade in the summer months. He entered through the side door. The interior was a smattering of cubicles, old desks covered with paperwork, computers. The interview rooms were on the opposite side. The lobby was in the front of the building, where Sharmaine held her own kind of court. The sergeant's office was in the corner, the blinds closed. Geena walked in behind him.

After talking with Sharon and her daughter, Parker and Geena had gone door-to-door up and down Second Street, looking for neighbors who might've remembered Lester. A few old-timers were still around. The ones they'd talked to said Lester had kept to himself mostly. A couple of them had brought up the fact that he'd fought with his wife, had probably drunk too much, but it had been none of their business. Yet, they'd mentioned it.

Lester's other neighbors, including Mrs. Sherwood, who had lived on the other side of the semiattached house, were deceased. Others had moved away, no forwarding address. A bunch of new families lived on the street now, moved in several years after Lester had disappeared.

"I guess this desk is as good as any," Geena said and took off her jacket, sat in the chair at one of the empty cubicles, her sidearm jutting from her hip.

"It's not so bad," he said and picked up the coffeepot, looked at the sludge on the bottom. "Although you'll want to bring in your own coffee, if you drink it."

"Noted," she said. "What's next?" she asked.

"I want to stop by the place where Lester was last employed, check it out, see if anybody is still around."

"Okay. What are your thoughts on the mother-daughter duo?"

"Something doesn't add up." He hadn't worked out what exactly.

"That was my feeling too," she said.

He stopped at his desk, pushed some paperwork around, checked for messages. "I think we should go back and have a chat with Linda Walsh." Her name was listed as someone the police had talked to, but she hadn't been home on their first pass through the neighborhood.

"We can try her on the way back, if there's time." Geena grabbed her jacket. She knocked on their sergeant's window now that the blinds were open. She poked her head in his office, checked in, let him know she was there, and they were on their way to Easton to check out Cal's Carpets and Flooring.

❧

They weren't two miles from the station when Geena turned her head away from Parker, looked out the passenger-side window. "You know why you got the cold woods, don't you?"

"Cold woods?"

"That's what I'm calling the case," she said. "Because we had to sit in the freezing-cold woods, all because Sayres is ticked at you."

"So you named it after me?" When would he get to name a case? His last one had been named "river bodies" before he'd taken it over.

She shrugged. "But honestly," she said. "You got this one because the body wasn't fresh."

"What's that supposed to mean?"

"I hear stuff. Sometimes the guys at headquarters ignore me, being the only woman, and they don't always include me in their conversations. But it doesn't mean I don't overhear everything they're saying."

"What did you hear?"

"They're concerned about how you're coping."

"Who's 'they'? The lieutenant? You?"

Geena shrugged. "This job's not easy. And seeing somebody blow their brains out," she said. "That's not easy."

"I'm fine," he said, not wanting to discuss it. His father had asked him a similar question. *How are you doing, son?* He'd wanted Parker to leave the motorcycle gang alone. When Parker had been a kid, the gang members had shown up at his house, banged on the door of his father's medical practice with knife wounds, busted hands, and broken bones. His father had treated them, but he'd also been afraid of them. Parker had thought if he solved the case against the same gang members, his father would've been proud of him, but instead, he'd gotten the impression he'd somehow disappointed him.

Geena must've picked up on Parker's reluctance to talk about it, because she was quiet the rest of the ride to Easton. The radio crackled with static. She checked her phone. Salt and cinders kicked up from the tires, melting the snow that had covered the roadways overnight. Parker pulled into the entrance of a strip mall and what was the new location for Cal's Carpets and Flooring.

From what Parker had gathered online, Cal's store had moved three times since Lester had worked there. It was a miracle the family business had survived at all. Most small businesses in the area had struggled once online shopping and supersize megastores began luring customers away with their promise of lower costs and faster deliveries. But the bigger stores and their so-called conveniences lacked a personal touch: the care and attention the old mom-and-pop shops had provided. Or that was Parker's take on it anyway.

The parking lot was mostly empty. Parker pulled into the closest space near the door of the carpet store. Maybe the snow had kept people away. The temperature was close to freezing. A bell clanged when they stepped inside, announcing their arrival, but no one was on the showroom floor to greet them. A male's voice came from the back of the building. They headed in the general direction, Geena in the lead.

They found a guy with wire-rim glasses on the phone behind a cheap metal desk you could pick up at any office-supply store. He held up his pointer finger, signaling them to wait. He was younger than Parker had expected. He'd hoped for someone much older, someone who'd remember Lester.

The guy hung up the phone. "How can I help you?" He looked back and forth between them. His gaze flickered back to Geena. He looked a little nervous: maybe it was her height, or quite possibly her striking good looks.

Parker opened his mouth to speak, but Geena beat him to it.

"I'm Detective Brassard, and this is my partner, Detective Reed."

The guy looked to Parker. "Is there a problem?"

"We're looking for the owner, Cal Rawlins," Parker said. He'd looked Cal up on the internet. Nothing online had indicated the old man had passed. As far as he could tell, the business was still owned and operated by Cal.

"I'm Eric, his son. What's this about?" he asked Parker, clearly avoiding looking Geena's way again.

"We have some questions about a former employee of his. You were probably just a kid around the time."

"Oh," he said. "Okay. He's in the back. If you give me a moment, I'll go and get him. He doesn't get around as good as he used to."

Eric disappeared behind the closed door that apparently led to the back office.

"Did you notice how he completely ignored me and directed his questions at you?" Geena asked. "Why do men do that, just assume you're in charge because you're a man?"

"Personally, I think it's because he's intimidated by you." Parker glanced around the desk—business cards, order forms, calendar, stapler, credit card machine, computer, phone—nothing out of the ordinary.

"And why do you think that?" she asked.

"I don't know. Some guys are intimidated by a woman in a position of power." He purposely left out the part that some guys might also be intimidated by a very attractive woman in a position of power. He didn't want her to take it the wrong way when, in his mind, it was a simple fact, nothing more.

She snorted. "Jerk-off."

"I didn't say I was one of them."

"So defensive." She smiled, and he realized she was kidding with him. Then she poked around the aisles, looked through carpet samples, wandered to the back of the store, where the warehouse was located.

When she returned, she motioned to two cameras mounted on opposite walls.

The office door opened. Cal shuffled toward them gripping a cane. The store's name was stitched on the pocket of his faded blue shirt. His khakis frayed at the cuffs. "What can I do for you?" he asked. Eric came to stand by his father's side.

"We have a few questions for you about a former employee, a Lester Haines," Parker said.

Cal nodded. "I remember him. Haven't seen him in years. I heard he went missing."

"Tell me what you remember about him," Parker said.

"I fired him sometime in December. It must've been in '86. I can't remember when exactly, but I remember we were busy. Folks like to remodel before the holiday. If I recall correctly, he didn't show up for work around that time for over a week. How was I supposed to know something happened to him? I had a business to run."

"No one is accusing you of anything, sir," Geena said.

"Do you recall the last time you saw Lester?" Parker asked.

"No, I can't say I do," Cal said.

"You never had a falling out? Argued with him about not showing up for work?" Parker asked.

"No, not that I recall. He worked in the back warehouse loading trucks and taking care of inventory. I don't think he liked the work, though. He wanted to be on the floor selling. But I couldn't have him talking with customers with alcohol on his breath. Lester liked to drink. Things were different back then. You gave people second chances. When he was here, and he was sober, he worked hard. I cut him a break when I could."

"Did he ever argue with a customer? Or any of his coworkers?" Parker asked.

The old man leaned heavily on his cane. "Lester was an odd duck. Did he get along with the other guys? Not really. Mostly, he kept to himself. I suppose when everything was said and done, it was just easier on everyone at the time to let him go."

"Any idea where he went when he didn't show up for work? Who he might've gone out with?"

"Like I said, he kept to himself. He wasn't the kind of guy who'd hang around after work and shoot the shit."

Geena made a point to look at Eric when she spoke, a fact that amused Parker. "Can we get a list of the employees' names who had worked with Lester?" she asked.

Cal answered for Eric. "I remember some of their names, but not all of them."

"Did you keep records?" Geena asked, again directing her question to Eric.

"Yes," Eric said. "It'll take some time to dig through the old files. Nothing was computerized back then."

"Can you send them to us? Thanks. What about these cameras?" Geena asked and pointed to the two she'd spied earlier. "When were these installed?"

"About five years ago," Eric said. "Some of the other stores in the strip suggested we get them. I guess there were some problems before we set up shop here."

"Did you have cameras when Lester worked for you?" she asked.

"We were in a different location then. Security was pretty lax in the eighties." Eric looked to his father.

"No cameras back then," Cal said.

"Okay," Geena said and handed Eric her card. "If you can send those names to me by the end of the day, I'd appreciate it. Mr. Rawlins, thanks for your time."

"I have one more question," Parker said. "Mr. Rawlins, did your employees happen to play on a baseball team? I know a lot of businesses have teams that play in local leagues."

"No. We didn't have any team."

"Okay, thanks again for your time."

Geena waited until they were out in the parking lot, getting into the cruiser, when she asked, "Baseball team, huh?"

"Just trying to figure out who might've been walking around carrying an aluminum baseball bat."

CHAPTER SEVENTEEN

Trisha slipped on the one jacket she'd packed, another designer label, the thin leather meant for desert nights, not Pennsylvania winters. But it was the closest thing she had to outerwear. She shoved a large wad of twenty-dollar bills into her jeans pocket along with her photo ID that she'd used to get into VIP rooms at the casinos. Next, she wrote down Sid Whitehouse's name on a scrap of paper and stuck that in her pocket too. Her ID would help the handsome young detective identify her body if she happened to turn up dead alongside the road; the scrap of paper with Sid's name on it would hand him the name of her killer.

Sid was never far from her mind. He was with her, always, his presence lurking in the shadows around every corner, hiding between her cracked, bruised ribs, a reminder with every breath she took. And yet there was a small part of her, a *sick* part, that ached to see him, touch and hold him. No matter how bad things had gotten between them, when the fighting was over, he would pick her up, clean her off, put her in that big fancy bed of his so that she could rest her battered head.

She often wondered why she'd put up with it. Maybe it was a Stockholm syndrome kind of thing, where she'd developed feelings for her captor. She didn't know. The best she could come up with was that a part of her believed she deserved to be punished, the flirty, dirty girl who had needed attention, good or bad, right or wrong. It was all she'd ever known. *Don't leave me,* her younger self had begged Sid. *Don't forget about me.*

It was an awful thing she'd gotten used to, the very thing her younger self had sworn she'd never let happen, and yet, here she was.

She stepped onto the porch to find her mother wrapped in a puffy winter coat, a cigarette in one hand, a can of beer in the other, a knit hat on her head.

"Isn't it kind of cold to be sitting outside?"

"Not for me it isn't," her mother said. "Besides, look at that moon. Evelyn would've loved that moon."

Trisha looked at the night sky, the moon on center stage. The stars sparkled along with the neighbors' twinkling Christmas lights. Her mother used to wrap white lights around the front porch posts and hang an evergreen wreath on the door. But her mother hadn't put up holiday decorations yet. Trisha would like her to, but she wouldn't ask her. She wouldn't ask for anything other than a roof over her head.

Two houses down, Carlyn and her mother stepped outside. They headed in their direction. Trisha was surprised to see them together. Linda sat in the chair next to Trisha's mother. She plucked a can from the six-pack that lay on the ground between them, a routine their mothers must've established in Trisha's absence. Carlyn stood on the sidewalk, stared up at Trisha, hands shoved deep inside her winter coat.

Trisha walked down the three steps and stood in front of her, a little closer than what convention dictated. "I hear the new owners of the hotel bar classed it up with linen napkins and tablecloths. I thought I'd check it out. Do you want to join me?"

"Okay," Carlyn said.

They walked single file, Trisha in the lead, the shoveled path on the sidewalk narrow and icy in spots. Their mothers watched them go without a word. They turned the corner at the end of the block, and Trisha slipped, her high heel catching a patch of black ice. Carlyn caught her with sturdy arms. Her muscled thighs kept them upright.

Trisha laughed, relieved. Imagined the pain in her ribs if she'd gone down. As it turned out, Carlyn had squeezed Trisha's waist, but not hard enough to make her wince. They separated.

"Your shoes are ridiculous," Carlyn said.

"Four hundred dollars' worth of outrageousness."

Carlyn shook her head. "Here," she said and pulled off her gloves. "Put these on. You must be freezing." She handed them to her.

"Thanks." Trisha took the gloves, tentatively, trying to figure out what Carlyn was up to: whether she was just being kind or whether she had some other motive. But Carlyn's kindness wasn't going to break Trisha down, so she did the only thing left and slipped the gloves on, the insides soft and furry and warm.

They continued walking at a slow pace for another two blocks. Trisha teetered in heels, Carlyn prepared to catch her, until they reached the bar on the corner.

Carlyn pulled the door open. "After you," she said.

The warm air smothered Trisha's face the moment she stepped inside. The smell of fried food wafted from the kitchen. The sparse crowd at the bar lifted their heads to see who had walked in but quickly turned away from the cold Trisha and Carlyn had carried in with them.

Trisha poked her head into the dining room. The lights were turned low. Candles flickered on top of white tablecloths. A Christmas tree was on display front and center. She followed Carlyn to the far end of the bar, away from the other customers.

They sat on stools. The bartender wiped down a splash of beer, then flipped the towel onto his shoulder. "What can I get you?" he asked, smoothing his goatee. Tattoos covered his arms like sleeves.

"Vodka on the rocks," Trisha said. "From the top shelf." She pulled off the gloves and dropped them next to Carlyn.

"Ketel One okay?" he asked.

She nodded. It was as top shelf as she was going to get here. The bartender looked to Carlyn.

"I'll have a glass of merlot."

They waited to speak until their drinks were in front of them. Carlyn offered a toast. "To old friends," she said.

"To old friends," Trisha said and winked.

Carlyn smiled, lifted her glass to her full lips, which were the softest shade of pink. Her hair was straight, cut in a bob that framed her face nicely. She'd aged well, a few lines by her eyes and mouth, but overall, Carlyn looked good in her black jeans and turtleneck sweater.

Trisha finished her drink and signaled the bartender for another. She expected Carlyn to tell her that she ought to slow down. She was prepared to lash out, tell her to mind her own business, when Carlyn asked, "So what have you been up to?"

Carlyn was full of surprises tonight.

"Not much. You?" she asked.

"Nothing changes around here—you know that," Carlyn said.

Trisha sensed a certain strength in Carlyn, a self-assuredness she'd lacked when they were kids. She seemed more confident, comfortable with herself. "Something must've changed. There's something different about you," she said.

"Time has a way of doing that to you," Carlyn said. "I work with kids who have a lot of problems. It tends to put your own life in perspective."

"What kinds of problems?"

"Most are behavioral. I can't talk about any of my cases specifically, but I help kids and their families work through their negative behavior, the kind that escalates above and beyond what is considered normal. Although I'm not a fan of the word *normal*, but don't get me started."

"You work with violent kids?"

"Sometimes, yes."

So Carlyn helped troubled kids. Well, wasn't that wonderful. But she'd never bothered to help her *best friend*. That was what they had been back then. It should've meant something, but obviously it hadn't.

Carlyn had given up on her, abandoned her. Trisha tossed back the rest of the drink and waved to the bartender. "Keep them coming," she said. The alcohol settled in her stomach, a hot, prickly comfort. Soon it would cloud her thoughts, numb the anger piling up in the back of her throat until it was nothing more than a dull taste in her mouth.

The bartender set another drink down in front of her. She wrapped her hand around the glass and brought it to her lips. It wouldn't be long now.

"I was surprised to see you with your mother tonight," Trisha said. "I didn't think the two of you got along."

"I think we've reached a place of understanding," Carlyn said. "It's not perfect, but we're trying."

"Good for you." Trisha's fingers and toes tingled. Soon she would feel nothing, zip, zilch, where not even Carlyn's wonderful life would be able to touch her.

❧

Trisha put down one drink after another. Carlyn sat quietly, sipping her single glass of wine, her silent disapproval thrashing in the space between them. Trisha didn't know how long they'd sat there, or how many drinks she'd had. She had to pee. Where the hell was the bathroom anyway? She tried to stand and knocked over the barstool. She stumbled. Carlyn caught her before she fell to the floor. The bartender yelled, refused to serve her, cut her off.

"Stupid shit!" she hollered back. Did he think she was an amateur? This wasn't her first rodeo.

"I'm going to have to ask you to leave," the bartender said.

Carlyn's hands were clasped around Trisha's upper arms, holding her up. "Don't touch me," she said and pushed Carlyn away. She tripped. Carlyn caught her again.

"Get her out of here," the bartender said.

"I have to pee. Can I at least fucking pee first?" she shouted at him.

"Get out," he said.

"Come on." Carlyn squeezed Trisha's arm, pulled her across the room and out the door.

The bitter cold hit her face, but she barely registered it. That was what was so great about being drunk. You just didn't care about things like below-freezing temperatures. She pushed Carlyn off her. Carlyn raised her arms and stepped back to prove she wasn't touching her anymore.

"Where were you? When I needed you, where were you?" Trisha hollered, staggered toward her. "You were supposed to be my friend." She hit Carlyn's shoulder. "We were fucking friends!" She shoved her, but Carlyn was strong, and her treaded snow boots kept her from slipping on the icy walk and toppling over. Trisha swung her arm to land another blow, but the ice beneath her stupid three-inch heels sent her to the ground. Her hip smacked the cold pavement. A warm gush spread between her legs, soaked her jeans. Her ribs ached, but the pain was dulled from the cushion provided by the alcohol. She pushed herself up to her hands and knees.

"Let me help you." Carlyn reached down. Trisha batted Carlyn's hand away. A siren chirped, and a police cruiser pulled alongside them.

"That's just great," Trisha said, falling to her butt. The bartender must've called the cops. She looked down at her jeans, where they were torn at the knee. Cinder and salt stuck to the scrape on her skin.

She was surprised when Scott got out of the car. He was taller than she remembered. His once-dark hair was now more salt and pepper. She was too drunk to feel ashamed, too fucked up to care that she was sitting on the cold sidewalk in her own urine.

"What's the problem here?" he asked.

"Ask her," she spat and pointed in the general direction of Carlyn. There were three of her.

The bartender appeared. Scott talked with him briefly before he disappeared back inside. The street was mostly dark, definitely blurry. Circles of light from the lamppost floated in front of her eyes. She could lie down. Here was as good a place as any. Scott's voice jolted her upright.

"Get in the front seat," he said to Carlyn. Then he stood behind Trisha and slipped his hands underneath her armpits, pulled her up. He put her in the back seat of the cruiser, his hand on her head so she wouldn't bump it when she crawled in.

She stuck to the vinyl seat, pulled at her wet jeans, tried to get them to stop clinging to the back of her legs, but her hands were thick and clumsy.

Scott talked to Carlyn, clearly avoiding having to talk with Trisha in the back seat. He kept his eyes on the road ahead. "There's a kid I'm concerned about," he said to Carlyn. "He's five. I wonder if you could check in on him for me." For the first time since they got in the car, he glanced in the rearview mirror at Trisha. She rolled her eyes.

He continued. "His mother is worried about him. He's been getting into some trouble. He brought a plastic gun to school. I thought maybe you could give her a call. Maybe you could help sort him out."

"Sure, send me the information. I'll contact the school and see if anyone has been assigned to him. If not, I'll gladly see him."

"Thanks, Carlyn. I appreciate it." He shot another glance at Trisha. She refused to look at him and stared out the passenger-side window, seeing her own reflection, the dark circles under her eyes, her tangled hair.

"You're a good copper, Scott," Carlyn said. Trisha got the impression they'd worked together in the past. She didn't know how she felt about it. Angry. Yeah, definitely angry.

"I try," he said. Was he smiling? He was acting all cozy with Carlyn. Was he trying to get Trisha jealous? Well, fuck him. He couldn't hurt her anymore. Nothing could. You had to have feelings to get hurt, and other than anger, Trisha hadn't had those in a long time.

Scott double-parked in front of Trisha's mother's house. Trisha tried to open the door, but it was locked. She sat with her arms tightly folded like a sulking teenager. Carlyn got out of the car with Scott. They exchanged a few more words before Carlyn headed in the direction of Linda's house. She didn't go inside but got into her car. She wasn't going to stick around, obviously. Well, fuck her too.

Scott helped Trisha out of the cruiser and walked her to the front door. "You're lucky he didn't press charges," he said. "Or you could be sleeping it off in a cell."

Carlyn's gloves. Trisha had left them on the bar. She had to go back for them. She wouldn't be in debt to Carlyn for anything, especially stupid gloves. She turned around, but Scott grabbed her arm before she could take one step off the porch. *God*, she could feel his heat through her thin leather jacket. It sent a shock wave through her. How was that possible? Was the alcohol already wearing off?

"Where do you think you're going?" he asked.

"Back to the bar."

"Not tonight you're not. In you go." He opened the door, which her mother hadn't locked. He gently pushed her inside. "Good to see you, Trisha," he called as he made his way back to his cruiser.

She looked at her hands to find she had been wearing the gloves the whole time.

CHAPTER EIGHTEEN

NOVEMBER 1986

Trisha found her mother unconscious at the bottom of the stairs.

"Mom." She shook her mother's shoulder. "Come on, Mom, wake up." She bent over her, smelled the cigarette smoke in her hair, the alcohol on her skin. She put her ear close to her mother's mouth, listened, heard breathing. She slipped her hand behind her mother's back, tried to hoist her up. Her head rolled to the side. There was a welt on her cheek, a black-and-blue mark on her neck.

Trisha heard a noise, what sounded like a floorboard creaking. She scrambled to her feet. She listened hard for something to alert her that Lester was still in the house. She didn't hear it again. Maybe it was just the house settling or the wind blowing outside.

In the weeks that followed Dannie's brush with Lester, he'd become agitated, his mood sour, as though even he knew he'd gone too far. It had been clear to Trisha that it had been a ruse from the start. He'd had no intention of repairing the damaged downspout or roof.

And now he'd put his hands on her mother's throat.

"Hang on, Mom," Trisha said, stepping over her to check that Lester wasn't in any of the rooms downstairs.

He wasn't.

She stepped over her mother again, then raced up the steps, down the hallway to the master bedroom. She didn't know what she was going to do if she found him. The bed was empty. She checked the other rooms upstairs. Empty. She ran back down the steps.

They were alone.

"Don't move," she said, having no idea if her mother could hear her or not. "I'm going to get help."

Trisha burst out the front door. The car Lester and her mother shared was gone. She sprinted down the sidewalk to Carlyn's house. She banged on the door.

Carlyn pulled it open. She was dressed in her winter coat. Her backpack hung off her left shoulder. "What's wrong?" she asked.

"Where's your mom?" Trisha pushed past her. "Mrs. Walsh?"

"She's upstairs sleeping," Carlyn said, chasing after Trisha as she darted for the stairs.

Trisha ran into the bedroom. "Mrs. Walsh," she said and stood next to the bed, shook Mrs. Walsh's shoulder like she'd done moments ago with her own mother. "Mrs. Walsh, wake up. Please."

Mrs. Walsh rolled over, looked up at Trisha's face. "What is it?"

Carlyn stood in the doorway, not making a sound.

"It's my mom," Trisha said. "She needs help."

Mrs. Walsh threw off the covers. "What happened?" She pulled on a pair of jeans and tugged on a sweatshirt over her pajama top.

"I'm not sure. I was in the bathroom. I heard yelling, a thump. And now she's on the floor at the bottom of the stairs. She's not getting up."

They rushed out of the room and down the steps. Mrs. Walsh called over her shoulder, "Carlyn, get to the bus. You're going to be late for school."

"I want to help."

Mrs. Walsh stopped in the living room, faced her daughter. "There's nothing you can do, and the last thing I need is for the school to get on my case for you skipping. Now go." She nudged Carlyn out the door.

Dannie was standing on the sidewalk in front of the house. "What's going on?" she asked.

"Get to school. Both of you," Mrs. Walsh said. "Trisha, come with me."

"Come on." Carlyn took Dannie by the arm, and they headed down the block toward the buses.

Trisha chased after Mrs. Walsh, pausing long enough to look back at her friends one more time before rushing through the door of her house.

Mrs. Walsh knelt next to Trisha's mother in the small space between the last step and the wall. "Sharon, can you hear me?" she asked.

Trisha's mother opened her eyes. She looked at Mrs. Walsh, then Trisha. She touched her neck where it was bruised.

"Don't move," Mrs. Walsh said. "Did you fall down the stairs?" she asked.

"No," she said and tried to pull herself up.

"You shouldn't move," Mrs. Walsh said.

"I didn't fall," she said. "I must've blacked out." She continued to pull herself up.

Mrs. Walsh helped her, leaned her against the wall for support. "Trisha, could you get your mom a glass of water, please?"

Trisha did as she was told.

"Maybe you should go to the hospital," Mrs. Walsh said. "Just to get checked out."

"I can't afford it."

Trisha returned with the glass of water.

Mrs. Walsh inspected the welt on Trisha's mother's cheek. "It doesn't look too bad. Some ice should take care of the swelling," she said. She moved Trisha's mother's head to the side, drew in a shaky breath when she saw the finger mark on her neck. Then she touched the bruised skin on her shoulder. She lifted up her arm. There were more bruises on her bicep where Lester had no doubt grabbed her. "This has to stop. This can't continue. You can't stay here any longer." She took the glass of water from Trisha, handed it to Trisha's mother.

Her mother didn't respond right away, took a sip of water. Then she said, "Where am I supposed to go? I don't have the money to go nowhere. And the cops . . ." She paused. "What good's it going to do if he sits in jail for a couple nights? Where's he going to go when he gets out? Right back here, that's where."

"What about a restraining order?" Mrs. Walsh asked.

"You think the cops are going to come around and check he isn't here? A piece of paper isn't going to protect me."

And there was the truth of it. Her mother was stuck here in this house with him. And that meant Trisha was stuck here with him too.

"What about Chicago?" Trisha asked. "We can go back. We can find Dad." The last she'd heard from him, over a year ago, he'd been released from prison.

"And what, beg him to take us back? To take care of us?"

"Yes."

"Your dad's in jail, Trisha. He can't help us."

Trisha stepped back, confused. "But he got out."

"Well, he's back in again," her mother said and touched her neck where Lester had left his mark. "What am I going to do?"

Mrs. Walsh put her arm around her. "I don't know," she said. "But we're going to think of something."

❧

Trisha found Carlyn sitting on the bench in the girls' locker room. It was the end of last period.

"What are you doing here?" Carlyn asked. "I thought you were home with your mom. Is she okay?"

"Yeah, she's okay," Trisha said, eyeing Carlyn's gym bag on the floor at her feet. It was big, long. Carlyn carried her cross-country gear in it. It always smelled a little funky, like sweaty socks and sneakers. They were the only two left in the locker room after the rest of the girls from gym class had fled to the buses that were parked in front of the school. "I need a favor." She pulled an aluminum bat from behind her back. She'd stolen it from the cage next to Miss Kline's office, where she kept the sports equipment. "Put this in your bag for me."

"What? No," Carlyn said. "That's stealing."

The door to the locker room banged open. Dannie appeared wearing her big puffy coat. "I thought I'd find you here," she said to Carlyn. "I thought you cut?" she asked Trisha.

"I did. I snuck in a few minutes ago. I'm trying to get Carlyn to hide this in her bag for me." She held up the aluminum bat.

"Why?" Dannie asked.

"I need it," she said.

Carlyn glared at her. "If I get caught stealing gym equipment, they'll kick me off the cross-country team. And they won't let me go out for track in the spring."

"I'd do it myself, but look at me," Trisha said. "Where would I hide it?" She was wearing jeans, a cropped winter coat. She had no place to hide a bat on her body, and it was too big for a backpack.

"Why do you need it anyway?" Carlyn asked.

"You know why," she said. "You both know why." She didn't have to explain any further. It was clear what she needed it for, who she needed protection from.

"Give it to me," Dannie said. "I'll put it in my coat."

"No," Carlyn said. "I'll put it in my bag." She held out her hand. "It'll be fine."

"No. I'll do it. You can get into trouble, kicked off the team," Dannie said. "What could happen to me? Besides, it should be me."

Dannie had become withdrawn, quiet, since that day on the side of her house with Lester. She'd spent more and more time alone in her house, in her room, distancing herself from both Trisha and Carlyn.

And lately, Carlyn had manipulated situations so she and Trisha would end up alone together, further isolating Dannie. Dannie had been feeling left out, put out by the other two. Trisha had known it, allowed it to happen. An invisible crack had found its way into their friendship, a fissure created by their silence over everything that had happened: not only to Dannie but to Trisha too.

Her friends continued arguing over who would hide the bat. Trisha didn't interfere. It was a curious thing to watch them fight over who would get to help her.

Carlyn gripped one end of the bat. Dannie held the other end. They pushed and pulled, tugged it back and forth. Carlyn kept glancing at Trisha.

There was a certain way that boys, *men*, looked at Trisha. She knew what they wanted, what was on their minds. Sometimes she'd want to shower, scrub their gaze from her skin. Sometimes Carlyn looked at her in that same way, but rather than wanting to wash it away, Trisha tucked it deep inside a place in her heart. She'd hide it there for safekeeping, let it linger in the back of her mind.

Dannie pulled the bat from Carlyn's hands. "I'm the fat girl. No one will notice if my coat is bulky."

"You're not fat," Carlyn said and yanked the bat from Dannie. She shoved it into her bag. "I want to do this," she said. "So let me."

Miss Kline appeared from around the corner of the lockers. "What are you three doing here? Shouldn't you be heading to the bus?"

"Yes, ma'am," Carlyn said and picked up her gym bag and backpack.

They rushed past Miss Kline and ran to the bus, jumped on board seconds before the doors closed. They didn't talk on the ride home. Carlyn stared out the window, gripped her gym bag in her lap. Dannie bowed her head. Trisha's heart thrashed inside her rib cage the closer she got to home.

When they were alone on Second Street, standing outside of Carlyn's house, Carlyn pulled the aluminum bat from her bag, handed it to Trisha, and said, "I hope you know what you're doing."

CHAPTER NINETEEN

Parker knocked on Linda Walsh's door for the third time in two days, only to find she wasn't home again. He was beginning to wonder if she was avoiding them, hiding somewhere inside the house.

Geena stood on the top step, looked up and down the street. "People are watching us from their windows," she said.

"You get used to it," Parker said. "It comes with living in a small town."

"What does? Nosiness? Paranoia?" Geena asked.

"Yes," he said.

They got back in the car, drove the few blocks to the hotel on the corner of First Street and Broadway. Their next stop was to check out the bar where Lester had hung out on occasion, according to Sharon. It was a long shot, but they didn't have any other leads at the moment, not since Parker had taken a call from the lab earlier that morning. They hadn't been able to find any hair in the shred of material they'd collected from the scene, although the fabric was made of polyester and spandex, similar to that of the material found in a common baseball hat. The rotted pieces of rubber they'd found in the soil were consistent with that of the sole of a shoe, but no other information could be obtained, other than Lester had been wearing shoes.

Parker pulled into a parking space in front of the hotel. They got out of the car. Geena fished around in her pockets for quarters, fed the meter. They walked inside the restaurant. The place was busy with the lunch crowd. Most of the tables at the bar were full. The formal dining room was empty. Christmas music played in the background. The TVs were turned to the sports channel. Geena checked for a hostess. Parker headed for the bartender. He flashed his badge. "I need to speak with whoever's in charge."

The bartender set a mug of beer down in front of a man in a thick flannel shirt, trucker's cap, heavy boots on his feet. He smelled like he'd been working outdoors, possibly shoveling snow, plowing.

"That would be me," the bartender said. He had tattoos of dragons, hearts, and arrows covering both arms.

Geena joined them, introduced herself.

The bartender motioned for them to follow him to the corner of the bar where they could talk privately.

"We need to see the hotel's guest log from 1986," Parker said. "I'm assuming you kept records."

"Does this have something to do with those bones they found on the mountain trail?"

Parker didn't answer, and Geena jumped in. "Do you think you still have those records?"

The bartender looked her over. "I'm not sure. We got rid of a lot of stuff when we bought the place a few months ago. Not to mention it changed hands a couple of times through the years. If they're anywhere, they're in the basement." He nodded to Geena. "You're welcome to check."

A local cop walked into the place. Some of the customers looked up, glanced around. He was older, more seasoned than both Parker and Geena combined. Parker didn't recognize him. It wasn't unusual, given how many small towns there were in the county and the number of law enforcement officers assigned to each.

"Excuse me," the bartender said and walked over to greet him. They exchanged a few words. The customers were more alert, checking out Parker and Geena, no doubt wondering what was going on.

"They're staring at us," Geena said.

"I told you," Parker said. "Small towns."

The local cop made his exit, and the bartender returned to his place behind the bar.

"We had a little trouble with one of our customers last night," he explained. "I'm supposed to call him if she shows up again."

Parker nodded. "Where's that basement?" he asked.

※

Parker and Geena stood over dusty boxes in the musty basement of the hotel. It was cold and damp and miserable work. They'd gone through six boxes of ledgers, none of which had been from 1986. There were old linens and centerpieces lying around as well as decorations for all the different holidays. There were a couple of framed pictures that must've hung inside the guest rooms some time ago.

Geena picked up two more boxes, dropped them onto an old table they were using as a desk. "There are three more boxes left," she said. "Might as well finish going through all of them."

Another hour later and in the second-to-last box, Parker pulled out the ledger they were searching for. He checked every page for the six months prior to and including December 1986. If Lester had stayed at the hotel during that time, it had never been recorded. He wasn't sure what he was hoping to find—something, anything, to track Lester's movements before he'd disappeared.

He tossed the ledger back into the box. "Now what?" he asked.

"Let's get out of here," Geena said. "And stop by Linda Walsh's one more time."

❧

Parker knocked on Linda Walsh's door yet again. The wind picked up, whipped around his shoulders. He pulled his collar up to ward off the chill. Men weren't supposed to show that the cold bothered them. They were supposed to be rugged outdoorsmen, tough enough to withstand the elements, blah, blah, blah. The whole idea of it sounded stupid to Parker as he stood with his shoulders to his ears doing his best to block the icy breeze from hitting the back of his neck. Geena didn't seem bothered by it.

"Nordic, huh?" he said.

She smiled, shrugged.

"Can I help you?" An older woman stood behind the storm door. Her white hair was cut to her jawline in a style that was fitting for her sharp features.

"Linda Walsh?" he asked.

"Yes."

"I'm Detective Reed," he said. "And this is my partner, Detective Brassard."

"What can I do for you?" She talked through the glass door. She wasn't going to make this easy. They were going to have to work for every little bit of information they needed from her.

"We have a few questions about Lester Haines. May we come in?"

She opened the door, stepped aside. Geena walked in first, followed by Parker. Mrs. Walsh motioned for them to sit on the couch. She took up a position in the armchair across from them.

The first thing Parker noticed was the smell of new carpeting. He looked down at the blue rug underneath his feet. "Cal's Carpets?" he asked.

"No," she said.

"Did you know Lester Haines?" Geena asked, getting right to the point.

"Yes," she said and folded her hands in her lap. "I knew him."

"How well did you know him?" Geena asked.

"I don't know what you're insinuating, but he was the husband of my good friend."

"I wasn't insinuating anything," Geena said and glanced Parker's way. He hid a smile. Mrs. Walsh was living proof of that small-town paranoia Geena had brought up earlier.

Parker jumped in. "You and Sharon Haines are friends, then?"

"Yes, we've lived on this street together since our daughters were kids. I've known Sharon a long time."

"What can you tell me about her relationship with her husband?" Parker asked. "Was it good? Did they get along?"

"I wouldn't say it was good." Her voice was flat, matter of fact.

"How would you describe it, then?" Geena asked.

"They had their problems." Mrs. Walsh stared at Geena. "Lester used to drink."

"We know the local police were called to Sharon's place on more than one occasion," Parker said. "But she refused to press charges," he added in a gentler tone.

"Does that matter? The fact he put his hands on her should be enough."

"Yes, you're absolutely right," Geena said.

Mrs. Walsh directed her question to Geena. "What exactly are you looking for?"

"We're just trying to figure out what happened to him," Geena said.

Mrs. Walsh looked back to Parker. "Did he break her bones? Put her in the hospital? Is that what you want me to tell you? Would that be better for your case, evidence that she was roughed up?"

"No, ma'am, we're not saying that at all," Parker said.

"Well, you won't find any evidence. She always refused to go to the hospital."

"Okay," Parker said. He seemed to be the bad guy here. No matter what he asked, she went on the defensive.

"Do you know anyone who might've wanted Lester dead?" Geena asked.

Mrs. Walsh smiled. It softened her features. "I'm sure there were numerous people who wanted him dead. He was that kind of guy. But if you're looking for specific names, I'm afraid I can't help you."

"Did you want him dead?" Parker asked. He'd never played bad cop before, never had to, but it was clear Mrs. Walsh might not like him, simply for being male. He might as well go with it, see if they could keep her talking.

She glared at Parker. "No, Detective, not me. But I was glad when he wasn't around anymore. And I can tell you that I didn't expend too much energy worrying about where he might've gone or what might've happened to him."

"What about friends?" Geena asked. "Family? Anyone he might've been at odds with around that time? Other neighbors? Fights? Disagreements?"

"Sorry," she said. "I can't think of anyone, but I wasn't around much. I was a single mother. I worked a lot to pay the bills. I do recall speaking to the police when Sharon first reported him missing. I'm sure you have my statement somewhere."

"We do," Parker said.

"Well, then, if I suspected anyone back then, I would've said so."

"Okay," Geena said and stood. "If you think of anything, anything at all, give me a call." She handed her a card. "Thank you for your time."

Parker nodded at Mrs. Walsh, then followed Geena out.

"What do you make of her?" Geena asked once they were in the car.

"I don't think she's fond of men in general."

"I don't know about that," Geena said. "But she definitely didn't warm to you."

"And she certainly didn't hide her dislike for Lester."

"He sounds like a real scumbag," Geena said.

"Yes, but whether we like it or not, our job is to find out who killed him."

Geena was silent for a while, checked her phone, then dropped it in her lap. "It's not always easy, though, is it, detaching yourself from a case." She looked out the passenger-side window.

"No, it's not," Parker said, wondered if she were talking about their current case or a past one. He was already invested in what Geena called the "cold woods." Maybe distancing himself was something he'd eventually learn how to do better after he'd spent more time on the job, to pull back, to disconnect, if only to be able to sleep at night. So far, he hadn't been able to do it.

There was something about these women, Sharon and Trisha and even Linda, that tugged at him, a silent strength they emanated, one that came from having endured something awful and survived.

CHAPTER TWENTY

DECEMBER 1986

Trisha played dead, or maybe she wasn't playing at all. Maybe she really was dead. She'd been lying still on her mattress underneath the comforter for so long that her arms and legs had gone numb. Her breathing was shallow—when she allowed herself to breathe—holding her breath for long periods of time as she strained to listen for any sounds.

A loud banging came from downstairs, Lester cursing afterward.

The blue numbers on the clock radio glared one a.m. Her mother wouldn't be home from her shift at the bar until well after two. She was late getting home on the nights she'd close up, leaving Lester a vast amount of time to get up to no good.

Trisha stared into the dark bedroom. She listened hard for footsteps on the creaky wooden stairs. The kitchen cabinets opened and closed. He was searching for food. He cursed some more. It was quiet after that. Another ten minutes passed. The kitchen chair scraped the linoleum floor. She smelled ramen noodles. He must've heated them on the stove. He didn't know how to use a microwave.

This was her chance to move. It was now or never. And still she continued to lie there. She needed more time to gather her courage. When had hiding under the covers ever worked? She'd tried everything when she'd been younger: cocooning in the sheets, curling into a fetal position, praying to Dannie's God to make the monster go away.

Nothing had ever worked.

She was seventeen and too old to be that frightened little girl anymore. If she didn't stop it now, if she let it continue, there would be nothing left of her to save.

Time ticked away. It was now 1:20 a.m. He would finish eating the noodles any minute. She counted to three and slid from beneath the covers, tiptoed across the room, tried not to make a sound. She reached her bedroom door and quietly closed it, careful to turn the knob so that it wouldn't click. The lock had stopped working years ago. Lester had seen to that. But with the door closed it would give her a few more seconds to prepare herself, to hide in the dark.

She sneaked back to the bed and dropped to her hands and knees, searched the floor for the aluminum bat that she'd kept next to the mattress. Scott had been pissed when he'd found out she'd stolen it. He'd begged her to return it to the gym and even offered to do it for her. She'd told him she couldn't; she needed it. He hadn't asked her again.

She picked it up. The handle was cold in her sweaty palms. She was wearing Scott's T-shirt, felt the cotton sticking to her back. She moved away from the bed and the window, crept to the corner of the room, disappeared in the shadows.

It had grown quiet downstairs. The bat at her side knocked against her leg.

Lester was on the steps, heavy footed and lumbering. He stumbled, mumbled something under his breath. He was in the hallway. Then her bedroom door opened. She pulled in a breath, raised the bat.

Lester stepped into the room. "Princess," he said and kicked the edge of the mattress.

Adrenaline forced her out of the shadows, or maybe it was pure hatred. She swung the bat in the general direction of his head. She missed and struck the wall instead, knocking one of her posters down, along with pieces of plaster.

Lester yelled, surprised. She swung at him again, missed him a second time, striking nothing but air, sending her careening forward. He grabbed her arm. She twisted away. The entire room smelled of him, sweat and alcohol and testosterone.

From the sliver of moonlight coming through the window, she could make out his bare chest, ropy arms, potbelly. She lowered her gaze, glancing below his waist, not wanting to, but she was unable to stop herself.

He grinned. "Like what you see, princess?"

Fear spread throughout her limbs, reaching as far as her fingertips and toes. "Leave me alone."

He lunged at her. He was quick, faster than she'd anticipated. He yanked the bat out of her hands, raised it high above his shoulders as though he were going to hit her with it. She threw her arms up to shield herself from the blow.

He didn't hit her.

Instead, he swung the bat wildly, back and forth, over and over again like a madman. Trisha didn't move, mesmerized by the craziness of what she was seeing. He finally stopped, his breathing heavy, his body drenched with fresh sweat. He took an awkward step back and then another one. He was swaying, looked as though he didn't know what to do next. He mumbled into his chest.

Trisha thought about running out of the room, but then he shook the aluminum bat under her nose. She inhaled sharply, her heart beating loudly in her ears.

"Stupid bitch." He made like he was going to hit her.

She flinched.

He laughed, and the bat dropped from his hand. She could just make out the shape of it as it rolled across the floor toward the dresser.

He said something. She didn't understand. His words were jumbled. He slurred. He was having trouble staying on his feet. He rocked forward.

Trisha lunged for the bat, her bare foot banging hard into the corner of the dresser. Pain shot through her little toe. Why was it always the little toe? She picked up the bat as Lester stumbled toward her. He tried to grab it from her hands again, but she pushed it toward him rather than pulling it away from him, and it knocked him off balance. He tripped on the mattress and fell to his knees. She ran out the door, down the stairs.

She didn't look back.

꙾

Trisha raced down the sidewalk toward Carlyn's house. The winter air assaulted her skin, the cold cement like sandpaper beneath her bare feet. Carlyn's mother wouldn't be home until sometime around seven.

Trisha knocked on the door. She shoved her hands underneath her moist armpits, along with the bat. She wondered if her mother would find Lester passed out in Trisha's bedroom when she got home. She wanted to tell her mother what he was doing, but she was ashamed, as though it were somehow her fault. How could she tell her when he'd convinced Trisha that she was partly to blame for walking around the house in tight pants and shirts, flaunting herself at him? "No, I don't do that," she'd yelled. "I don't do any of those things." He'd forced her down. "Yes, you do."

"Carlyn!" she called and knocked harder.

"Trisha?" Carlyn's voice rang out from the open window on the side of the house.

"Open the door," she said.

Within a few seconds, Carlyn pulled the front door open.

"Did I wake you?" she asked.

"That's okay; come in, come in. What happened?" Carlyn took Trisha by the elbow, led her to the kitchen. She flipped on the light. "Sit," she said and put Trisha in a chair at the folding card table. Then she grabbed two sodas from the refrigerator and sat across from her.

Trisha leaned back in the chair and lit a cigarette, her arms and legs trembling.

Carlyn got up and opened a window. Mrs. Walsh didn't like when people smoked in her house. She believed the warning label on the pack that said cigarettes were dangerous to your health.

"Talk to me, Trisha. Tell me what happened," Carlyn said.

Trisha shook her head, unable to speak. There were some things she couldn't talk about, put into words, the fear of reliving them too strong. She rubbed her eyes, took a drag from the cigarette, and blew the smoke toward the open window. A night breeze sucked the polluted air outside, pulling the yellow curtains against the screen.

"Did you hit him?" Carlyn asked, motioning to the bat.

"Missed," she said.

"Too bad."

Trisha smiled. "Yeah."

"Where is he now?"

"I don't know. I wish he'd just go away." She looked at Carlyn's messy brown hair, wide-set eyes. "Is it okay if I stay here tonight?"

"Of course it is."

Trisha popped the tab on her soda, took a sip. She picked at the scrape near the top of the bat where it had struck the wall, putting a hole in the plaster. The blue dye had chipped away to reveal the silver metal underneath. "You got a knife?" she asked.

"In the drawer."

She got up and put the cigarette out in the sink, then searched through the silverware drawer, found a steak knife.

"What are you planning to do?" Carlyn asked.

"You'll see," she said, and with enough pressure, she was able to etch the initials *S. S.*, for Slate Sisters, their childhood club, onto the sweet spot in the center of the bat. She inspected the engraving. "It's missing something."

"Put a heart around it," Carlyn said.

Trisha scratched a heart into the aluminum. "There." She showed it to her.

"Is that Scott's shirt?" Carlyn asked.

She looked down at her chest. "Yes."

Carlyn fiddled with the can of soda. She wouldn't look at her.

"Don't be mad. It's not what you think."

"I'm not mad. Why would I be mad?"

Trisha sighed. "Do you mind if we just went to bed?"

She followed Carlyn upstairs.

"There's an extra pillow in the closet," Carlyn said and crawled into bed. "Do you want my sleeping bag?"

Trisha shook her head. All the other times she'd slept in Carlyn's bedroom, it had been on the floor with her own blankets and pillows. But tonight, she didn't want to be relegated to the floor. Instead, she slipped into the bed next to her friend, tucked the bat safely by her side. The sheets smelled like Carlyn, a little bit like a locker room. Or maybe that was her dirty running gear piled high in front of the closet door. She reached for Carlyn's hand, turned to face her on the pillow.

"What are you doing?" Carlyn asked.

She couldn't see her eyes. There wasn't enough moonlight to reach her face, but she sensed Carlyn's nervousness. "I see the way you look at me," she said.

"I have no idea what you mean," Carlyn said.

"I know how you feel about me."

"I don't know what you're talking about."

"It's okay. You don't have to be embarrassed." Trisha brushed a strand of hair away from Carlyn's cheek.

"Don't do that," Carlyn said and pulled her hand away.

"Don't do what?" Trisha searched for Carlyn's hand under the covers once again, found it, held it firmly.

"Don't tease me," Carlyn said.

"I'm not teasing you," she whispered and rolled toward her, leaned in close. "Do you want me to stop?" Trisha didn't know what she was doing, why she was toying with her friend's emotions this way. She thought it had something to do with trying to take back the power that Lester had stripped away from her, even if it meant hurting someone she loved. It was as though she craved control, needed it, to be the one in charge, when she felt so helpless in every other aspect of her life.

"If you don't mean it," Carlyn said, "then yes, I'd like for you to stop."

Trisha turned away, stared at the ceiling.

"You don't mean it, do you?"

She could hear the desperation in Carlyn's voice. Trisha didn't know what made her say what she said next. "Do you touch yourself when you think of me?" she asked.

"What? No," Carlyn said.

"Ever yell out my name?"

"Shut up, Trisha." Carlyn rolled to her side, put her back to Trisha.

"Oh, come on. I'm just teasing you. Don't be that way." Trisha laid the bat on the floor. She didn't know what had come over her, but now that she'd started down this path, she couldn't seem to stop. She curled her body around Carlyn's, spooned her. "I know you *like* me."

"You're so full of yourself."

"Maybe I am. Maybe I'm not," she said and squeezed her tightly.

"I'm not talking to you." Carlyn wiggled free and flipped onto her back.

"I saw what you wrote about me in Dannie's slam book. Do you remember? Back in seventh grade?"

"I didn't write anything about you. Those things were stupid."

"I know your handwriting, Carlyn. You think I'm perfect."

"Perfectly certifiable."

She very well could be. She didn't know who or what she was, but she decided she wasn't someone who'd intentionally hurt her friend. She needed her. Maybe they needed each other. Maybe she could give Carlyn what she wanted. She leaned over her again, hovered an inch above her face. "I'm sorry for being a jerk," she said.

"It's okay," Carlyn whispered.

The game she'd started playing with Carlyn didn't feel like a game anymore. She pulled Scott's T-shirt off, tossed it to the floor.

"What are you doing?" Carlyn asked.

"No more talking," she said and rolled on top of her, kissed her neck, her lips.

CHAPTER TWENTY-ONE

Parker sat at his desk at the station in front of the computer, researching the last thirty years of Trisha Haines's life. There wasn't much online. She didn't have a Facebook account, or any account for that matter, on any of the tell-all, oversharing social media sites. It took some real digging to find something, and then it was only that she was married. He redirected his search under her married name. It was as though she barely existed, which was saying something in the internet age. All he came up with were a few society pieces. The photos were the grainy black-and-white kind that could've been anybody if you didn't look closely enough. She was overshadowed by her husband in most of the shots, a much older man by the name of Sid Whitehouse, whose own face had been turned away from the camera in every single shot. There wasn't much information about him, either, other than he was a businessman, but what kind of business wasn't clear. He was described simply as a high roller.

There was a reason Trisha had kept a low profile. There usually was. She'd turned up in the system, a couple of misdemeanor offenses for disturbing the peace, specifically public drunkenness, as recently as six months ago.

From what Parker gleaned off the little information he'd found of her high-society profile, minus the misdemeanors, Trisha lived the kind of lifestyle most people dreamed of when they were on the outside looking in. It was when you were on the inside that nothing was as it seemed. Or it appeared that way to Parker.

Sharon Haines was a little easier to pin down. She hadn't left the area ever since moving to the Slate Belt in 1979. She'd worked nights as a bartender at a place called Foxy's when Lester had disappeared, and later she'd managed the service station downtown until retiring. She lived off social security checks. She never remarried. She'd claimed to be sleeping the day Lester disappeared, tired from her previous shift at the bar. Her alibi was flimsy. No one had seen her until she'd shown up for work around seven p.m. Nothing in the file from her coworkers mentioned anything about seeing fresh bruises on her arms or face. But that didn't mean she didn't have any. Most battered women knew how to hide them.

To Parker's way of thinking, the most remarkable piece of information about Sharon Haines was that she had a clear motive for wanting Lester dead.

He checked his watch. He'd been here all night. Around three a.m. he'd thought about going home, but sleep hadn't appealed to him. Sleep meant dreaming. The last time he'd had a few hours of sleep, he'd woken in a pool of sweat. He'd had another nightmare, the one where the guy's brains were on Parker's face rather than on the autumn leaves. His father had been in the shadows, yelling, *What have you done?* as though it had been Parker who had pulled the trigger.

The morning shift had come in about an hour ago. Sharmaine was sitting at the front desk. The smell of coffee was strong. Geena walked in carrying two cups from a coffee shop.

"Traffic was a nightmare," she said. She commuted from Bethlehem, where she'd told Parker she owned a condo close to headquarters. She set one of the cups on Parker's desk.

"Thanks," he said. No one had ever brought him coffee before. None of the guys ever had, that was for sure. He was touched by the gesture. This was a perk of having her as a partner. She took a sip from her cup.

"What have we got?" she asked, sitting across from him at her new desk.

"Not much," he said. "I think Sharon's our best suspect, given her history with her husband."

"Agreed, but what evidence do we have to support it?"

"None yet." He leaned back in the chair. "I think it's time we set up a tip line. Maybe someone will come forward with some new information."

She nodded.

His phone went off. The lab's number flashed on the screen. "Reed," he said. Five minutes later he hung up.

"What is it?" Geena asked. "Spill."

"That was Cheryl," he said. "She made a cast of the bat, matched it to the depressed fracture on Lester's skull. She can't say the bat was the exact weapon used, but she can confirm that the bat is consistent with the specific pattern of the injury. She's sending the report over. Also, the location of the depression on the left temple leads her to believe that whoever had struck Lester was standing in front of him. So we're looking at someone who is right handed."

"Okay," Geena said. "Now we're getting somewhere."

"There's more. As it turns out, the bat isn't a baseball bat but actually a softball bat. Some official size that meets some standard."

"In other words, there's a chance it belonged to a girl."

"That's what I was thinking." He stood, grabbed his jacket.

"Where are you going?"

"To talk to my old coach at the high school. Just a hunch about something."

"You want me to ride along?"

"Nah, it might turn out to be nothing. But do me a favor and run out and pick up a pack of cigarettes and a pink lighter. I got one of the daughter's friends coming in to talk later this morning." He tossed Carlyn Walsh's statement from the old paper file onto Geena's desk. "I'll be back in time. We'll see what she knows."

⁊⸱

Parker pulled into the high school's parking lot. He checked in with security before heading to the gymnasium. Coach Friedman was in his office in the back of the boys' locker room. Parker poked his head inside.

"Hey, Coach," he said.

"Parker." Coach motioned for him to enter. "It's good to see you," he said. "I was surprised when I got your call. Did you know you still hold the record for most receiving yards?"

"No one's broken it yet?" Parker smiled. His old football coach and gym teacher looked good. His hair was mostly gray now and his face a little weatherworn, but overall, he hadn't changed much in the last decade or more.

"No one's come close," Coach said about Parker's record. "What brings you by?"

Parker pulled out his phone and showed him the picture of the softball bat. The bat had once been bright blue with a red logo, but now the colors were faded, dulled from years of being buried on the mountain. "Do you recognize this? I thought it looked similar to the old softball bats in the gym."

Coach looked closely. "It's in pretty rough shape. I can't say for sure, but it's possible. We've got about a dozen or more of the old aluminum bats in the cage. Let me make sure the girls' locker room is clear." Coach called the female gym teacher—a name Parker didn't recognize—and asked her to check the girls' locker room.

Parker waited for Coach in the gym. He picked up a stray basketball, tossed it at the net, watched it bounce off the rim. It wasn't his sport. Memories flooded him: time spent with friends, football drills, sweat, basic screwing around. Becca used to hang around after practice, leaning against the wall outside the locker room, her big gray eyes finding him in a crowd of jocks. He'd been young, blind, not seeing the way she'd looked at him, who she was, what she'd meant to him. He supposed it was what some called hindsight. Either way, it didn't do him much good now.

"All clear," Coach said and joined him by the locker room door.

Parker had never been inside the girls' locker room during his time in high school. It wasn't much different from the boys' locker room, other than the lack of urinals. It had the same outdoor carpet, lockers, graffitied benches, open showers. Coach grabbed a set of keys, unlocked the cage, where balls, bats, and bases; jump ropes; and hockey sticks had been more or less thrown in organized piles. He pulled a couple of softball bats out of a bag buried in the back. The girls wouldn't have their unit on softball until spring.

"They do look similar," Coach said and handed a bat to Parker. "It's the same logo."

Parker agreed. "Any chance I can look at your inventory records?" He followed Coach back to the office.

"I'm not sure how far back you're looking to go, but it's only been in the last decade that we've gone digital."

"1986," Parker said.

Coach hitched his thumb to a large filing cabinet behind him. "You'll want to search in there, then. It should be listed by the school year. We keep a report of what equipment we had at the start of the year and what we ended up with at the end. You'd be surprised how much of it disappears or gets damaged and tossed out."

"Disappears as in stolen?" Parker asked.

Coach threw up his hands. "Kids will be kids," he said. "Well, I have a health class in a couple of minutes."

"Understood."

"I'll leave you to it." On his way out, Coach said over his shoulder, "It was good seeing you, Parker. Don't be a stranger."

"You too, Coach," he said, feeling a thousand years younger. Like it or not, for better or worse, Parker wasn't the same easygoing kid he used to be, but every now and again, tucked somewhere inside the man he'd become, his younger self emerged. *Don't lose sight of that,* he said to himself, worried what impact the job had already inflicted on him.

Parker opened the top drawer, worked his way down to the 1986–87 school year, Trisha's senior year. Kids were constantly going into the cages for equipment, which led him to believe that Trisha would've had access to the bat. And if she'd stolen one and brought it home, wouldn't that also mean her mother would've had access to the murder weapon?

※

"Have a seat," Parker said.

Carlyn Walsh sat across from him and Geena in the small plastic chair in front of an old table in one of the interview rooms. She kept her coat on and her scarf tied around her neck. She was sending a signal that she didn't expect to be here long.

"Thanks for coming down," Parker said. "Do you know why we asked you here?"

"I assume it has to do with Lester Haines. I read about it in the paper."

"How well did you know him?"

"Not well. I only knew him as Trisha's stepfather."

Parker pulled out the pack of cigarettes and pink lighter Geena had picked up for him. He dropped them on the table.

"Do you smoke?" Parker asked and offered her a cigarette.

"No," Carlyn said.

"Ever?"

"I tried it once when I was a kid. I didn't like it."

She seemed nonchalant about it. He put the pack and lighter back into his pocket. It probably wasn't her lighter that they'd found at the scene. "You mentioned you had appointments today. What is it you do?"

"I'm a clinical psychologist. I specialize in children with behavioral disorders."

The last person Parker wanted to be questioning was a psychologist. What would she think if he told her about his dreams—the blood, the brains stuck to leaves and sometimes spattered on his face. He wiped his cheek, scratchy with stubble. He wasn't going to see a shrink, no matter what Geena may or may not have overheard the lieutenant or anyone else say about him. "How long have you been a psychologist?" he asked.

"Twenty years."

"I bet you've seen it all," Geena said.

Carlyn looked back and forth between the two detectives. Her hair was straight; the ends brushed her shoulders. She wore little if any makeup. She had a strong jawline, and her eyes were set wide apart. She appeared calm. The only clue Parker could discern that she was nervous was the way she gripped the leather case in her lap. "There are very few surprises in life. Wouldn't you agree?" she asked Geena.

Geena didn't answer her one way or the other.

"People surprise the hell out of me every single day," Parker said.

The corners of Carlyn's lips turned up slightly.

"I know you gave a statement back when Lester first disappeared," he said.

"I was just a kid then. I don't remember exactly what I said."

Parker nodded. "Can you tell me what you do remember about that time?"

"I didn't keep tabs on my friend's stepfather, if that's what you're asking. We were teenagers, too wrapped up in our own world to pay much attention to the adults around us. If anything, we stayed as far away from them as possible, and especially from Lester."

"Why is that?"

"I don't have any proof, but you just know things. He was a mean drunk. I don't think there was a person on our block who didn't know this about him."

"We know the local police were called a few times. Other than that, did anyone ever confront him?" Parker asked. "Did you ever see him arguing or fighting with any of the neighbors?"

"No, I didn't," she said. "It's not like it is today. Back then, people minded their own business and kept to themselves for the most part. There wasn't a whole lot of meddling or *sharing* like there is today. Honestly, I'm not sure which is worse: respecting people's privacy or blabbing it to the whole world on social media sites. I suppose the answer lies somewhere in between."

"Did you ever see Lester fighting with Sharon?"

"Sure, they argued, but I'd never witnessed him hitting her." She paused. "I do remember seeing bruises on Sharon's arms and face, and this one time, there were marks on her throat." She touched her neck.

"That must've been hard to see," Geena said.

"I worried about Trisha and her mother living there with him, so yes, it was hard. I think I can say we—Dannie and I—were afraid of what he'd do, how far he'd go. It was obvious he was out of control when he was drinking." She hesitated. "I suppose that's the adult in me talking. I'm not so sure I could've articulated what I was seeing or what was happening when I was a teenager."

Parker nodded. "Who is Dannie?"

"She was a friend who lived across the street from Trisha. The three of us were good friends. Best friends," she added.

Parker flipped through his file, finding a Danielle listed as a person who'd been questioned. "Dannie is short for Danielle?" he asked.

"Yes. Danielle Teagan, although she goes by Danielle Torino now."

"Okay. Do you remember where you were the day Lester went missing, December fourth, 1986?"

Geena was taking notes. She looked up, waiting for Carlyn to answer.

"I imagine I was in school."

"And after school?"

"I spent a lot of my free time at the library most days. Or I was home. I don't remember exactly, but it should be in my original statement."

Parker flipped through the folder again. He pulled out a couple of sheets of paper. "It says here that Trisha stayed at your house the night he disappeared."

"If that's what it says, then it must be true."

"Was your mother or father home at the time?"

"My father left when I was five years old. My mother worked the night shift at the hospital. Trisha stayed with me a lot during that time."

"Didn't she like being home?"

"You'd have to ask her."

"Do you know what Sharon was doing that day? Or that night?"

"She might've been working. She worked nights as a bartender. But I don't know if she worked that night. Like I said, we were teenagers. We were wrapped up in our own lives."

"One more question," he said and pulled a photo of the softball bat from the folder. He'd learned from the files in the coach's office that three bats had gone missing during the 1986–87 school year. He'd sent the serial numbers to the forensics lab to see if one of them was a match. "Have you seen this before?" He passed it to her.

She glanced at it. "No."

"Take another look. Does it look familiar to you?"

She glanced at it again. "No, it doesn't look familiar."

"It's the same kind of softball bat the high school used."

"I was on the cross-country team. I didn't play softball."

"What about gym class?"

"Could be, I guess. It was a long time ago."

"Okay," Parker said and put the photo back inside the folder. "I appreciate you coming down and talking with us."

Geena pushed her chair back. They stood and escorted Carlyn to the front desk. They watched her walk to her car, put her leather case on the passenger seat. Then she got in on the driver's side and started the engine. As far as Parker could tell, she never checked her phone for messages, which was unusual these days. She pulled out of the lot onto Route 191. They continued to watch her drive away until she was no longer in sight.

"What do you think? Is she telling the truth?" Geena asked.

"Honestly," Parker said, "I'm not sure."

CHAPTER TWENTY-TWO

Trisha's head felt as heavy as a slab of slate, her mind dull and gray. Her memories of the events of the last couple of nights were like tiny slivers of rock peeling from the edges before flaking away. She was somewhere between waking and dreaming. She could sense someone in the room with her, someone who was close, wheezing. There was a hand on her shoulder, shaking her, trying to wake her up.

"Go away," she mumbled into the cushion. Foam stuck to her dry tongue.

"Get up," a deep, scratchy voice said. "You've been sleeping all day."

"So?" she asked, but it was too late; she was up. She could tell by the pounding behind her eyes.

"We missed you today. Dannie could've used your help. There's still a lot of sorting and packing to do."

Right. Evelyn's funeral. Dannie putting the house up for sale.

"Carlyn stopped by, but she couldn't stay. She had appointments or some such."

Trisha rolled over.

"Whoa." Her mother stepped back.

Trisha covered her eyes with her forearm. This was what a drunk smelled like. How could her mother forget?

"Were you with Carlyn again last night?"

"No. Just me, myself, and I," she said, having gone to a seedier joint on the south end of town, where she'd spent the last forty-eight hours, or so she thought. It was all a blur. The only thing that stood out was when she'd been with Carlyn at the hotel bar on that first night, how Trisha had peed her pants, how Scott had shown up, driven them home. It could've been worse. Scott could've arrested her. She could've woken up in a jail cell. Instead, she'd woken up in her mother's house the next day and had gone straight to another bar.

Trisha's mother stood over her, arms crossed. "Did you two have a nice chat the other night?"

"Who are we talking about?" Trisha asked, having a hard time following the conversation.

"You and Carlyn. Did she tell you she bought a place on Garibaldi Avenue up from the fire station?"

"She didn't mention it."

"She's come a long way, you know. It wasn't easy growing up around here in this small town, given her proclivities."

"Proclivities?"

"You know what I'm talking about."

"Sure," Trisha said.

"Anyway, she's done a lot of good, helping kids everybody else has given up on. It makes Linda very proud."

"Okay," she said. She had no idea where her mother was going with this.

"But even after everything she's accomplished, she's still lonely."

Trisha didn't know how to respond, so when she didn't say anything, her mother said, "Try not to hurt her."

Interesting for her mother to think Trisha still had that kind of power over Carlyn. From what Trisha had seen, she would've guessed otherwise.

"Let's get you cleaned up."

She allowed her mother to help her off the couch. She stumbled into the chair. Her mother grabbed her arm before she fell over.

"We need to dry you out." She continued helping Trisha up the stairs and into the bathroom. She filled the old claw-foot tub with water and then left Trisha alone to undress.

Trisha pulled off her jeans, stiff from dried urine, from wearing them two days in a row. She yanked off her top, sending one of the pearl buttons flying across the room. She didn't care where it went. She wasn't going to look for it. She stepped into the tub, sinking into the hot water. Her ribs ached, but her head hurt more.

The bathroom door opened, and her mother stepped inside. She gathered the soiled clothes from the floor, paused when she glanced at Trisha in the tub. Trisha covered the bruise with her arm.

Her mother looked away. "When you're done getting washed up, I'm taking you shopping. You need winter clothes. You're lucky you didn't freeze to death in these things." She left Trisha alone again.

Trisha sank in the tub until the water came up to her chin, replayed her mother's comments about Carlyn over and over until she was angry. So what if Carlyn was lonely? That was her choice. She'd pushed Trisha away. She'd ended their friendship back in high school. And yet the more she thought about it, another feeling emerged, one that wasn't familiar. What was it? Could it be Trisha was feeling empathy for her friend?

Trisha understood the pain of loneliness. She was forever lonely—in the penthouse suite, in the corner of the room at lavish parties, at the bar while Sid played cards in the back rooms of casinos. She'd spend long hours alone binge-watching the latest series on Netflix, waiting for Sid to come home, let her out of the room, pay attention to her. It was sad, pathetic even. No, she didn't like to think that Carlyn had suffered from the same affliction.

She grabbed the bar of soap, rubbed her neck, careful to lift her arm next to her sore ribs.

But at least Carlyn had Dannie. All these years they'd had each other, a friend a phone call away. It had been Trisha they'd abandoned, they'd left friendless.

But the hardest part for Trisha to accept about losing her friends, being lonely, was that it was her own fault. She was the only one to blame.

※

Trisha followed her mother down an aisle in some chain store where designer clothes were sold for less. She checked the price tag on a sweater with a label she recognized: $84, marked down to $29.99. She inspected the seams, the cable stitching, the percentage of wool to cotton. Polyester. Cheap. She was a label lover, a clothing snob, what she'd become since she'd married Sid. She grabbed the sweater from the rack. She picked out four more sweaters, two "designer" flannels, and a pair of black faux fur–lined winter boots with heavy tread. On the way to the checkout counter, she grabbed a black puffy winter coat, also with faux fur on the hood—a perfect match with the boots.

She paid in cash.

Her mother helped her carry the bags to the car, limping alongside her through the parking lot. The cold wind whipped around their shoulders.

"What did you do to your hip?" Trisha asked, showing a level of compassion, concern. She wasn't used to caring. She didn't know where it had come from, but there it was.

"Arthritis," her mother said.

"Do you take anything for it?"

"Yeah, I take that stuff you see on those commercials during the football games. You know, the ones with those big horses. What's it called?"

"The beer commercial?"

"Yeah, that's it. Beer. Works like a charm."

Trisha laughed. "I bet it does."

Within twenty minutes they were back home again. Trisha slipped on her new boots before getting out of the car. The sidewalks were covered in salt and ice. The temperature remained at freezing. She grabbed the packages from the back. Her mother stopped short of stepping through the door.

"What is it?" Trisha asked and pushed her mother aside. The front door was ajar.

"I could've sworn I closed it," her mother said.

Tentatively, Trisha pushed it all the way open and walked into the house. She put the bags on the couch. Her mother stood behind her.

"Stay here," she said and checked the dining room and kitchen. She smelled the faint scent of expensive cologne. *No. No. No.* Slowly, she made her way up the steps. By the time she reached the top stair, she felt as though a leather strap had tightened around her throat. She looked left and then right into the shadows of the hall. None of the lights were turned on. The winter days were short, dusk dropping its curtain as early as four o'clock.

She stopped just inside the doorway of her bedroom. She searched for the light switch, found it, turned it on. On top of the mattress was a pile of poker chips. Something like a gasp escaped from her lips. Her hands wrapped around her neck, pulled the imaginary noose at her throat.

Her mother came up behind her.

"He found me," she choked.

"Who found you?"

"My husband."

꩜

Her mother touched the blouse by Trisha's ribs. "I saw the bruise," she said. "You have the same taste in men as your mother."

She might've laughed if it wasn't true. Deep down she'd always known she'd never get away from Sid. He wasn't the kind of man who let something go, not when that something belonged to him. He wouldn't give her up, allow her to escape. Not without consequences. Anything else would've been too easy. And nothing in this life was easy.

Her mother picked up a chip, turned it over. "They're from the casino right here in Bethlehem," she said.

CHAPTER TWENTY-THREE

DECEMBER 1986

Trisha woke up alone in Carlyn's bed, heard the sound of Christmas music coming from the kitchen downstairs. She dragged herself out from under the covers. School would start in less than an hour. She dreaded going home, wondered if Lester would be there.

The toilet flushed in the upstairs bathroom, which meant Mrs. Walsh was home. Carlyn had to be the one who was downstairs. She was the only one who would play Christmas music. Mrs. Walsh didn't make a fuss around the holidays, no decorations or even a tree, although, according to Carlyn, they were Christians. Mrs. Walsh wasn't a sentimental or emotional woman. And yet, she was a nurse. There had to be some compassion inside of her somewhere, an instinct to heal and care for others. Trisha had seen tenderness when she'd taken care of Trisha's mother, a kindness she'd shown to both of them.

Trisha tiptoed into the hall and down the stairs. She peeked in the kitchen. Carlyn was up and dressed, sitting at the table. Her anatomy book was opened in front of her. The pages were covered with images of human body parts stripped of skin, muscles exposed, each one labeled. Carlyn had started taking honors courses three years ago when they'd entered high school. Trisha was barely passing basic biology class, the remedial one for students who would not be going to college next fall.

The bathroom door upstairs opened. Carlyn looked up from her book. Trisha blew her a kiss, then jetted to the door in a hurry to escape Mrs. Walsh's questions. Trisha had slept over more times than Mrs. Walsh had been made aware of. Her rule was no sleepovers during the school week. Weekends were different, of course. But what Mrs. Walsh didn't know wouldn't hurt her.

Trisha slipped out the front door and into the cold. The sky was gray, a kind of pewter. The air was still and quiet. A couple of inches of snow had fallen sometime after Trisha had gone to Carlyn's. She shivered and hurried down the sidewalk in bare feet. All she was wearing was the clothes she'd slept in: shorts and Scott's T-shirt. She hadn't thought about shoes or a coat late last night when she'd fled from home.

The car her mother and Lester shared wasn't anywhere on the block. She looked up and down the street, double- and triple-checked. Maybe her mother had come home last night and Lester had already taken off with it. Trisha glanced across the street at Dannie's house, saw Dannie in the upstairs window looking down at her. Dannie would now know that Trisha was coming from Carlyn's house. She'd been caught, and Dannie would sulk the rest of the day, hurt because she hadn't been invited too.

Sometimes Trisha resented being stuck between the two. Other times she liked the attention: the friend in their threesome who was never left out. She could've run to Dannie's house last night, spent the night there, but she didn't want to. Dannie's mother was always home. The woman never left the house. Dannie did all the grocery shopping, the cooking and cleaning. Trisha didn't know how Dannie could stomach it, taking care of her fat, lazy mother. Dannie had to resent it, although she'd never admit it. She'd told Trisha she got her frustrations out by praying. Trisha had laughed. Dannie hadn't. Dannie hadn't thought it was funny at all.

Dannie stared at Trisha a moment longer, and then she pulled the blinds closed, everything but her silhouette disappearing from Trisha's view. She knew that neither one would mention they'd seen each other. Trisha didn't know why, but it had something to do with the day she'd caught Lester with Dannie on the side of the house, a wound that refused to heal.

She pulled open her front door and stepped inside. The house wasn't much warmer than the outside. Her mother had complained about the high electric bill last month. She'd turned the heat way down to save a few bucks.

Trisha rubbed her arms for warmth as she made her way upstairs. The house was silent except for her mother snoring. Lester was nowhere to be found.

She plopped onto the mattress in her bedroom. The poster that had been knocked down last night lay on the floor with the pieces of plaster. She put her head in her hands. What now? She didn't want to go to school. What was the point? She was failing most of her classes. She wasn't going to college. She was never getting out of here. She didn't know what she was going to do, what would happen to her. She couldn't stay in her own home. Not with Lester.

She pulled off her shorts and slipped on jeans. She tugged a heavy sweatshirt on over Scott's T-shirt. She laced up her snow boots.

Anywhere was better than here.

On her way out the door, she grabbed her winter coat. Then she plucked the cigarettes and the pink lighter she'd stolen from her mother and hidden in the empty flowerpot on the front porch and shoved them in her pocket.

CHAPTER TWENTY-FOUR

Trisha had her mother pull into the parking lot of the gun shop.

"Wait here," she said.

"You don't want me to come in with you?" her mother asked.

"No," Trisha said and got out of the car. She didn't want her mother involved any more than she had to be. She was only here because Trisha had needed a ride.

Trisha looked over her shoulder, then pulled open the glass door and stepped inside. Everywhere she looked there were rifles and handguns and every kind of weapon you could imagine. Some women might've been intimidated by the sheer firepower surrounding them. Trisha breathed it in as though she tasted fresh air, as though she'd shed her old skin and slid into a new one.

She leaned on the glass counter, checked out the display of handguns.

A man appeared from behind a closed door. "What can I help you with today?" He was short and round. His cheeks were full. His beard was red.

"I'm looking for a handgun," she said.

"Okay. Any idea what kind you're looking for?"

"No."

"Well, first you'll have to fill this out," he said and handed Trisha a form. "I'll need to do a background check. It shouldn't take more than a few minutes, unless you were charged with a crime." He smiled, an attempt at a joke, but they both knew he wasn't kidding.

Trisha faked a smile back as she looked over the application, pausing when she came to the questions about misdemeanor offenses. None of her previous convictions were related to anything on the form. They were nothing, really—disorderly conducts, disturbing the peace. Sid had bailed her out, paid the fines, then locked her in the closet in their suite, her own private cell.

She filled in her name, wrote down Second Street as her home address. When she got to the next box asking for her driver's license number, she stopped.

"I don't drive," she said. What did she need a driver's license for when she didn't own a car and Sid had a car service? It was another way he'd controlled her, another way she'd let him. It was the reason her mother had had to drive her here in the first place.

The guy pointed to another box on the form. "Make sure you put your social security number down, and let me see what I can do," he said.

She did as she was told, worried the misdemeanors would show up now, but there was nothing she could do about it. When she finished, the guy plugged the information into a computer. He tapped on the keyboard, played around with something, trying to get it to go through. Several minutes passed before he finally looked away from the screen and down at her.

"I lived in Vegas," she said, knowing he was looking for an explanation about her prior offenses. "You know the saying 'What happens in Vegas . . .'"

He seemed to consider her explanation. He struck a couple of keys on the keyboard, then turned to her again. "You'll want to pick something you're comfortable with. It has to feel good in your hand. It's all about how it feels to you. Guys tend to choose their weapons based on firepower. Women choose what feels comfortable. At least, that's been my experience working here."

Trisha nodded. "Okay. What do you suggest?"

He pulled out a small SIG Sauer with a rosewood grip. "Try this."

Trisha held it in her hand, turned it over. "It's lighter than I thought." It was okay, but it didn't feel quite right.

For the next thirty minutes, Trisha held more guns in her hand than some people would ever hold in their lifetime. In the end, it was the "Baby Glock" that fit snugly in her palm like it had been customized for her small fingers, like all the clothes Sid had had made special for her petite frame. She paid cash. Sid's money. How poetic.

The guy behind the counter suggested she take the three-hour classroom lesson on safety, then another hour of live fire on the range. She declined.

"Just show me how to load it," she said.

�§

Trisha sat on the floor in her bedroom turning the gun over in her hand. Every now and again she held her arm out straight, aimed, pretended to shoot. The gun was loaded and would remain that way. The only problem was that she wasn't feeling secure, safe, not like she thought she would. If anything, it felt more dangerous.

Her mother was sitting on the front porch in the freezing cold drinking beer with Linda. It was ten o'clock at night.

Trisha had to leave now, or she'd be late. *She'd be late. She'd be late.*

An image of the white rabbit in *Alice in Wonderland* flitted across her mind. It was fitting. She was headed down her own proverbial rabbit hole. She shoved the small Glock underneath the mattress. She couldn't take it with her. The guy at the gun shop had made it clear she'd need a license to carry a concealed weapon, and that could take up to several weeks to process. If she got caught without the license, she could be charged with a felony. Home protection was entirely different, though, and perfectly legal.

Her new snow boots were by the front door. She stuffed her feet into them and stepped outside. "Holy crap, it's cold," she said and pulled the hood up on her new puffy winter coat.

Linda chuckled. "You forgot what winters are like around here."

"I guess I did," she said.

Her mother looked her over. "You going to be okay?"

Trisha nodded. "I'll be fine."

In the next minute, a black sedan rolled to a stop in front of the house, like Trisha knew it would.

"I'll see you later," she said to both women and got into the car.

CHAPTER TWENTY-FIVE

Parker hung up the phone, shook his head at Geena, signaling that the call that had come in on the tip line wasn't anything they needed to follow up on. They'd taken a couple of calls in the last several hours, but nothing that had given them any new leads.

Something Carlyn had said stuck out in Parker's mind. She'd mentioned seeing bruises on Sharon Haines's neck. He'd read somewhere in cases of domestic abuse that when the violence escalated to choking the victim, the next step had often led to killing them.

He thought back to the first time he'd met Trisha in her mother's living room. She'd kept her right arm close to her side, as though she'd been protecting her ribs. He hadn't realized it then, but the reason she'd sat so still was because it must have hurt to move. He'd dismissed the marks on her neck as shadows. Now he wondered if they'd been bruises. It was enough to get him to dig further into Sid Whitehouse. He learned he was in town. Parker supposed that wasn't so unusual, given his wife was here.

Geena got up from her desk, picked up her keys and phone. "I'm heading to Benny's. I could use a drink," she said. "You coming?"

"I'll meet you there," he said.

Parker met Geena at Benny's, a local pub the guys in their troop frequented. He used the bathroom, then sat at the bar. It wasn't like he had anything better to do. He'd texted Becca, but she'd replied she was working late at the clinic. The thought of going home, sleeping, only to toss and turn in a nightmarish frenzy, wasn't appealing.

Geena saddled up next to him. She took her hair out of the ponytail. The long blonde waves cascaded down her back. Her hair smelled good: something sweet, like strawberries. For the first time, he wondered what her life was like outside of the job. He didn't know if she had a boyfriend, a roommate, hobbies.

"Don't you have any plans tonight?" he asked.

"Like a date?"

"I guess. Yeah," he said.

"I don't have much of a social life."

"No one at home waiting for you?" he asked and immediately regretted it. It sounded cheesy, like a pickup line. It wasn't his intention.

"No one at home," she said. "You?"

"She's working tonight."

"What does she do?" she asked.

"Veterinarian."

"Cool job," she said, then motioned to Benny. "Two drafts. And keep them coming."

Benny set two cold ones on the bar. "Never knew you to drink beer," he said to Parker.

Parker hadn't touched a drink in years, not since he'd graduated college. It was a choice. He just didn't like who he was when he was drinking. He didn't like the way it made him feel as though he'd given up some of his control over his decision-making ability. But he didn't think a beer or two tonight could hurt. Maybe it would help him sleep, knock the nightmares right out of him. He was willing to give it a try. Nothing else seemed to be working, short of taking pills, and he wasn't there yet.

But after a while, two beers had turned into three, then four. The hockey game that had been blaring from the television had ended. Most of the guys, other cops, had gone home. A few stragglers sat around a table in the back, a couple of detectives from headquarters. Geena got up, strolled to their table, joined them. They were working a fresh case that had turned up two days ago. A body of a young woman had been discovered in a ditch on the side of the road in Allentown, her corpse burned beyond recognition. Her car had been dumped not three miles from where she'd been found. It was a major case. It had attracted the local news media. It had demanded urgent attention.

Parker and Geena hadn't been asked to help with it, not since they'd been handling the cold woods on their own. Even the media had left them alone. No one was interested in a thirty-year-old case when the victim had reportedly been a lowlife.

Rick Smith, the retired detective who'd helped Parker on his first case as lead, sat on the stool next to him. Rick was in jeans and a sweatshirt. His hair was clipped short. He may have been retired for a few years, but it was hard to shed the look of a cop. It was the kind of job that was ingrained in your skin, a permanent part of your core.

"Surprised to see that beer in your hand," Rick said.

"Me too," Parker said, burped into his fist.

"I've been watching you put them away since you got here. Everything okay?"

"Just one of those days."

"You want to talk about it?" he asked and drank from his own beer.

"Nope. I heard you were getting into the PI business," Parker said.

"You heard right. I'm picking and choosing which jobs I take at the moment. Nothing too involved. You ever need something from me, you let me know."

"Will do," Parker said.

Rick looked over his shoulder at Geena; then he turned to Parker and kept his voice low. "Your new partner is easy on the eyes. Not many guys would want to work with someone that good looking. Could complicate things. I don't imagine too many wives or girlfriends would be happy about it either. I hear that's why Albert partnered up with her. He was old enough to be her father. I was surprised to hear he retired. Guess we're all getting old."

Parker only nodded, stared straight ahead at the rows of bottles on the shelf behind the bar. This was precisely the reason he hadn't told Becca about his new partner. Before Becca and Parker had gotten together, the guy she'd been living with had cheated on her. Her father had cheated on her mother. She had trust issues. And since her and Parker's relationship had recently moved from friendship into something more, he didn't want to say or do anything to derail it.

Geena walked up to them. "Nice to see you again, Smith," she said to Rick.

"Hear anything from Albert?" Rick asked.

"He's enjoying working in his garden," she said, smiling, shaking her head as though it were hard to believe.

"Tell him I said hi next time you talk to him," Rick said and stood. He headed to the back table.

Geena leaned over Parker, touched his shoulder as she signaled Benny for another round.

"Parker."

Both Parker and Geena turned when they heard his name.

CHAPTER TWENTY-SIX

Trisha looked around the crowded floor of the casino. It was similar to Vegas casinos but smaller, this one built on land that was once owned by Bethlehem Steel. She'd walked through security not five minutes ago. They'd checked her ID for her age, which was laughable. "Standard procedure," the guard had said. When he saw her name, he looked her up and down as though she weren't anything like what he'd expected. He was right. But she nodded anyway, affirmed she was who the VIP ID had said she was. Another guard approached. "This way, Mrs. Whitehouse," he said and escorted her to the tables in the back, where the casino's special guests received preferential treatment.

She stood off to the side, near the corner where Sid could see her but far enough away where she couldn't interact with him or anyone, for that matter. He glanced in her direction, but otherwise he didn't seem to pay much attention to her. Was it possible he didn't recognize her? She hid a smile and took a drink off the tray of a young waitress with a tight skirt and tattoos on her fingers. A live band played at the front of the casino, where the general public overpaid for drinks at the bar. The music thrummed through Trisha's chest, a cover band, a song she didn't recognize. Smoke from cigars and cigarettes filled the room.

Sid looked in her direction again some ten minutes later. A kind of realization spread across his face as he locked onto her. She was wearing her winter coat, the shabby sweater, faux fur–lined boots. He would expect three-inch heels, a designer cocktail dress, salon-styled hair, and makeup.

Not the middle-aged woman in cheap clothes.

He rearranged his face to disguise his surprise at her appearance. He returned his focus to the cards on the table. He could be winning or losing. It was impossible to tell from the stacks of chips in front of him. A tall blonde appeared, clung to his arm. She was half Trisha's age, a third of Sid's age. If Trisha could, she'd beg the young blonde to steal him away. *Please, take him. He's yours. Become his pet, his caged animal.* Trisha was done. Overdone. But she couldn't bring herself to let that happen to an innocent woman, even a stupid, gold-digging, prostituting one.

She stood in one place, lifted the vodka to her lips, washed her self-loathing down, one swallow at a time. Whenever the waitress passed by, she replaced her empty glass with a full one. The minutes ticked by. She swayed on her feet, but at least her skin had stopped prickling. She was comfortably numb, waiting for her punishment, not knowing when it would come.

And it would come. Perhaps not tonight. But it would come.

Knowing Sid the way she did, he would want to draw it out, let her terror take a firm hold. There was nothing more satisfying to him than seeing fear in her eyes.

It was close to midnight by the time Sid got up from the table. Heinrik, his henchman, gathered the chips and held on to the arm of the young blonde. Later, while Sid cashed in his winnings, Heinrik would show the girl to one of the suites, where she would wait for Sid and eventually perform the most degrading acts with an old man.

She would do it for money or the promise of money, expensive clothes, jewelry, fine dining, trips around the world. Sid would promise all these things, with no intention of keeping any of them.

Everything Sid had was meant solely for him. Trisha knew it, lived it, breathed it. She'd been one of those girls many years ago.

❧

Sid made his way through a throng of people. He stood in front of Trisha in his black pin-striped suit, starched white shirt, and polished shoes. "Well, I never expected this," he said and flicked the faux fur on her hood.

"Winters are cold in Pennsylvania."

"Yes," he said. "I never liked the cold."

She didn't reply.

"Still." He looked her over. "There's something about this hillbilly look on you."

When she didn't respond a second time, he asked, "Did you miss me?"

"Yes," she said and turned her head away. She couldn't look at him, and not because she was lying but because that *sick* part of herself was telling the truth.

He stepped closer, so close his stale breath was warm in her face. He closed his eyes, breathed her in. He'd told her once that her scent, her skin, was like a drug to him.

"How did you find me?" she asked.

"You're a drunk, Trisha. You don't remember everything you say."

He was right, of course. How could she have been so stupid? She'd probably told him herself, how she'd escape from him one day, where she'd go when she did. He'd probably laughed out loud when he'd found her gone from the penthouse suite six days ago. He'd known all along where to find her. It was her own fault, everything that would happen to her from here on out, or so he'd convince her. She was her own worst enemy. She'd created the situation she was in. She deserved whatever she got. Eventually, you heard these things about yourself often enough that you began to believe they were true.

"Do you know why I came home?" she asked.

"It has something to do with your stepfather."

She stared at a spot over his shoulder. The music was muffled, the chatter at the tables subdued. "I was instructed by the police not to leave town." A lie, but one she knew he'd believe.

He smiled, but not the kind of smile that reached his eyes. "Did you do it?"

"No. I'm innocent." Her voice was flat. Deadpan.

"There is nothing innocent about you." He looked around the room. "I guess I could stay for a while. I don't have to be anywhere anytime soon. This place could grow on me, as long as I have my luck."

She didn't say anything. Of course he wouldn't fly back to Vegas without her.

"Will you stay with me?" he asked. "Here at the casino."

"No," she said. She wouldn't stay with him willingly. If he wanted her, he'd have to drag her kicking and clawing.

He nodded, leaned in, whispered in her ear, "You're going to pay for this."

God, she knew she would.

He laughed. "You're such a tease," he said, lifted her chin with his finger. "Go and play with your cop friends." He started walking away but stopped, turned back around. "I'm never going to let you go. You know that, right?"

She held her breath and didn't release it until he was gone, Heinrik and the blonde two steps behind him.

When she was sure he wasn't coming back, she searched the crowded room, found an artificial tree in the corner, retched into the pot.

⁂

Sid's driver dropped Trisha off in front of her mother's semiattached house. The street was dark. The Christmas lights that had lit up the porches and windows had been turned off, most likely when the neighbors had gone to sleep hours ago. A light snow was falling. The driver waited as he was instructed to do, the engine idling, until she went into the house and closed the door behind her. The kitchen light was turned on in the back room. She found her mother sitting at the table smoking a cigarette. A pink lighter sat next to the ashtray. Her mother had a thing for cheap pink lighters.

"How'd it go?" her mother asked. "You don't look any worse for the wear."

Trisha paused at the bottom of the stairs, her head down. "Why do you care? Why now?" she asked. "When I was a kid and I needed you, where were you? Where were you when I relied on you to protect me?"

"I've always cared. Always. You have to believe me. I just didn't know. I didn't know until after he was already gone."

"How could you not have known? It was happening right under your nose." But even as she said it, she understood sometimes a person couldn't see beyond their own circumstances, even if it involved their own daughter. And what she finally realized was that her mother hadn't been able to see past the bills, the bruises, her own pain.

"I swear I didn't know," her mother cried. "Why didn't you tell me?"

"I was a kid. I was scared and ashamed. I thought it was my fault."

"It wasn't." Tears rolled down her mother's cheeks. "I'm sorry."

"Yeah," she said and headed up the stairs, whispering, "that makes two of us."

CHAPTER TWENTY-SEVEN

After hearing his name, Parker turned on the barstool where he was sitting at Benny's to find Becca standing behind him. He opened his mouth, mumbled something that sounded like "Hey." Geena stuck out her hand.

"Geena Brassard," she said.

"Becca Kingsley." She looked at Parker, her expression indecipherable. He used to be able to read her eyes, the twist of her mouth, to know what she was thinking. He no longer understood the woman in front of him. She looked beautiful, even though he was a little drunk and her features blurred.

Geena picked up the beer Benny had topped off. "He's all yours," she said to Becca and walked away.

Becca waved to Rick across the room.

"He called you?" Parker asked.

"He's worried about you," she said.

Parker looked her in the eye. "What did he say to you?" he asked, noticed Geena had rejoined Rick and the others.

"Not much," Becca said. "Other than you might need a ride home."

Parker supposed this was Rick's way of looking out for him, making sure he didn't do anything stupid tonight like go home with his partner. It had never crossed Parker's mind. He picked up his mug to take another drink, but Becca gently put her hand on his arm, stopped him before it reached his lips.

"Why don't you let me take you home?" she said.

His stomach was full, his head fuzzy. The room was hazy. She was probably right. He shouldn't be driving.

"You can get your car tomorrow," she said.

He followed her out to her Jeep. They drove with the windows cracked, the icy air sobering him up a bit. Next to him, Becca shivered. She was a runner, her body lean, taut. What she needed was some fat on her bones to keep her warm.

He rolled up his window so she wouldn't be cold. The heat from the dashboard vents blew in his face. The winding, bouncing roads made him feel sick. His tongue was slick, the taste bitter. He forced it down.

"She's my new partner," he said, not knowing how else to explain Geena's presence with him at the bar. He wanted to put Becca's mind at ease. He didn't want her to think there was something going on between him and his partner.

"Oh" was all she said.

They were quiet on the rest of the ride to his place. He closed his eyes and didn't open them again until Becca had pulled into his driveway.

She helped him into his cabin, walked him straight into his bedroom. He might be a bachelor, but he kept his place tidy. *Rustic chic*, Becca had called his style, with his gourmet kitchen, barnwood floors, flat-screen TV. Behind the cabin the river flowed. His place was too far away from Dead Man's Curve to hear the raging rapids. The stretch of water off his dock was as calm as a lake. He fumbled with the buttons on his shirt.

"Let me help you," she said.

She was a lot shorter than he was; her head barely reached his shoulders. She smelled nice, citrusy. Her cold fingers brushed his chest. He tried to get her to look up at him. He bent down to kiss her. She moved away. He tried again, but she turned her head a second time, stepped back, put too much distance between them.

She watched him closely.

He yanked his shirt off, dropped it on the floor. Then he unbuttoned his pants and pulled down the zipper. He kicked off his pants one leg at a time, having to reach for the dresser to keep from falling over. He stood in front of her wearing nothing but his briefs and socks.

She didn't even take off her coat.

"Into bed," she said and turned down the comforter.

He was too drunk, tired, to do anything other than what she asked. He crawled into bed, closed his eyes as soon as his head hit the pillow.

"Sleep tight," she said and kissed his forehead. He didn't hear her leave. He should've asked her to stay. He wanted her to stay. "I miss you," he mumbled to the empty room.

కర

Hours later Parker's cell phone went off. He rolled over, searched for it on the nightstand. His head pounded. His mouth was dry. The room had the hazy feel of morning.

"Hello." His voice cracked.

"We got something." It was someone from the lab. Maybe Mara, the tech who had helped him on a previous case. His brain was slow waking up.

She continued. "Someone scratched initials onto the bat. It's actually not that hard to scratch aluminum."

"Anything on the serial numbers?"

"No. They're too worn to read clearly."

"Okay. Send a picture of the initials to my phone," Parker said, pressed the heel of his palm into his eye where the headache throbbed behind it.

"Will do," Mara said. "Any idea who S. S. could be?"

Parker ran through his short list of suspects. Nothing jumped out at him. He'd have to comb through the file, see if there was a name with those initials. "Not yet," he said.

"Oh, hey, we got nothing on the lighter other than it was pink," she said. "I'll get those pics to you ASAP."

"Thanks," Parker said and hung up.

He sat up. His stomach rolled. He might get sick. He had to get to the station, call Geena, figure out whose initials were *S. S.* and what their connection to Lester might be.

His clothes had been thrown on the floor haphazardly. Then he remembered Becca driving him home from the bar, refusing to kiss him, putting him to bed. He could already feel the regret moving through his insides, settling in his chest, and he wasn't even out of bed yet.

He dragged himself to the shower, let the hot water run down his back. He dressed. His car was in Benny's parking lot. He called Uber. His phone went off again. Mara had sent a close-up of the softball bat with the engraving—*S. S.*, surrounded by a heart.

CHAPTER TWENTY-EIGHT

DECEMBER 1986

Trisha hid against the side of the house, watched Carlyn and Dannie walk down the sidewalk in the direction of the bus stop. Dannie was wearing her long puffy coat that made her look three times heavier than she was. Carlyn had tucked her hair underneath a knitted hat, her backpack stuffed full of books. Their heads were down. They were careful where they stepped, avoided the patches of snow and ice covering the walkway. They weren't talking, as far as Trisha could tell.

Trisha scooted around the back of the next house and slipped up the side yard unnoticed. She didn't know why she was spying on her friends. She didn't know why she'd done half the things she'd done lately. But she wasn't going to school today, not after last night, swinging the bat at Lester's head, sleeping in Carlyn's bed. She hadn't bothered asking Carlyn to skip with her. She hadn't played hooky with Trisha in weeks. And Dannie had been missing so many days lately, staying home and taking care of her mother, that if she missed any more, the school had threatened to hold her back a year, not allow her to graduate.

Her friends made it to the end of the block. Trisha scurried behind two more homes, pressed her back to the wall of the last house on Second Street. The cold aluminum siding cut through her layers of clothes. Other kids emerged on Broadway. No one saw her. No one was looking for her.

Not even her friends.

Trisha waited until the buses pulled up. She spied Scott in the crowd. He was looking up and down the street. Perhaps he was looking for her. Then he climbed on the bus with Carlyn and Dannie and everybody else. Once the buses started pulling away, Trisha stepped onto the sidewalk in full view, wondered if Scott would notice, if her friends cared.

It was Carlyn who looked out the back window and saw her, put her palm against the glass as the bus rolled down the street.

¤§

After the buses had gone, Trisha shoved her hands into her coat pockets. She wrapped her fingers around the pink lighter, squeezed it in her fist. She walked fast, head down, breathing into the collar of her coat, which she'd zipped all the way up to her chin. The air was so cold it stung her skin. The occasional car drove past, but other than the sound of traffic, the town was quiet.

She continued walking toward the woods and the trail that would take her up the mountain. Four inches of snow had fallen. The streets were wet, salty. But the woods were untouched by plows and traffic and people. The snow was so bright it hurt her eyes to look at it directly. The branches drooped with the weight of the ice. The woods were silent. It was the kind of silence that buzzed in your ears, the quiet before the storm. They would get more snow tonight. The weatherman had forecast a blizzard, over a foot of snow coming their way. It wasn't expected to hit until this evening. Trisha had all day to waste before it became too dangerous to be on the mountain in the freezing-cold temps in the middle of a winter storm.

She found the trail and ascended the hill. Snow seeped into her jeans around the tops of her boots. She stopped to pick the bigger chunks of ice out so her feet wouldn't get wet. Somewhere behind her twigs snapped. Her head shot up. She looked around, listened.

It must've been an animal, a squirrel. She lit a cigarette, stuffed the lighter in her jeans pocket. The smell of smoke would drive whatever it was away. She took several steps before stopping. The hairs on the back of her neck bristled. She had the feeling of being watched. She looked behind her, then all around.

"Who's there?" she called, her voice echoing, bouncing off the rocks and trees.

She dropped the cigarette and took off up the trail. She didn't know why she went up and not down the mountain. She wasn't thinking. Her only thoughts were to get away. She was out of breath. Sweat soaked her hairline. She climbed onto the large rock that was underneath the tree with the *Kilroy was here* carving. She looked down the mountain through the bare branches, the fallen logs, the rocky, snow-covered terrain.

Not far in the distance she spotted him walking up the trail. She recognized the Phillies baseball cap, the insulated flannel jacket, the bottle of whiskey swinging from his hand.

Lester.

He staggered, took two steps forward, one step back. He was drunk. She had a better chance of getting away from him when he was drinking. She was sure she could outrun him. But her feet weren't moving. Fear spun in her stomach like the blades of a helicopter. Her breathing came in rapid bursts. She couldn't believe he'd followed her.

"What do you want?" Trisha's voice rose, knowing he could hear the panic in her tone. She was already crying. *Please, no. Please don't,* she begged silently.

"Don't yell, princess. I'm drunk, not deaf. Shouldn't you be in school?" he asked.

"Yes," she said. "They'll be looking for me. I should go."

Before she could move, he took a step toward her.

"What are you doing here, anyway?" he asked. "You meeting a boy? Is that what you're doing?" He stuck his tongue out, wiggled it in a lewd gesture.

"You're disgusting." She lost her footing on the rock and slid. Lester reached out, caught her. The pack of cigarettes fell from her coat pocket.

"What do we have here?" He put the whiskey bottle down and picked up the pack of smokes. He plucked one out and put it between his lips, patted his pockets in search of a lighter.

He was blocking her way, but maybe she could get around him. She stepped to his side. His arm shot out.

"Where do you think you're going? Thought we were going to have us a little party." His rancid breath hit her face.

She winced.

He grabbed her arm.

"Let go of me."

"Come on, now." The cigarette dangled from his lips. "Where are you hiding that lighter?"

He shoved his hand into her coat pockets. Then he searched the back pockets of her jeans, smiling as his hand lingered on her ass. She twisted away, but he pulled her close. He was so much stronger than anyone gave him credit for. Even when he was drunk, he was so darn sturdy. He put his hand deep into the front pocket of her jeans. His fingers closed around the pink lighter.

"Aha," he said and pulled it out. He squeezed her arm tightly while he lit the cigarette.

"Let go of me," she said again.

He pulled her closer. "Now see what you've done." He took a long drag, then blew the smoke in her face. "You've gone and got me all worked up."

"I didn't do anything." Trisha tried to wriggle from his grip. She knocked the pink lighter from his hand. It sank in the snow and disappeared.

Lester reached around the back of her neck, pushed her head down. "Come on, don't fight me," he said, dropping the cigarette in his struggle to control her.

She clenched her jaw, her mouth closed in a tight line as she tried to break free from his grasp. Her senses heightened: the sound of his raspy breath, the rise of his Adam's apple when he swallowed, the scent of sweat on his skin.

She wouldn't do it. He couldn't make her.

She spotted the whiskey bottle on the ground by her feet, reached for it, twisting, turning, stretching, straining, until her fingers wrapped around the neck. She pushed back with all her strength and brought her arm up. She swung as hard as she could. The bottle struck him on the side of the head. The glass broke in her palm. Whiskey sprayed.

The hand he'd wrapped around the back of her neck dropped to his side. He tilted backward as though in slow motion, falling, falling, falling. His body hit the ground, the sound echoing through the woods. She stared at the broken bottle in her hand, watched as it dropped from her fingers.

Blood dripped from her palm, stained the snow at her feet. She watched it fall as though it were coming from someone else's hand and not her own. There was blood around Lester's head.

He wasn't moving.

She wasn't moving. Time became a hazy thing while her mind tried to catch up to what she was seeing, what she'd done.

He still wasn't moving.

She wasn't aware of backing away from him, her palm now soaked with blood, her fingers sticky.

Run.

Trisha turned and ran. She didn't think about anything but getting away.

She slid down the snowy trail. She didn't look back. Oh, how she hated him, how every inch of her hated him.

CHAPTER TWENTY-NINE

Trisha knocked on the late Evelyn's door before she stepped inside. The furniture in the living room had been taken out, thrown into the large dumpster Dannie had rented that now sat in front of the house. A couple of neighbors had complained to Trisha's mother and Linda about how it looked trashy having a dumpster on the street. Dannie had promised it would be removed within forty-eight hours.

The couch where Evelyn had lain for the last four decades was the first item to be tossed. The cushions were stained beyond cleaning, greasy from the oils seeping from Evelyn's skin and hair. The end tables and entertainment center had been donated to family services. Dannie's oldest daughter had confiscated the television set for her bedroom.

Trisha walked across the worn carpet into the dining room. The table was covered with boxes, mostly the kitchen items they'd packed the other day. There were voices coming from the basement, her mother's and Linda's. Upstairs a door opened. Trisha headed up the steps. She found Dannie in the spare room next to the bathroom: the room they hadn't been allowed to enter when they were teenagers. Dannie had said it was a junk room, storage room, old clothes and knickknacks, nothing worth seeing.

But everywhere Trisha looked there were statues and images of Jesus, the Virgin Mary, the Last Supper, the Resurrection. Oh, this was definitely something worth seeing. Crucifixes decorated an entire wall. There was an altar in the corner where several candles had been burned, the wax dripping onto the wood. A small bench was placed at the foot of the altar, where someone was meant to kneel. Dannie's back was to Trisha.

"Hey," Trisha said.

Dannie jumped. "I didn't hear you come in."

Trisha picked up a figurine of the Virgin Mary. "Was this why you kept us out? You didn't want us to see all of your mom's stuff?" It was as good an explanation as any as to why the room had been off limits. Never mind the sheer creepiness of it.

"No," Dannie said. "I didn't want you to see it because it was mine."

"Really? Wow." Trisha said the only thing she could think of. "I mean, wow."

"I know," Dannie said. "I was obsessed with it back then. I guess I went overboard." She glanced at Trisha. "But I needed to. It helped me cope with a lot of things."

"Like your dad leaving?"

"Yes, that was part of it."

Trisha didn't have to ask what the other part was, knowing it had to do with Lester. "What are you going to do with all of this stuff now?" she asked.

"I'm going to keep some of it. The rest I'll take to the church. They can sell it at the bazaar."

Trisha nodded. She was sure there was something more she should say, but she couldn't think of anything.

Dannie picked up a bust of Jesus. She stared at his face when she said, "The police left me a message this morning. They want to talk with me."

Trisha had expected this. She moved to stand at Dannie's side. "You're going to tell them exactly what I tell you to."

Dannie nodded, kept her eyes on the bust. "What is it you want me to say?"

"You don't know anything about what happened to Lester. We were at Carlyn's. There was a snowstorm. We didn't leave her house."

Downstairs the front door banged open. Voices carried up the stairs. "Mom," one of them called. "Where are you?"

"Up here," Dannie said. "My girls." A panicked look crossed her face.

"Tell the police exactly what I said," Trisha whispered and turned when two teenage girls entered the room. They were both wearing their Catholic school uniforms: plaid skirts, knee-high socks, button-down shirts with matching varsity band jackets.

"Ugh, Gram's Jesus room," one of the girls said.

Trisha turned to Dannie. "*Gram's* Jesus room?"

"Yes," Dannie said, shooting Trisha a look. "Girls, this is an old friend of mine from school. Trisha, this is Jenny and Marie."

Jenny, the taller of the two and the one who looked to be the oldest, said, "Hi." Marie cowered behind Jenny without saying a word. It was something Dannie might've done back in high school.

Carlyn appeared in the doorway. Her face registered surprise at the sheer quantity of religious figurines scattered around the room. "Wow," she said, having the same reaction as Trisha.

"Okay," Dannie said, trying to usher everyone out. "I'm not going to have you make fun of me. I mean, *Gram*," she said to her girls. "I need more boxes before I can pack this stuff up, anyway. Scoot. Out you go."

"Jeez, Mom, don't get so defensive," Jenny said from the hallway. The girls waved to Carlyn as they passed by her.

It bothered Trisha that Carlyn knew Dannie's kids. It was just one more thing, another twist of the knife her old friends had stuck in her back. She picked at the skin on her forearm. It was about time for another drink.

"I've got some more boxes at my house you can use," Carlyn said to Dannie. "I can go get them. Want to come with me?" she asked Trisha, touching her fingers to Trisha's elbow.

Trisha jerked her arm away out of habit.

"Sorry," Carlyn said.

"Please, don't take it personally," Trisha said. "I'll ride along with you." She'd do anything to get out of the Jesus room. Her mere presence was one big stain on its holiness. She waited for Carlyn to go ahead of her. When she and Dannie were alone again, she said, "Your girls are really great."

Dannie nodded.

"You'll tell the police what I told you?"

"I don't remember it any other way," Dannie said.

⁂

Trisha looked up at Evelyn's house before getting into Carlyn's car. Dannie stood in the window, watching them go.

"Feeling better?" Carlyn asked once they had turned off Second Street and were heading down Broadway.

"About what?" Trisha watched the houses as they drove past, the blur of holiday wreaths hanging on doors, blinking lights, Christmas trees in windows.

"Since the last time I saw you," Carlyn said and glanced at her. "The other night at the bar. Scott."

"Right," she said, which wasn't an answer, but she refused to rehash the embarrassing evening. Nothing she could do about it now, anyway.

They were quiet, sitting at a traffic light.

"I see you went shopping," Carlyn said and pressed on the gas when the light turned green. "I'm glad you bought some warmer clothes to wear."

Trisha continued staring out the window. "I have your gloves," she said. "They're back at my mom's somewhere."

"Keep them," Carlyn said. "I have another pair."

"Right," she said again. She wasn't some charity case. Carlyn had no idea the kind of money Trisha had at her disposal.

Within minutes Carlyn had pulled down an alley and parked alongside a garage that appeared to have been converted into an apartment. They got out of the car. Trisha followed her down a narrow sidewalk, past what looked to be a garden, but it was hard to tell with all the snow in the yard. They walked underneath a pergola where grapes would grow, the vines climbing, stretching, bearing fruit waiting to be picked, fermented into wine. They crossed a patio, the chairs covered in plastic to protect them from the weather during the winter months. Finally, they reached the back door, stepped into the kitchen.

"This is it," Carlyn said. "My crib."

Trisha walked around, ran her fingertips across the marble countertops. She moved into the small living room, where a flat-screen TV was mounted on the wall in front of the softest leather couch Trisha had ever felt. The hardwood floors looked to be the original, creaking when she stepped on them the way old floors do. However, they had been refinished recently, the scuff marks buffed out, shiny new stain on top. The home might be old on the outside, but Carlyn had updated every inch of the inside. Shrinks must make decent money.

"The boxes are upstairs in the bedroom," Carlyn said.

Trisha took her coat off, sat on the couch. "How about a drink first before you show me your room?"

"That's not what . . ." She broke off, gave a nervous laugh. "All I have is wine."

"That'll do."

Carlyn disappeared into the kitchen. "Red or white?" she called.

"Whatever."

She came back with two glasses of red, handed one to Trisha. "It's homemade. I made it right here in my basement." She sat at the opposite end of the couch.

"That explains the pergola." She took a sip. "It's good."

"Thank you."

Neither seemed to know what to say next.

Trisha swallowed more wine. "If you're hoping I'm going to talk to fill the silence, you're wrong. I'm not falling for any of your shrink tricks."

"I work with children, not adults," Carlyn said. "Besides, that's not what I'm doing. To be honest, I don't know what to say to you."

"Oh, I think you know exactly what you want to say to me."

"Maybe I do," Carlyn said. "But that doesn't mean I'm going to."

Trisha laughed. "Do you see patients here?"

"Sometimes, yes. I remodeled the garage we passed and turned it into an office. I do see a lot of patients in their homes, too—whatever fits their needs."

"You always were good with kids. Me, I can't stand them." She drank some more wine. "I was pregnant once, though. It didn't work out."

"What happened?" Carlyn asked.

"Sid didn't want kids." She hadn't thought about her baby girl in years, but now she'd gone and opened the door, allowed her grief to walk in. Sometimes that was all it took: for her to make a stupid comment without thinking what it would cost her. She'd spent a lifetime shutting down, disconnecting. Then one remark had the power to bring back memories that made her vulnerable, human, her mind and body thirsty for thoughts and feelings after a long drought. She'd never told anyone how she used to touch her belly, felt the tiny fluttering underneath her palm, the joy it had brought to her hard days. She'd fallen in love, head over heels, with her baby. It had been the first time she'd ever felt an overwhelming, crushing love for another human being.

It had also been the last.

She'd been young, twenty-five years old, drinking more than her share by then. She'd forgotten to take her pill, hadn't noticed she'd skipped her period for three months. She'd told Sid. She'd been so young and naive, believing he'd be happy, but of course he hadn't been. He'd become increasingly disgusted by her growing belly, calling her fat, lazy. Ugly. She'd been hurt, back in the days when she'd cared about what he'd thought, when she'd have done whatever he'd asked to please him. As the weeks passed, she'd cared less about him and more about the life growing inside her. She'd stopped smoking, had tried her hardest to give up drinking, but that demon had been too hard to kill. Still, she'd hoped to make it to term, to change her habits. But Sid had had his own agenda. He'd come home from a late night, cross after a particularly long losing streak. He'd found her in the bathroom, peeing. The baby had been pressing on her bladder by then. She'd had to get up every three hours to use the bathroom. He'd grabbed her by the hair, pulled her off the toilet, pee dribbling down her leg and onto the floor. It hadn't been an ordinary rage, where he'd hit with abandon. His fists had purpose, the heel of his foot on her abdomen, intent. Afterward, she'd lain on the cold tile floor, unmoving, bleeding out.

Now, she rested her hand on her stomach, the scar so much deeper than the one from the hysterectomy.

Carlyn leaned forward, cradled the wine with both hands between her legs. "What did he do to you?"

"It doesn't matter. It's in the past."

"Why do you stay with him?"

"Why indeed."

Carlyn waited her out, wanted something more from her. A better explanation perhaps.

"I told you it doesn't matter," Trisha said.

"Your mom told my mom she saw bruises on your ribs."

Karen Katchur

Trisha looked away, couldn't stand seeing the sympathy on Carlyn's face.

"You don't deserve to be punished," Carlyn said. "You're not to blame."

Trisha crossed her legs, folded her arms, wagged her foot back and forth. "I stay for the same reasons every woman stays."

"And why is that?"

"Money. And I don't have anywhere else to go." She uncrossed her leg and stood. Wine splashed on her wrist. She downed what was left in the glass. "Where are those boxes anyway? Dannie's waiting."

CHAPTER THIRTY

DECEMBER 1986

Trisha was lying on the mattress in her bedroom. She was curled on her side, knees tucked under her chin. Carlyn was lying next to her, wrapped around her. The sun was up, melting the icicles hanging off the slate roof outside the window, the water dripping onto the sill. Drip. Drip. Drip.

Downstairs, Trisha's mother paced, the cheap linoleum floor creaking under her weight. The refrigerator door opened and closed. Next came the pop and spritz of a tab being pulled off a beer can.

Trisha counted six cans that had been opened in the last two hours since she'd been awake. She'd been hiding in her room ever since she'd left the woods yesterday, lying on her filthy mattress, where Carlyn had found her early this morning.

"Why weren't you in school yesterday?" Carlyn had asked. "Where did you go?"

Trisha had told her everything, the words tumbling out in a monotone voice as though she were reading a phone book. Her tone had been unapologetic, but she hadn't been able to stop from shaking. Carlyn had held her, was still holding her.

Trisha's palm throbbed where the glass shard from the broken whiskey bottle had cut through her skin. She'd covered it with a bandage to stop the bleeding sometime last night—she didn't remember when—to prevent the blood from staining her sheets.

Her mother had come home late, close to three a.m., after her shift at the bar had ended. She'd stomped around the house, talking to herself, mumbling about what a crappy husband she was stuck with, and where was he, anyway?

A million plus one reasons why Lester hadn't come home raced through Trisha's mind, but only the last one screeched and clawed at her conscience. She could do nothing but cradle her head in her hands and wait for the thrashing to stop.

When she couldn't stand to think about it any longer, she ripped the big white bandage off her hand and threw back the covers. She couldn't hide the bandage, but she could conceal the cut in her fist.

Carlyn untangled herself from Trisha. "What are you going to do?" she asked.

"I have to know," she said. "Wait here." She crept down the hall, poked her head into her mother's bedroom. She had to check, make sure Lester wasn't here. The bed looked slept in, but it was empty now. The sheets were twisted, her mother's pillow indented. Lester's pillow was plumped, untouched.

Trisha tiptoed downstairs. Her mother was standing in the middle of the kitchen with a cigarette in one hand and a beer in the other, her bleached hair teased and piled high on her head. She was wearing her work clothes: the tight black skirt and top. She must've slept in them.

"Everything okay, Mom?" She took a tentative step toward her. Up close, her mother looked haggard and worn, a woman too young to look the way she did, possibly from stress, but more likely from working late nights, drinking, and smoking.

"Your dad didn't come home last night," her mother said and put the cigarette to her lips.

"He's not my dad." How dare her mother say he was? Lester was a monster. He was no father to her.

"You're right. He's not. Stepfather." She wiped her eye with the back of her hand, careful of the cigarette between her fingers.

"He's done this before, off on a bender," Trisha said, steadying her voice. "He'll be back once he sleeps it off or runs out of money." The lie came easily. How many more would she have to tell?

Her mother drank from the can, followed by a drag of the cigarette. "Did he say where he was going last night?"

"No. How would I know?"

"I don't know. It was a stupid question." Her mother turned away, stared at nothing. She brought the cigarette to her lips. Her nails were painted fire red, her fingers stained yellow with nicotine.

Trisha's stomach burned, the old familiar anger searing inside. "You're worrying for nothing," she said, trying to sound calm, even reasonable.

When it was apparent her mother wasn't going to respond, Trisha scurried out of the kitchen and climbed the stairs back to her bedroom. She closed the door, the one that didn't lock.

"Well?" Carlyn asked. Her hair was stuck flat to her head. She rubbed her arms. The house was cold, the heat turned down low even though the weather outside was close to freezing.

"She doesn't know where he is."

"You don't think you . . ." Carlyn stopped.

"I don't know. But I have to go back. I have to be sure." Trisha put her arms around Carlyn, rested her head on Carlyn's shoulder. Fresh blood dripped from Trisha's palm. She was scared. She wanted her friend by her side. She couldn't do this alone. She clung to Carlyn, nuzzled her neck. "You'll help me, won't you, Car?"

Carlyn pulled in a breath. "What do you need me to do?"

CHAPTER THIRTY-ONE

Parker typed a text message to Becca. I'm sorry about last night. He hesitated before hitting send. Becca must think he was a first-class jerk, which of course he was. What had he been thinking? The throbbing behind his eye subsided after three aspirins, which was probably one too many, but whatever worked. He deleted the text before hitting send. Maybe this was something he should apologize for in person. He struggled navigating the whole social/technology thing, what you should or shouldn't text when you were in a relationship. He leaned against Geena's desk, considered asking her for advice. But was that crossing a line? He didn't know, said nothing.

"Don't get comfortable," Geena said and stood. "We're going door-to-door, seeing if anybody knows anything about this guy." She held up a mug shot for Parker to see. The guy's head was shaved. Tattoos climbed up his neck. He had a large scar under his right eye. "Goes by the nickname Boonie. He's the possible doer in Angel's case."

"Angel?" Parker followed Geena outside to the car.

"The girl this guy allegedly burned and left on the side of the road. It's the case everyone's working, including us, apparently. Sayres wants us to sweep her neighborhood for any witnesses, for the third time. Yeah, you heard me: two other teams already worked it. He told me you'd know why we got this detail."

They stopped by the car, talked over the roof.

"This have anything to do with your last case?" Geena asked.

Parker ran his hand across his brow. "Yeah, that would be my guess."

"What exactly did you do to get on his shit list?" She looked up, peered at the sky, the thick gray clouds.

"I got involved with a witness."

"Involved how?" Geena asked as they climbed into the car.

He didn't answer.

"Shoot, Parker." Geena looked at him. "I'm assuming this witness is the same girl from last night? What was her name? Becca?"

"It is."

"Please tell me she's worth it so this sucky assignment in the freezing-cold rain will actually be worth our time."

"She's worth it."

"Okay, then," Geena said. "You look like crap, by the way."

"I feel like crap."

Geena pulled onto Route 191, heading in the direction of Allentown. "So how did it go with her last night, anyway?" she asked.

"With who? Becca? Not so good."

"Sorry to hear it," Geena said. "I hope I didn't have anything to do with it."

"You didn't."

"Are you sure? I'm not blind or deaf to what goes on. I know some of the guys' wives complain about me working with their husbands."

"It's not that," Parker said and made up his mind: he didn't want to talk about it. He felt bad enough about his behavior last night. He pulled up the image of the softball bat on his phone, held it up for her to see. "Check this out," he said.

Geena looked at the photo, taking her eyes off the highway for a brief moment. Parker zoomed in on the spot where the initials *S. S.* had been engraved.

"There isn't anyone in the file that matches the initials," Geena said.

"You're sure?" Parker asked. He hadn't had a chance to look.

"I'm sure," she said.

"Okay, well, we still have two people we haven't talked to who gave statements back then. A Danielle Teagan. She lived across the street from Lester. Her mother passed about a week ago. I left a message for her to contact me."

"You mean Danielle Torino," Geena said. "Carlyn Walsh said Danielle changed her name when she got married."

"Right." He'd forgotten that detail. "The other one is Scott Best. Turns out he's the same cop we saw at the hotel." Parker had searched for him online, found a picture of him in uniform.

Sleet pelted the windshield. Geena pressed on the gas. "We better get moving. I don't want to be traipsing around in the freezing rain all day."

⁂

Parker and Geena returned to the station after walking up and down Fourth Street in Allentown, knocking on doors, searching for witnesses in the Angel case for the last three hours. No one was willing to come forward, although Parker bet every single one of the neighbors they'd spoken to had known something about the man in the photo. Geena called Sayres, told him they hadn't found anyone who'd been willing to talk.

Parker threw his rain-soaked jacket onto the chair. His fingers were white, numb. He blew on them. Most of the patrol was out dealing with the icy roads, auto accidents. "Did you ever get the list of names of Lester's coworkers from Cal's son?" he asked.

"He finally emailed it late last night. I made a couple calls, but so far nothing." Geena sat at her desk, checked her messages. "Hold on. One of them got back to me," she said. "Says he has some information about Cal that we might find interesting."

"Let's check it out," Parker said.

⳨

Parker and Geena sat across the table from Ron Schneider at a diner off Route 191 in Nazareth. Ron was a thin man in his seventies. He had a long face and bulbous nose that was covered in pockmarks and veins. He sat in front of a plate with a half-eaten open-faced hot turkey-and-gravy sandwich.

"I didn't know Lester that well," Ron said, talking while he chewed. "He worked in the back, in the warehouse. I was in the front of the store with Cal when I wasn't out on sales appointments."

"You mentioned something in your message about Cal and Lester's wife, Sharon," Geena said.

"That's right," he said, stabbed a piece of turkey with his fork, ran it through the gravy before shoveling it into his mouth. "I'd sometimes see them together in the store. But I think Cal used to visit her at her house, if you catch my drift."

"You think Cal and Sharon were having an affair?" Parker asked.

"I can't say for sure, but I had my suspicions."

"Did Lester know?" Parker asked.

"I don't think so. I don't know. Like I said, he worked in the back. I didn't have much opportunity to talk to him."

"Why did you think they were having an affair?" Parker asked.

"A married man doesn't go to another married man's house when he isn't home. Not unless something's going on with the wife."

He had a point.

"Okay," Parker said. "Thank you for your time. If we have any further questions, we'll be in touch." He picked up the check, paid for the man's lunch.

Back in the car, Parker said, "Sharon has another motive for wanting her husband dead."

"Yeah, and maybe so does Cal," Geena added.

CHAPTER THIRTY-TWO

DECEMBER 1986

Trisha and Carlyn slipped into their winter parkas and pulled on their boots. A foot of snow had fallen overnight. School was canceled. The weatherman forecast another few inches coming their way before nightfall.

"We have to do this quick," Trisha said, shoving her hands into her gloves. If she thought about it for too long, she'd lose her nerve.

Carlyn pulled her knit hat on. She'd been awfully quiet in the last ten minutes since leaving Trisha's bedroom.

"Mom," Trisha called. Her mother was still in the kitchen, pacing, drinking. "We're going sledding. Be back soon." She turned to Carlyn, looked in her eyes, searched for courage.

Carlyn nodded.

Trisha opened the door and stepped onto the porch. Most of the neighbors on the street were already busy at work, wielding shovels, digging out cars, clearing the snow from the steps and sidewalks. Some of the snow was still fresh, the white so bright it stung her eyes. Other piles were covered in a dirty grit kicked up from the plows and slate mines.

Across the street, Dannie was shoveling a section of sidewalk in front of her house. She stopped, stared at them. There was something sad about her expression, a kind of puppy-face look.

Trisha ignored her, headed for the middle of the road, where the plow had gone through at least twice during the night. The road wasn't completely cleared, but the packed snow made for easier walking. The wind picked up in the open space, gnawed at her ears.

It seemed to Trisha that Carlyn hesitated. A second later she was by her side.

Dannie ran to catch up to them. "Where are you going?" she asked. Her big puffy coat came down to her knees. It was a little too small and was pulled tight across her chest.

"The trail," Trisha said.

Dannie grabbed Trisha's arm. "Why?" she asked.

Trisha shrugged her off. "Because I have to."

They stopped at the end of Second Street. A couple of boys on their block were in the midst of a snowball fight. Two little girls worked on a snowman in their patch of yard. The older kids, classmates, were walking up Broadway's steep hill, dragging their sleds behind them. Trisha searched the street, squinting against the bright-white snow, looking for Scott's black jacket with the silver racing stripes. She didn't want to see him. He was the last person she wanted to bump into. He would know something was wrong.

"You can't go," Dannie said. "There's too much snow. You'll never find the trail," she insisted.

"I have to try," Trisha said.

"I don't understand why," Dannie pleaded.

"Something happened," Carlyn said. "Something bad."

Dannie shook her head, her lips clamped, her eyes watery.

Trisha started walking again. Whatever Dannie's problem was, she didn't have time to deal with her. Not now. Carlyn followed.

"Please," Dannie said and rushed to catch up to them. "You'll never make it through the woods in this much snow."

Trisha spied Scott halfway up Broadway. He turned her way. He saw her. "Hurry," she said and took off running, although she knew he wouldn't follow them. She didn't know how she knew, but she did.

Carlyn chased after her. Dannie tried to keep up but fell several paces behind. They kept to the side of the road. Once they had to jump in a snowdrift to get out of the way of the plow.

Trisha's jeans were soaked up to her knees. Her legs were cold and numb. She continued jogging. She wouldn't stop, even though the air burned her lungs and the wind stung her cheeks. When she reached the edge of the woods that would take them to the trail, she stopped and bent over, tried to catch her breath, work up her nerve. Carlyn was used to running; she was barely winded. Dannie finally caught up to them.

"We can't go up there," Dannie said between gulps of air.

"We have to," Trisha said. "We have to check on something." She kept her head down. Phlegm clung to the back of her tongue.

Carlyn put her hand on Dannie's shoulder, explained why they had to go up the mountain. Trisha didn't stop her. Dannie had to know. She was a part of it now too.

"He never came home last night," Carlyn said.

Dannie was shaking her head. "No, no, no, no." She looked back and forth between them. "He must have. You just didn't see him."

"I have to know for sure," Trisha said. She didn't think beyond that. She wouldn't be able to wrap her mind around what she'd done until she was certain she'd actually done it.

"I can't go up there. I can't." Dannie covered her face.

"You don't have to," Trisha said. Dannie was too slow. She'd only hold them back.

"You can wait right here for us," Carlyn said.

"Okay," Dannie said. She nodded, as though it wasn't okay at all. Her cheeks were windburned, her lips blue. "Okay," she said again.

Carlyn turned to Trisha. "Ready?"

Trisha stepped from the road into the woods. It was a small step but a momentous one. She pushed through the thigh-high snow in search of the trail. A small red dot blossomed in the palm of her mitten.

❧

Trisha shivered underneath her parka. Snow leaked inside her boots, her jeans now soaked to her thighs. The mountain looked different under a foot of snow, with its rolling white hills, frosted trees. It was desolate, colorless, beautiful. She had to guess where the Appalachian Trail was: a path she'd walked a hundred times over but was now playing a game of hide-and-seek beneath her feet.

"Are you sure we're heading in the right direction?" Carlyn asked, trekking a few steps behind, pausing every couple of seconds to look around.

"Just follow me," Trisha said over her shoulder, jumping when a bird screeched, scolding her for the intrusion. She searched the woods, tried to get her bearings. She continued upward, stopping when she spotted the tree with the *Kilroy was here* carving. She looked back the way she'd come. Carlyn stood next to her, teeth chattering. No one was behind them. Their solitary footprints were evidence they were alone. An uneasy feeling tightened her chest and throat.

Think. Think about where she'd seen him fall. She looked to her left. She didn't want to look but couldn't stop herself. It was as though she were drawn to the horror of what she might find, what she expected to see. Next to a large maple tree, she spied a red baseball cap bleeding through the snow, and underneath, Lester's head, his body slumped, buried in white.

She covered her mouth, breathed into her mittens. The coppery smell of her own blood soaked the fabric, filled her nose.

Carlyn saw him too. She turned her head away.

Trisha stepped toward him, unable to resist this strange, strong pull toward the morbid.

"Where are you going?" Carlyn asked, her words distant in Trisha's ears.

Her legs quaked as she pressed through the snow, a wet blanket around her thighs, weighing her down, holding her back. She stopped a few feet from his body. The area around his head was stained pink. Something dark and sticky had plastered his hair by his brow. A fallen branch poked through the snow. Hanging from the branch was a bloody icicle.

She wasn't fully aware of Carlyn coming up behind her, putting her arm around her, leading her away.

They hiked down the mountain, pushed through the heavy snow, followed their tracks out of the woods. Trisha's legs and feet were numb. Her limbs moved as though they belonged to someone else. Carlyn's arm was warm around her waist. The next thing Trisha remembered was standing on the side of the road. Dannie was there, hollering.

"What is it? What happened? Did you see him? Was he there?"

"Shut up!" Carlyn yelled.

"Was he there?" Dannie shrieked. "Was he? Was he?"

"Shut up, Dannie!" Carlyn grabbed Dannie by the collar of her puffy coat. "Get a hold of yourself," she said.

Dannie nodded, kept nodding until Carlyn let her go. Trisha watched her friends, but it was as though she were seeing them through a dirty glass window. She raised her arm to wipe it clean, her hand floating in front of her like a balloon.

Carlyn took hold of Trisha's wrist, lowered her arm. "Come on, Trisha. This way," Carlyn said. "We'll get you home."

They were walking again.

She recognized some of the side streets: neighborhood yards she'd cut through when she'd been a ten-year-old kid. When they reached Second Street, they stopped. Carlyn kept her hand on Trisha's arm.

"Don't talk," Carlyn ordered. "No one say a word."

Trisha was having trouble thinking, her mind fuzzy around the edges. She looked up and down the street. Two smaller boys whom Carlyn had babysat on occasion played in the snow in their yard. Others were sledding down Broadway.

"Let's take her to my house," Carlyn said to Dannie. "My mom's working a double shift. Some of the other nurses couldn't make it in on account of the snow."

They were moving again, one foot in front of the other. Dannie was quiet. Trisha was vaguely aware of walking up Carlyn's porch steps. Carlyn threw open the front door, pushed Trisha inside, led her straight to her bedroom, Dannie in tow.

"Let me help you," Carlyn said and pulled off Trisha's boots, unbuttoned her jeans, tugged them off Trisha's cold pink thighs. "Here." She handed her sweatpants, but Trisha didn't take them, and they dropped to the floor.

"What did I do?" Trisha asked.

Carlyn picked up the pants, handed them to her a second time. "You protected yourself," she said.

Dannie cried.

Trisha slipped on the sweatpants. Carlyn changed into dry clothes, then scooped up their wet ones in her arms.

"Follow me," she said and carried their soggy clothes to the washing machine in the basement, tossed in their jeans and socks. They could hide some of the evidence that they'd been to the woods, but they couldn't hide the footprints they'd left behind.

On rubbery arms, Trisha hoisted herself on top of the machine. The washer hummed beneath her. Cobwebs dangled from the ceiling. An empty container of laundry detergent had been knocked over, dripping what was left onto the cement floor. A clothesline ran the length of the room.

Carlyn leaned against the dryer, arms crossed, head down.

Dannie stood in front of them, rocking on her heels, hands in prayer. "Oh my God. Oh my God. Oh my God," she whispered over and over again.

Trisha couldn't concentrate, focus, with Dannie's constant rambling in her ears. *Shut up!* she wanted to scream. She tried to think, devise some kind of a plan, an alibi, but her thoughts scattered, crumbled, dropped to the concrete floor.

The room, her friends, were blurry in her mind's eye. But one image remained clear: Lester's body. One feeling: the cold.

She was so cold.

CHAPTER THIRTY-THREE

After Parker and Geena had left the diner, they'd tracked down Scott Best and asked him to meet them at the station.

"Officer Best," Parker said, shook Scott's hand, then introduced him to Geena.

Scott had the salt-and-pepper hair of a man in his forties. It was quite possible he was closer to fifty than not. He was a big guy, fit for his age. They moved into one of the back rooms where they could talk privately.

"Thanks for coming in," Parker said, instructed Scott to have a seat at the small table where countless other witnesses and the occasional victim had sat before. The room was friendlier than the other interview rooms. It had a potted plant in the corner, tissues on the table. The walls were the same bland beige as the rest of the building.

Parker asked Scott questions, the conversation casual. Scott said he'd been a cop in Bangor for the last twenty years. He'd served overseas in Iraq during Desert Storm, returned and attended four years of college on the GI Bill before becoming a police officer in his hometown. You couldn't help but like him. He had an air of confidence about him. You could tell just by looking at him that he was one of the good guys. He was the real deal.

But even good guys had their limits, made mistakes.

"I didn't know Lester Haines personally," Scott said. "But I knew he was Trisha's stepfather. Trisha and I were friends. I'd go as far as to say she was my girlfriend—well, for a little while, anyway." He shrugged. "She was more or less my girlfriend, as much as anyone is anyone's girlfriend at that age. It ended after all the trouble started when her stepfather went missing." Scott cracked his neck, lifted his chin.

"Did she talk to you about Lester? Did she tell you what she thought might've happened to him?" Parker asked. Geena remained quiet, letting Parker take the lead.

"No, she didn't know," Scott said. "Or if she knew, she never told me. She stopped talking to me after that."

"How was her homelife? Did she ever mention Lester fighting with her mother? Did you ever hear her arguing with Lester, complaining about him?" Parker asked. Sharon and Lester had gone rounds, he knew. Sharon had a motive for wanting Lester dead.

Scott stared at the empty corner of the room. "I never heard them argue. She didn't talk about her family," he said. "None of us did. We were too involved with other things to pay much attention."

"Did you ever go to her house, hang out there?" Parker asked.

"No, she never invited me. Whenever we'd meet, it was always out with other friends around."

"You never went to her house? Ever?" Geena asked.

"No." Scott leaned back in the chair, rubbed the leather belt where he carried his weapon. He was wearing the standard-issue bulletproof vest underneath his uniform, pulling his shirt tight across his chest.

Parker referred to Scott's original statement. "It says here you were in school that day. After school, you went to an indoor baseball practice at the school gym, and then you went straight home." It was the mention of baseball practice at the school gym that had piqued Parker's interest.

"Sounds about right. If I remember correctly, we had a pretty big snowstorm that week. We got like a foot of snow. I think we might've missed school because of it."

Parker nodded. He made a note to check the weather reports. He pulled up the image of the softball bat on his phone and handed it to Scott. "Does this look familiar to you?"

Scott brought the phone close to his face. He nodded. "Yeah, it looks familiar." He swallowed. "It looks like the bats from the high school gym." He handed the phone back to Parker.

"That's what I thought too," Parker said. "Do you know anything about this particular bat?"

Scott stood, ran his hand across the top of his head.

Parker and Geena looked at each other.

"Maybe I do," Scott said after a few seconds had passed.

Parker was under the impression that Scott and Trisha's relationship might've been more than he was letting on.

Scott continued. "Trisha stole a bat from gym class. I know because we argued about it. I wanted her to return it. I don't know. She was always doing these stupid things to get herself into trouble. She was her own worst enemy sometimes." He rested his hands on the back of the chair. "But look, it could be anybody's bat. I'm sure she's not the only one who took equipment from the gym and didn't return it."

"Do you remember when she stole the bat? Was it before Lester disappeared? After?"

"A couple of weeks before, I think," he said.

"Take a look at this." Parker zoomed in on the S. S. initials with the heart around the letters. He handed the phone back to Scott. "Do you know who or what it stands for?" Parker asked.

"Yeah," Scott said. "I know what it stands for." He dropped into the chair, his whole body crumpling as though he were under a tremendous weight.

CHAPTER THIRTY-FOUR

DECEMBER 1986

Three days after seeing Lester's body on the mountain, Trisha walked the halls of the high school. Faces blurred, voices carried, spinning around her, over her, through her. Dannie had avoided her, made the sign of the cross, cried whenever they'd crossed paths. Carlyn had sequestered herself in the library, studying, preparing for exams before Christmas break, keeping her own form of distance.

Scott had approached Trisha six times that morning. She kept count: six times. He'd made several attempts to get her to talk, to tell him why she was ignoring him. The last time he'd asked her to please tell him what he'd done wrong. She opened her mouth, but only a strange guttural whimper came out. He strode away from her then, tears in his eyes, gripping the straps of his backpack.

The bell rang. She slid into a chair in Mr. Cleaves's history class.

"You're not dumb, Trisha," Mr. Cleaves said and dropped a graded quiz onto her desk. *D+* in red ink was at the top of the page. "With a little effort, you can pass this class. It's up to you."

Trisha grabbed the quiz, picked up her books, and left the room. She went to the nurse's office, lay on the cot. Her head throbbed. She was cold and she was sweating.

The nurse stuck a thermometer under Trisha's tongue. After three minutes she held it up, scowled. "You don't have a fever."

Trisha shivered, wrapped her arms around her waist.

"Let me see your hand," the nurse said.

Trisha tucked it between her knees. The nurse coaxed it out, examined the cut on Trisha's palm. "This looks pretty deep. Did you see a doctor?"

"No," Trisha said.

The nurse frowned. She cleaned the cut, applied antibacterial ointment before wrapping it in a clean bandage. "How did you get this, anyway?" she asked.

"I don't remember," Trisha said and grabbed her books. "Just call my mom and have her come pick me up."

⁂

It was now two weeks since Trisha had seen Lester on the mountain, and she still wasn't sleeping. She was barely eating. The only time she left the house was when she had to go to school.

Today, after getting off the bus and walking home alone, she'd lain in bed, staring at the ceiling. It wasn't long before she'd heard her mother talking to someone downstairs. Her voice carried up the steps, down the hall, buzzed like a gnat in Trisha's ear. Trisha slid from the mattress, went to see what was happening.

She crept into the dining room, slipped into a dark corner unnoticed. Two police officers stood in the living room, their heft usurping the space, siphoning the air.

"When was the last time you saw your husband, ma'am?" the officer asked. He was broad shouldered, the bulk of his upper body teetering on ostrich legs. He held a notepad and pencil in front of his expansive chest. The other officer, leaner, shiftier, eyeballed their home, not inconspicuously but blatantly, tossing his head from side to side, taking in his surroundings. His expression screamed what he thought of them, none of it good.

"Two weeks ago. I'd seen him in the morning before he was supposed to go to work. I was trying to get some sleep." Her mother took a drag from the cigarette, exhaled, snuffed the butt out in the ashtray. "I work nights at Foxy's, bartending and stuff. You know it." She pointed to the shifty cop. "I think I've seen you there."

"No, ma'am. Never been." He exchanged a look with his partner before asking, "Do you know what day that was when you last saw him? Wednesday, Thursday?"

"Two weeks ago, Thursday. So that was what, December fourth, I think."

"And where is your husband employed? Has he been to work in the last two weeks?" Ostrich Legs asked.

"He works at Cal's Carpet and Flooring. He works in the back warehouse. But they called two days ago looking for him. I'm supposed to tell him not to show up for work no more." Her voice cracked. "So you see, he hasn't been to work either. Nobody's seen him. It's not like him to be gone for more than a couple days."

The shifty cop spotted Trisha hiding in the shadows in the corner of the dining room, said nothing.

Her mother continued. "I talked to someone, I can't remember who, about reporting this when he didn't show up after the first week." She lit another cigarette. "They told me there was nothing anybody could do, unless there was a crime or something."

"Was there a crime?" The shifty cop pinned his eyes first on her mother before sliding them to Trisha, his gaze like seaweed, slippery and slimy on her skin.

"No," her mother said. "He just hasn't come home."

Ostrich Legs closed his notepad. "We'll ask around, see if anyone knows where he is." He rested his hand on his gun belt. "If he doesn't turn up and you're still worried, you can file a missing persons report down at the station."

"That's what I'm doing," her mother said. "I'm filing a report." There was an edge to her tone.

"I understand you're upset, ma'am. And if it were a minor missing, we'd get on it right away. But adults are free to come and go. Why don't you give him a couple more days?"

"You think he ran out on me." Her mother inhaled, then blew the smoke in the direction of Shifty Cop's face.

Shifty Cop stepped toward her mother. "It happens all the time, ma'am. And we can't chase after every husband who skips town. Do you understand what I'm telling you?"

"Yeah—you think he left me." Her voice pitched higher.

Trisha stepped out from the shadows. "He wouldn't be the first," she said. All eyes turned to her. If she could get them to believe Lester had taken off of his own accord, they wouldn't go looking for him. "Lester, I mean. He's not the first husband to skip out on her." Trisha's father had walked out on Trisha's mother more than once. It wasn't until he'd landed in prison that they'd split permanently.

Her mother shot her a look.

Another call came in on Ostrich Leg's radio. He responded that they were on their way and strode toward the door. "We'll file a report," he said, shrugging at Shifty Cop like they didn't have a choice. "We'll check around and see what we can find out." They headed out, hopped in their cruiser.

Trisha watched the flashing lights as they raced down Second Street. Once they were out of sight, she walked out the front door. Her mother didn't try to stop her.

❦

Trisha found Carlyn lying on her bed with an open book in front of her. Christmas was in six days. On top of Carlyn's nightstand sat a miniature

Christmas tree with red balls and cheap tinsel. A real tree, a Douglas fir, was downstairs in the living room. Even Mrs. Walsh had been acting funny the last few weeks, trying to get them into the holiday spirit when she'd never cared about Christmas before. She'd even offered to buy a tree for Trisha's mother. Maybe it was an attempt to cheer her up since Lester had disappeared. Her mother hadn't accepted the offer. Although she had hung the wreath on the door and strung the bright lights around the porch posts, but that had been done before Lester had made his great escape.

Mrs. Walsh wasn't home. She was at the hospital working another shift. Carlyn was alone, studying.

Trisha leaned against the doorjamb. She cleared her throat to get Carlyn's attention. Every conversation she'd had with Carlyn in the last two weeks had been abrupt, awkward.

"What do you want?" Carlyn asked.

Trisha entered the room and sat on the bed, moved a strand of hair out of Carlyn's eyes.

Carlyn smacked her hand away.

Trisha was stunned. She'd never hit her before. "Why'd you do that?" she asked.

"I don't know," Carlyn said and kept her eyes on the book in front of her.

"What did I do?" she asked.

"I would've gone with you to the trail, because we're friends. You didn't have to, you know, lead me on."

"What is that supposed to mean?"

"Stop toying with me, Trisha. I'm not some kind of experiment you can try and then just walk away from when you don't like the results."

"What are you talking about?"

"Forget it." Carlyn slammed her book shut. She wiped her eyes. "Why are you here, anyway?"

"The cops were at my house," Trisha said. "We have to get our story straight."

"Fine." She swiped her cheek. "What do you want me to say?"

"That I slept at your house on Wednesday night, December third. We went to school on Thursday. We were here on Thursday night, the whole night during the blizzard. We were out sledding the next day when school was canceled." This way Trisha was covered. She was never alone, never in the woods, didn't do what she'd done. She'd have witnesses, an alibi.

"What about Dannie?" Carlyn asked.

"Dannie was with us the entire time."

"Okay."

"Okay, that's what you'll tell them?"

"Sure, why not. Although, you weren't in school on Thursday. And Dannie wasn't with us Wednesday night. It was just you and me in my room, alone."

Oh, now she understood what Carlyn had meant earlier, why she was upset. Trisha had slept in Carlyn's bed, she'd kissed her, touched her in places she never had before. She'd forgotten. She'd pushed so many thoughts, images, out of her mind, she wasn't sure anymore what had happened and which order they'd happened in. Her lies had become truth. The truth had become lies. It all made sense now. "Of course I remember being here with you," she said.

"Do I mean anything to you?" Carlyn's lashes were wet with tears. "Or am I just a game to you? Something you tried and didn't like?"

The easy thing for Trisha to do right now would be to lie. Lying came naturally. But no matter how badly she wanted to tell Carlyn that it had meant a great deal to her that they were more than friends, she couldn't. She couldn't because what she realized was that she cared for Carlyn more than she'd ever cared for anyone in her life. She'd do anything for her, and that included not lying to her. She loved her, but not in the way Carlyn wanted her to.

"Well?" Carlyn asked.

"I . . ." Trisha searched for the right words.

"What?"

"I'm sorry," she said.

"That's it? You're sorry?" Carlyn wiped the tears spilling onto her cheeks.

Trisha reached for her.

"Just leave," Carlyn said and moved away. "Please. Just leave me alone."

Trisha hesitated. She couldn't think of what to do, what she could say, to ease her friend's pain. Maybe the best thing she could do was what Carlyn had asked of her.

She left.

CHAPTER THIRTY-FIVE

Parker leaned forward, his forearms resting on the small table between him and Scott, giving Scott his full attention.

"Look," Scott said, appearing extremely uncomfortable for the first time during the interview. "I can't say one hundred percent I know what *S. S.* stands for, but I have a pretty good idea."

"What do you think it stands for?" Parker asked.

"'Slate Sisters,'" Scott said. "It sounds kind of stupid now, but it was a friendship club—you know, the kind you make up when you're kids."

"Who was in this friendship club?" Geena asked before Parker could.

"Trisha Haines, Carlyn Walsh, Danielle Teagan—or Dannie's married name now is Torino, I believe."

"Any other members in this club that you know of?" Parker asked. Geena took notes.

"No, it was always just the three of them."

"Do you know who carved the initials on it?" Parker asked.

"I assume Trisha, although I didn't see her do it. But she's the one who stole it. As far as I know, she kept it with her in her house." He paused. He looked as though he was going to say something else but then changed his mind.

"We found the bat next to Lester's remains," Parker said. "We believe it's the weapon that struck him in the head and killed him."

Scott stared at Parker.

"What?" Parker asked.

"It's just . . . I was reluctant to say anything earlier because I don't have any proof, but I believe Lester used to hit Trisha's mother," Scott said.

Parker nodded. "We have records of a couple domestic complaints from the neighbors. Sharon never pressed charges."

Scott ran both his hands through his hair this time, exposing more gray strands underneath. "I think Lester abused Trisha too," he said.

"Abused her how?" Geena asked.

"I'm not sure. I mean, I don't know how far it went. I saw bruises on her arms."

"Did she ever tell you Lester hit her?" Parker asked.

"No. She wouldn't talk about it with me, but one time I asked her straight out. She didn't confirm it, but she didn't deny it either."

"What did she do?"

"For one, she stole the bat from gym class. I got the impression she wanted it to protect herself."

"Anything else?"

"She cried." Scott got up, paced the small room. "I always suspected it was so much worse than she ever let on. But I was a kid. I wasn't sure what to do. I wanted to help her. And then . . ."

"And then what?" Parker asked.

Scott hesitated. "And then Lester was gone, and I admit a part of me was glad. We all know the system isn't as effective as it should be in these types of cases. I was happy he was gone, and she wouldn't be thrown into the system. I don't think I understood that at the time, but as I got older, I did."

"How did she act after Lester disappeared?" Parker asked.

"What? Do you mean did she act guilty?" Scott asked. "No, but she wasn't the same. She stopped hanging out with her friends. She wouldn't talk to me. She was, I don't know, distant," he said. "After a while, I gave up trying. I guess we all did."

"Meaning?"

"By the end of our senior year, none of us hung out together anymore. And then I heard Carlyn went off to college. Dannie got married. I enlisted."

"Where did Trisha go?"

"I have no idea," Scott said.

Parker nodded. Trisha had gone to Vegas, as far as he could tell, and that was where she'd stayed.

"One more question before you go," Geena said. "We found Lester's remains near the Appalachian Trail." She pulled out the photo of the trail for Scott to see. "Does this look familiar to you?" She slid it across the table to him.

Scott picked it up, looked at it. "Sort of," he said. "We used to hang out on the mountain doing stupid kid stuff: drinking, smoking. We had a spot where we would sit on this big rock underneath this tree with *Kilroy was here* carved on the trunk."

Geena passed Scott the photo with the Kilroy tree.

"Yeah, that's it," Scott said and handed the photo back to her. "That's the tree."

For what seemed like the hundredth time, Parker and Geena exchanged a look.

"He was found about five yards away," Parker said.

෫§

After Scott left, Parker and Geena went through their notes.

"Here's what we know," Parker said. "Trisha stole a softball bat from the school gym. The same kind of bat found near Lester's remains and believed to be the murder weapon. At some point after stealing said bat, she carved into the aluminum the letters *S. S.* with a heart around it: a symbol of a friendship club she belonged to with her two best friends, Carlyn and Danielle."

Geena checked off the points in her notebook.

Parker continued. "Scott confirmed they used to hang out on the trail not far from where Lester was found. And if Lester was abusing Trisha, then she also had a motive for wanting him dead."

"Sounds about right," Geena said. "Let's say Trisha is our lead suspect. How does she end up with the bat and Lester in the woods?"

Parker gave it some thought. "What about this. One day in December, Trisha and her friends are hanging out on the trail. She brings the bat with her for what purpose?"

"Maybe they're afraid of bumping into a bear or some other animal, like Sharon was going on about, and they bring the bat with them for protection," Geena said. "But instead of a bear, Lester shows up. They argue. She hits him with it."

"Okay. And then Carlyn and Danielle lie for her," Parker said, recalling his conversation with Carlyn. He wasn't totally convinced she'd been honest with him, and now it seemed likely that she'd recognized the bat and lied about it. Maybe she was lying about other things as well.

Geena added, "What if Trisha lured Lester to the woods with the intention of killing him, and her plan worked? Then she wouldn't need to rely on her friends to keep her secret. Otherwise, it seems like a pretty big favor to ask of your friends."

Parker scratched his chin. "Who else do we know had access to the bat?"

"Sharon, for one. And Cal, if he was in fact hanging out at Sharon's house. I suppose Trisha's friends could've had access to it. I think we can rule out Scott. He never went to the house."

"What did he say again?" Parker checked Geena's notes. He noticed she didn't need to refer to them, not even once.

"Scott said that Trisha kept the bat in her house. For protection," Geena said. "As far as motive, we've got Sharon and Trisha, possibly Cal," she said. "They all had the strongest motive for wanting him dead."

"Right. But what would Sharon or Cal be doing in the woods? Neither one of them would have a reason to be there," Parker said. "The body wasn't moved, so that makes the woods our crime scene."

"And whoever did it buried him. Otherwise, if kids hung out there all the time, someone would've found him a long time ago," Geena said.

"Someone definitely buried him—deep enough that the animals hadn't even dug him out."

"We need to check on those weather reports," Geena said. "It'd be awfully hard to dig with a foot of snow on the ground."

"Near impossible," Parker said. "Who do you think is our main suspect?"

"Based on what Scott told us, I think it's Trisha. It was her bat, her hangout on the trail, her stepfather."

"I agree. Let's bring her in for a chat, and we'll go from there."

CHAPTER THIRTY-SIX

At her mother's request, Trisha carried up the box full of Christmas decorations from the basement. She set it on the floor next to the tattered couch in the living room. The foam from the cushion crumbled onto the worn carpet. Her mother came up behind her, handed her a beer.

"Cheers," Trisha said after pulling off the tab. She took a long swallow. "I'm going to buy you a new sofa," she blurted, wondered where that had come from. Why was she feeling so generous all of a sudden?

"You got some money off that no-good husband of yours?" her mother asked.

"Yeah, I got some money off him." More than some. She wasn't the only one who had talked too much when intoxicated. She'd listened, learned, skimmed hundreds of thousands of dollars from his winnings and assorted businesses through the years. The cash she'd lifted was hidden, locked away in a safe-deposit box in a bank. She was the sole proprietor.

She'd earned it.

Her mother laughed. "Well, at least you got something for it."

Trisha opened the box of decorations. The wreath she remembered from her teen years was on top. It looked a little shabby, but after she straightened the red bow, blew the dust off the plastic needles, it was decent enough to hang on the door.

"Where's the hook for this?" she asked and searched through the box, found strings of blinking white lights, a tree skirt, a star.

"Here." Her mother turned the wreath over. The hook was taped to the back. "So I wouldn't lose it."

"Clever." Trisha opened the door. She noticed a police cruiser was parked down the street. Scott got out of the car.

"Great," she mumbled and hung the wreath on the front door while Scott made his way up the narrow path of the sidewalk. The snow was piled high on either side of him, but his dark-blue uniform was hard to miss against the white backdrop. He crossed the street and stopped in front of her house; he saw her standing on the other side of the storm door looking out at him. She stepped onto the porch, met him halfway.

Trisha's mother joined them.

"Mrs. Haines," Scott said, nodding hello.

"It's nice to see you again, Scott." She handed Trisha her winter coat with the faux fur–lined hood along with a string of blinking lights. She gave Scott the rest of the strings of lights. "Well," she said. "I'll let you two catch up." She went back into the house.

Trisha pulled the coat on. "I guess you're helping me," she said, motioning to the lights, and started wrapping a string around the porch post. Her ribs ached when she raised her arm.

Scott leaned against the railing. She hadn't gotten a good look at him the other night when he'd given her a ride home from the bar. It had been dark. She'd been drunk. But in the daylight, she could see him clearly. He'd aged well. The gray flecks in his sideburns, the lines by his eyes, made him more handsome than she'd remembered. She bet underneath that uniform was a body that was slapped together with nothing but muscle. He even smelled good: some kind of aftershave she couldn't place. It had to be a brand you'd buy at a local drugstore. He wasn't the type of guy who would drop a couple of hundred dollars on designer cologne.

"You look a lot better since the other night," he said.

"I should hope so." She was almost at the end of the string of lights and held out her hand for him to pass her another one. His fingers brushed hers, causing her pulse to react, her body responding the same way it had the other night when he'd touched her. She'd been so certain she'd been wiped clean—or rather that she'd been beaten out of any romantic feelings she'd ever had or might possibly have—that she didn't fully trust what she was feeling now.

"I shouldn't be here talking to you," he said.

"Why not?" she asked. "What's her name?"

He shook his head, smiled. He was so easy to amuse. "I'm divorced. I've got two kids, though. Trevor is seventeen, and Ainsley, sixteen."

"You? Divorced? And with two kids? I thought you of all people would've been the kind to marry and live happily ever after."

He shrugged, an obvious sore spot. "I have joint custody. I'm with my kids every chance I get. I'm not some deadbeat dad. Everything I do is for them. Every single thing."

"Well, that's great, Scott."

"They're great kids."

"I'm sure they are."

He passed her another string of lights. She wrapped them around the post. She would need an extension cord at some point in order to plug them in.

"Look, I'm here because I need to warn you about something."

She hesitated. "About what?" She'd left her beer in the house. She scratched the skin by her wrist.

"I talked with two detectives today."

"And what does that have to do with me?" Would he think it strange if she suddenly went back into the house and returned with a beer? She glanced at the door.

"They were asking a lot of questions about you and me. About us."

"Us? There's an us?"

"There used to be, as I remember it."

204

Ah yes, she recalled why she couldn't be with him, why any romantic feelings she might've had would've eventually shriveled up and died. He was just too good. He wore his kindness like a halo around his head. Meanwhile, her head sprouted horns. Their last conversation before he'd enlisted, she'd all but told him this to his face.

"I'd be good to you," he'd said. "I'd never hurt you."

"I know you would. But I'd hurt you," she'd said. "It's what I do."

The way he looked at her now, she almost wanted to believe she was wrong and that it could work out for them after all. Maybe he cared for her as much as he had then. Maybe she could be a different person. Wouldn't that be something? But while she permitted herself these fleeting thoughts, there was something else she sensed from him. Was it pity? She fought the urge to spit on him.

"They're going to want to talk with you," he said.

"What did you tell them?"

"The truth, as best I could."

"You mean the truth as you saw it."

"Yes, that's fair."

"Did you tell them everything?"

"I told them what I suspected Lester had done to you."

Trisha glared at him. The winter air could've been a hot day in the desert compared to the ice pick he'd plunged into her heart. "You had no right."

"Maybe I didn't."

She fisted the string of lights, threw them at him.

He caught them before they hit him. "I'm sorry," he said. "I just want you to know that I'm really sorry."

Trisha's mother appeared at the door. "Everything okay?"

"Officer Best was just leaving," Trisha said.

Scott set the string of lights on the chair. "Take care of you," he said, then nodded at her mother. "Mrs. Haines."

Trisha watched him get into the cruiser, drive away. When he was gone, her mother came outside and handed Trisha a beer. They sat on the chairs on the porch, drinking, not talking for some time.

"That man still cares for you," her mother said of Scott. "He was a good kid back then, and he turned into a good man."

"Yes, well, that's always been the problem, hasn't it?"

Her mother laughed.

They sat in silence again.

Her mother motioned across the street to Evelyn's house. "I miss her," she said. "I don't know what I would've done without her and Linda. I don't know what I did in this life to deserve such good friends. I'd do anything for them."

Trisha nodded, hesitated. "Would you do anything for me?" she asked.

"Anything," her mother said.

They watched as a black sedan turned onto Second Street. It stopped in front of their house. The back window went down, and Sid's face appeared, gray, skeletal.

"Go in the house," Trisha said to her mother.

Her mother stared at Sid for a long second; then she got up, touched Trisha's shoulder before going back inside.

"Get in," Sid said.

Trisha set the beer can down on the porch. Sid's driver opened the rear passenger-side door for her. She climbed in. She'd followed Sid's orders for so long that it had become automatic. Her brain shut down; her emotions locked up tight. No matter what happened next, she'd survive.

He'd trained her well.

The driver got back behind the wheel, drove down the street, taking his time on the icy surface. The freezing rain had stopped some time ago, but a cold mist dotted the windshield. The wipers groaned, screeched across the glass.

"I have some business in Atlantic City," Sid said. "I'll be gone for a couple days." He smelled of expensive cologne, cigarette smoke, but it didn't mask the old-man smell underneath, his rotting insides, his blackened heart.

"I'm not supposed to leave. The police," she stammered. She'd told him the same lie the other night at the casino.

"So you said," he snapped.

Trisha flinched, then went still, robotic.

The driver stopped at the stop sign at the end of the street. He seemed hesitant to interrupt. "Where to?" he asked finally.

"Drive around the block," Sid said in a normal voice. He waited to speak again until they were back on Second Street, stopped in front of her mother's house. The windshield wipers continued screeching.

"I'll be back in two days," he said and adjusted his tie. Then he leaned in close, smelled her, his lip rising, taking in the scent of her. "You have two days, and then you're coming with me. And I don't give a *fuck* if you're allowed to leave or not."

CHAPTER THIRTY-SEVEN

MAY 1987

Trisha leaned over the back of the couch, stared out the front window, watched the cars drive down Second Street. Carlyn and Dannie had left in Dannie's mother's station wagon over an hour ago. They hadn't invited Trisha to go along. They'd avoided her at school and hadn't knocked on her door in five long months.

Trisha pulled on the cigarette, played with another one of her mother's lighters, flicked it on and off. She brought the flame within an inch of the curtain. She could burn the entire house down, herself included. Would anyone care? Wouldn't their lives be easier without her in it? Her friends wouldn't have to think up excuses to blow her off or go out of their way to avoid her in the halls. They could forget they'd ever known her and what she'd done, what she'd asked them to do. They'd lied to the police, protected her, and it appeared they'd gotten away with it.

She brought the flame closer to the ugly pea-green cotton fabric. She no longer knew who she was, now that she was no longer the girl who lived with a monster. She should've been happy. She was free of him. Instead, she found that she was still angry all the time, although she couldn't find a reason for it. She lashed out at her mother, at her friends, searching for anyone to take it out on. She rarely slept. And on the occasions when she did sleep, she'd wake in the middle of the night, expecting to find Lester standing over her. She hated who she was. She hated the feel of her own skin. What had he done to her?

The flame flickered. At the last second, she pulled the lighter away. A part of her, the fighting part, wouldn't give Lester or her friends the satisfaction of knowing they'd gotten to her.

She picked up the beer from the end table. Her mother had an endless supply of cigarettes, lighters, and beer. Sometimes she'd even let Trisha drink a six-pack with her at the kitchen table over a frozen dinner, neither one talking much. Their silence had become comfortable, if not boring. Deep down in a place Trisha rarely allowed herself to go, she ached for the excitement, the adrenaline-pumping fear, the fighting, that for years she'd wanted to end. But now that it had, the silence that followed filled every corner in the house until the rooms buzzed with it, a constant drone inside her head. The dark sleepless nights, the long days, had become unbearable. If she stayed here much longer, the quiet was sure to drive her mad.

Outside a car door slammed. Dannie's mother's station wagon was parked in front of Dannie's house again. Carlyn stood next to it. Dannie took a little longer to pull herself out of the driver's seat. She'd put on more weight recently. If she wasn't careful, she'd end up like her mother.

Trisha sprang from the couch, spilling beer on the carpet. She rushed outside. "Hey," she called, stomping down the porch steps and across the street. "Where were you?" she asked accusingly.

"I got my driver's license," Carlyn said. "Dannie let me use her car for the test."

"I didn't even know you knew how to drive," Trisha said.

"Dannie's been teaching me."

That hurt. When had they been going out driving? After school? Weekends? "How about you teach me too?" Trisha asked.

Dannie's face was flushed. "Sure, some other time, though." Her eyes drifted to the beer in Trisha's hand. She pointed to her house. "I have to go check on my mom. I'm sure she's wondering where I've been." She didn't wait for either Trisha or Carlyn to comment. She made the sign of the cross, as if talking to Trisha was a sin, and then she ran up the steps, disappeared behind the front door.

"Well, I should get going too," Carlyn said and turned to go.

"Wait," Trisha said. "I've got a couple of beers inside. Want to hang out?"

"I can't."

"Why not?"

"I have stuff to do."

"What kind of stuff?" Trisha asked.

"I don't know, just stuff."

"Oh, well, can I join you?"

"I don't think so," Carlyn said and headed in the direction of her house.

Trisha called after her. "What about tomorrow? Or the day after that? Or are you busy then too?" she spat.

Carlyn stopped. There was an expression on her face Trisha hadn't seen before, something like disappointment. "Yeah, Trisha, I'm busy then too."

Trisha took a swig of beer, then pulled on the cigarette. "Screw you!" she said. "And screw Dannie too!"

※

Trisha lay on the bathroom floor next to the toilet. She'd been sick most of the night. Her mother had found her passed out on the living room couch, beer cans scattered across the floor. She'd helped her to the bathroom, put a blanket on her, told her to sleep it off in here. Her mother must've known the retching was coming.

Trisha pulled herself off the small area rug in front of the sink and looked at her reflection in the mirror. Her cheek was creased with stripes from the pattern on the rug. The dark circles under her bloodshot eyes would make the most die-hard goth kids envious. Beyond that, she looked like she'd lived a thousand years. It was hard to believe she was eighteen years old.

Carlyn and Dannie had made it clear they were no longer her friends. The Slate Sisters were nothing more than sharp slivers of the memories they were made of.

"Happy birthday to me," Trisha said before kneeling in front of the toilet again.

It was time she disappeared, started over, made some changes.

CHAPTER THIRTY-EIGHT

Parker knocked on Sharon's door. Geena stood behind him, checked the time on her phone. They'd get one shot at pulling information, possibly a confession, out of Trisha. The evidence they had against her was circumstantial, but after a brief conversation with the DA, he'd said that if they could get Trisha to admit that she was on the trail and the bat was in her possession (combined with Officer Scott Best's statement, the key word being *officer*), he believed he could get a conviction.

Or maybe if Trisha were pressed, she'd give up her mother or someone else.

There was also the problem of the timeline to consider. They hadn't been able to pin down Lester's movements around the time he'd disappeared and when the report had been filed. Maybe Trisha would be more forthcoming than previously and fill in the gaps.

Either way, a lot was riding on this interview.

Geena put her phone back in her pocket. Parker knocked on the door again. The raw air bit at his ears. His thoughts jumped to Becca. He still needed to apologize for his behavior the other night, but if his case broke wide open in the next few hours, there was a good chance he'd have to work late, which would mean he wouldn't get an opportunity to stop by her place, not without having to wake her up. What if she had surgery scheduled in the morning—remove a cat's claws, neuter a dog? He shivered at the thought.

He knocked a third time. "Mrs. Haines," he called. "It's Detective Reed and Detective Brassard." He heard movement from inside the house. In the next moment, Sharon opened the door.

"Detectives," she said and stepped aside to let them in.

"Is your daughter home?" Parker asked.

Trisha walked into the living room. She carried a can of beer. Her dark hair was draped over one shoulder. Her jeans were tight. The cable-knit sweater she wore hung on her, the fabric stretched, ill fitting for her small frame. Her snow boots were nothing fancy, the typical kind everyone wore around here. It appeared as though she'd officially swapped the tailor-made clothes she'd worn when he'd first met her for something more casual. She must've decided the three-inch heels were no longer functional. It also meant that she planned on staying for a while. This was good news.

"I need you to come down to the station," Parker said to Trisha. "And answer a few questions for us."

"What's this about?" Sharon asked.

Trisha's face remained neutral. She didn't show any sign of being surprised by his request.

"It's just a few questions," he said. "Why don't you get your coat?"

"You don't have to go with him," Sharon said.

Parker kept his eyes on them, his mouth shut. Geena stood quietly next to him. Sharon was right. Trisha didn't have to go to the station with them. She didn't have to answer any of their questions, not unless he was arresting her and not without a lawyer present.

"No, it's fine," Trisha said and set the beer can on the end table. She pulled on her coat. "I'll go."

"You don't have to answer anything he asks you," Sharon said. "Not without a lawyer."

"Your mother's right," he said and proceeded to read her her rights.

"Got it," Trisha said.

Parker stepped back, allowed Trisha to go ahead of him. They walked to the unmarked cruiser. He opened the back door for her.

"Am I under arrest?" Trisha asked and slipped into the back seat. Her voice was level, not a hint of concern, as though he were taking her to the grocery store for milk.

"We'd just like to ask you a few questions," he said and closed the door.

They were quiet on the ride to the station. Parker was hoping Trisha would have more questions for them, but she didn't seem to mind the silence. Gray clouds soaked the sky, threatening to dump several more inches of snow on the town, or quite possibly more of that awful freezing rain. He couldn't remember the last time they'd gotten so much snow in December. According to the weather reports he and Geena had searched in the archives, the last time they'd had a particularly snowy December had been in 1986, when almost two feet of the white stuff had fallen in those three weeks before the holiday. Scott had been right about the storm.

⁂

At the station Parker escorted Trisha to interview room one. It was a different room from the one where they'd talked with Scott, where there were tissues and an artificial plant. This room contained a small table bolted to the floor and two chairs. The walls were a grungy beige. A camera was mounted in the corner. They'd agreed ahead of time that Parker had established a kind of rapport with Trisha and that he would do the interview. Geena was in another room watching on the CCTV.

Parker directed Trisha to sit in the chair, facing the camera. "Can I get you anything? Water? Coffee?" he asked. "Cigarette?" He dropped the pink lighter and pack of cigarettes onto the table.

"No, nothing. Thank you." She sat straight, still, her hands in her lap, the pink lighter not having any effect on her that Parker could see.

"Do you know why I asked you to come here today?"

"No," she said in a monotone voice. Her eyes flickered to the camera.

He was surprised by her response. He expected her to say that it must have something to do with her stepfather. "It has to do with your stepfather, Lester Haines." He reminded her of her rights, advised that the interview was being recorded.

"You can ask me whatever you want," she said. "But it doesn't mean I'm going to answer you."

"Fair enough," he said. "Do you remember where you were on Thursday"—he checked his notes for the exact date when Lester was reported to have disappeared—"December fourth, 1986?"

"School," she said.

"Actually, you weren't. You were marked truant that day." He'd found the information in the original file, made a note of it.

"If you say so."

"You don't remember?"

"I skipped school all the time. Hard to say exactly which days I was there and which days I wasn't."

"You weren't in school on December fourth. Do you remember where you were?"

"No, I don't. Like I said, I thought I was in school."

"Could it be that you were on the trail where you used to hang out with your friends?"

She gave no indication whether or not she knew what he was referring to.

He pulled a photo of the trail from the file, the one that clearly showed the large oak tree with the *Kilroy was here* carving in the trunk. "Does this look familiar?" He slid it across the table for her to see.

She looked at it, her body static, her hands unmoving in her lap.

"The woods around the trail tend to blend together," she said.

He pointed to the carving. "Do you see that?"

"Yes."

"Your friend, Officer Scott Best, said you and your girlfriends used to hang out by this tree. It's a little more than halfway up the mountain."

"Yes, that sounds like something we used to do."

"Take another look. Does it look familiar to you now?"

"Yes, it does look a little familiar."

"Were you on the trail Thursday, December fourth, specifically in this area right here?" He tapped the photo.

"I can't say for sure."

He was frustrated, but he tried hard not to let it show. He pulled another photo from the file. This one was the image of the bat. "Do you recognize this?"

"It's a baseball bat."

"Technically, it's a softball bat. Do you know what these initials stand for?" He showed her another photo, the blown-up image of the bat where the initials *S. S.* with the heart around them were easily identifiable.

"Yes," she said. "It stands for 'Slate Sisters.' It was a friendship club I was in when I was a kid."

"Did you carve the letters with the heart into this bat?"

"Yes, I did."

His heart pounded. "And this is your bat?"

"*Technically*, it was the school's bat. I stole it from gym class. What does this have to do with anything? I can't imagine you brought me in here for stealing a twenty-dollar bat."

"This bat, your bat," he said and pointed to the photo.

"Yes, so?"

"It's the weapon that struck and killed Lester." Parker butted up against the table, watched her reaction closely. Her face was unreadable.

"The softball bat," she said. "This is what killed him?"

"Your bat," Parker said. "Why don't you tell me what happened?"

She seemed confused, or was she surprised; he couldn't be sure. Then she laughed. She covered her mouth and *laughed*.

"Do you want to tell me what's so funny?" he asked.

She continued laughing, holding her side as though it hurt.

Her behavior was unsettling. He was firm when he asked, "How is it that the softball bat you stole from the school, carved initials in, is the same bat that struck and killed your stepfather?" And then in a quieter voice, he said, "I know why you did it. I know why you killed him. I know he abused you."

She stopped laughing, looked at him.

He continued. "Do you want to know what I think happened?" he asked. "I think you hit Lester in the head with this bat because of what he was doing to you. And then you buried him in the woods to cover it up."

She sat back in the chair, looking more relaxed now than ever. "It wasn't me," she said. "I didn't do it."

She sounded so confident. It wasn't the reaction Parker had been expecting. He pressed on. "You can talk to me, Trisha. I understand what he did was wrong. It was the worst thing he could've ever done to you. Maybe you thought he had it coming to him. Maybe you believed he deserved it. I can understand how you might've felt that way. I can understand how it happened."

She leaned across the table, looked him in the eye, and said, "It wasn't me. I didn't do it."

He stared back at her, tried to get a read on her. Was she that good of a liar? "Then who did?" he asked.

"I honestly have no idea," she said, a smile playing on her lips.

"What happened to your ribs?" he asked.

"Excuse me?"

"I noticed you were holding your side like you were protecting your ribs. What happened?"

"I fell down the stairs."

"I don't believe you," he said.

"I don't care what you believe."

"Do you have a good relationship with your husband?" he asked. His phone went off, Geena texting, What are you doing?

"That is none of your business, Detective." Her eyes darkened, glazed over.

His phone chirped again, Geena texting, Get out here now.

"Wait here," he said and left the interview room. He went to where Geena was watching on the CCTV.

"What's with the husband questions?" she asked.

Parker turned in circles, scratched his chin. "I don't know," he said. He had to focus on their case. "What do you think? Do you think she's telling the truth?"

"She's pretty convincing," Geena said.

"Yeah," Parker said. "It still doesn't explain where she was on December fourth and why she lied about being in school."

"Maybe it's as simple as she just doesn't remember."

"Maybe."

"What do you want to do?" Geena asked.

"Let's let her sit in there for a while. Keep the camera on her. Give her a chance to think things over."

CHAPTER THIRTY-NINE

JUNE 1987

Carlyn dropped her graduation cap onto the kitchen table, kicked off her shoes. She rubbed her foot where a blister had formed. She'd left the park where the graduation ceremony had been held. She'd walked down Broadway in heels. She cursed herself for not wearing her running sneakers like she'd wanted to. She thought wearing a dress with nice shoes was required. As it turned out, the kids in her class had worn all kinds of crazy stuff underneath their gowns—cowboy boots, bathing suits, shorts, and flip-flops.

Carlyn's name, Walsh, had been one of the last to be called. She'd hurried onto the platform, shook the principal's hand. She hadn't bothered looking into the stands, believing there was no one there to clap for her, no one for her to celebrate with, to acknowledge her academic achievements. Dannie hadn't even shown up. She'd picked up her diploma in the principal's office on the last day of school. And Trisha, well, Carlyn hadn't seen Trisha in weeks. They'd stopped hanging out together, the Slate Sisters. The burden of their secret had driven them apart.

High school was over, finished. All Carlyn had had to do was exit the stage, but she'd hesitated, heard the faint sound of her name. There on the bleachers, she'd found her mother, standing, clapping, calling to her. She'd shown up. Carlyn had waved the diploma in her mother's direction, smiled her first genuine smile in months.

Now she played with the yellow tassel on the cap. She'd graduated with honors, third in her class. With the help of a scholarship and high SAT scores, she'd been accepted into a private college in Easton. She was all set, her future going as planned. So why did she feel miserable, as though a heavy weight pressed down on her shoulders? Why did her heart feel empty?

She raced upstairs and changed into gym shorts and running sneakers. She'd go for a run, clear her head. She stepped outside. Two houses down, her mother sat on the porch with Mrs. Haines. She found herself walking toward them. Her mother was supposed to be working the night shift. Had she taken off work for the ceremony?

They were drinking beer, their feet up on the railing. Seeing their mothers together like this, chummy, felt like a kick to the gut when she was missing her own friends.

"Is Trisha here?" she asked Mrs. Haines.

"Gone," Mrs. Haines said. "She took off a couple days ago. Took some clothes, all my tip money I'd saved in a jar—about five hundred bucks she took from me."

Carlyn's mother touched Mrs. Haines's arm, left her hand there.

"Where did she go?" Carlyn asked.

"She didn't say."

"You don't know?"

"No, I don't. She's eighteen now. I couldn't stop her even if I wanted to."

"Maybe it's for the best," Carlyn's mother said and gave Mrs. Haines's arm a squeeze. "When you love someone, you let them go." She glanced at Carlyn.

"I guess she didn't tell you where she was going either?" Mrs. Haines asked Carlyn.

Carlyn shook her head. "Did she leave a note?" she asked.

"I didn't see any," Mrs. Haines said. "You're welcome to check her room if you'd like."

Carlyn rushed inside, passed the torn couch, the washed-out dining room, and raced up the stairs to Trisha's room. She stopped inside the doorway. The sheets and comforter were rumpled, half on the mattress, the other half on the floor, as though the bed had been slept in recently. The closet door was open. Carlyn searched for some of Trisha's favorite clothes: the black leggings, the torn jeans, the oversize gray sweatshirt that hung off one shoulder. They were gone. She opened a dresser drawer and pulled out Scott's T-shirt that Trisha had slept in. She brought it to her nose, inhaled Trisha's scent on the cotton. She was sorry for walking away from her, for putting so much distance between them these last few months.

She needed to tell her she wasn't mad at her. Not anymore. The thought of going away to college, leaving Second Street and her only true friends behind, had sneaked up on her—how she still needed them, wanted them in her life. It couldn't wait. It was urgent she find her friend before she lost her forever. But where would Trisha have gone? There was one place that came to mind. When Trisha had first moved to their street, she'd mentioned her real father living back in Chicago. That was where Trisha would go. She'd seek out the only other person she knew in the world.

Carlyn was sure of it.

⁂

Carlyn blew most of her babysitting money on a plane ticket to Chicago. It hadn't been easy finding Frank Ciccerone. The biggest help had come from Mrs. Haines. It appeared she'd been in touch with him on and off through the years. The last she'd heard from him had been a couple of months ago, which meant it was highly likely he'd been in contact with Trisha too.

Carlyn had taken an early-morning flight, the cheapest flight she could find from Philadelphia to O'Hare International Airport, then boarded a bus. She'd paid for the round-trip bus ticket with the few bucks Dannie had given her. "Take it," Dannie had said. "Bring her home." Even Carlyn's mother had offered to help by giving her a credit card. "Only use it if it's absolutely necessary," her mother had said.

In a little less than an hour, Carlyn was dropped off at the Stateville Correctional Center. She went through a security checkpoint. She'd brought her driver's license and birth certificate as proof of identity. She'd read that female visitors had to dress appropriately for prison, which meant they had to wear a bra, no underwires, and nothing that showed a lot of skin. She looked at her jeans, her sneakers, tugged at the cuff of her long-sleeve T-shirt. It was June. It was hot. But her body was covered.

She jumped at the sound of the gate locking behind her. The prison had a sweaty, disinfectant smell to its walls and floors, the scent of being institutionalized. The guard escorted her to the visitors' room, where a long glass wall separated the prisoners from their guests. All along the glass there was a string of small booths, each containing a chair and phone. She was instructed to sit in one of the booths. She sat in the small chair, tapped her foot against the metal leg. She didn't know what Frank Ciccerone had done to land in a maximum security prison. She'd once heard Trisha mention something about armed robbery. She wasn't about to ask him.

He was brought in by another guard. Frank was wearing a jumpsuit and chains. He sat across from her. He was small like Trisha. He had short clipped hair that had once been dark but now had turned gray. They both picked up their phones.

This might've been the stupidest thing she'd ever done. Now that she was here, staring at the man through the glass window, she wasn't sure he'd be any help at all.

"You don't know me, but I'm a friend of your daughter's, Trisha," she said.

He didn't respond. His face showed no reaction to the mention of Trisha's name.

"I'm worried about her. She left home and didn't tell anyone where she was going. I was wondering if she came to see you."

"You say you're a friend of hers?" Frank asked. The tattoos on his forearm blended together in one black splotch due more to his age than craftsmanship.

"Yes. A good friend."

"If you're such good friends, why didn't she tell you where she was going?"

"It's complicated."

Frank smiled.

Carlyn saw Trisha in his face, or an older version of what Trisha would look like when she aged. Carlyn had always imagined them growing old together: friends, maybe more, sitting on the porch with their feet up, drinking beer like their mothers. Or maybe they'd be sitting on a beach somewhere warm, feet in the sand, fruity drinks with umbrellas in their hands. Wherever they ended up, she thought they'd be together, they'd find their way back to each other. A girl could dream, couldn't she? She went to put her hand on the glass to touch the resemblance, the dream, but stopped herself when Frank laughed at her.

"Was Trisha here or not?" she asked.

"What's your name?" he asked.

"Carlyn."

"Well, Carlyn, she came to see me two days ago."

Carlyn's pulse spiked. She was right. "Where is she now?"

"I hooked her up with a friend of mine on the outside. I figured she needed some work—a little money to get wherever it is she was going."

"What kind of work?"

He leaned forward. He might have been old, but she saw in his eyes that he was dangerous.

"The kind of work you young ladies are good at," he said.

Carlyn almost dropped the phone. Then she gripped it tight, her lips close to the receiver. "You pimped out your own daughter?"

He didn't respond, kept staring at her with those menacing eyes.

"What's in it for you?" she asked.

He laughed.

"I'm her best friend, Frank. Where is she?" she asked, her jaw set.

"I can't tell you that. If she wanted you to know where she was, she would've told you herself."

"Tell me how to find her."

He hung up the phone, motioned for the guard.

"You piece of . . ." She slammed her phone down and turned to the guard on her side of the glass partition. "Get me out of here," she said.

※

Carlyn took the next bus back to the airport, not any closer to finding her friend. Trisha could be anywhere on the streets of Chicago, or maybe she'd already left the state of Illinois to work the streets in some other city. How could she ever find out? How could she know if what Frank had told her was true? She couldn't. Her only hope was that

Trisha would contact her to let her know she was okay. But somehow, deep down, Carlyn knew she wouldn't. She was gone. She wasn't coming back.

Everything Carlyn owned was shoved in her backpack. Her stomach growled. She dug in her jeans pockets for loose change. She was out of money, and her flight wouldn't leave for another two hours. She went back and forth about whether she should charge dinner on her mother's charge card. In the end she ordered a cheeseburger, fries, and small drink—a $2.60 meal.

When she finished eating the burger and fries, she licked the salt from her fingers. She didn't want to believe Trisha had faked the time they'd spent together. You couldn't fabricate the kind of tenderness she'd shown, the yearning in the touch of her skin. Carlyn clung to the memory. Trisha was the only one who knew Carlyn had a secret of her own. And now what would happen? Where would she go from here? Who would she love?

She didn't sleep on the plane or on the bus ride back to Bangor. She was exhausted by the time she reached Second Street. Dannie was waiting for her on her front porch.

"Did you find her?" she asked.

"No," Carlyn said. "She's gone."

Dannie got up to leave, paused. "It's not your fault, you know. She would've left no matter what."

"I guess."

"Maybe it's for the best. Maybe she can start over and put everything behind her. Maybe she'll finally be happy."

"Maybe," Carlyn said, holding back what she'd learned from Frank. Dannie needed to believe it was better this way, for Trisha, for all of them. Only Carlyn would know the truth: another burden she'd carry for her friend, because that was what friends were for, best friends.

"See you around," she said to Dannie and went into her house, up to her room. She dumped the backpack on the floor. She'd spend the next two months working, saving what little babysitting money she could make for college, and come August, she'd leave.

No one would ever know she'd loved a girl and lost her.

She reached in her jeans pocket and pulled out a pink lighter. She turned it over in her hand and made a promise to herself.

She'd take her secret to the grave.

CHAPTER FORTY

Trisha sat on the hard plastic chair in the interview room for what seemed like a very long time. Her skin was tacky. She picked at the underside of her wrist. There wasn't a clock anywhere in the small holding tank, and since she'd tossed her phone before she'd left Vegas, she had no idea how long she'd been waiting for the detective to return. It was likely his plan to leave her here for an uncomfortably long time, hoping her body language would reveal her guilt, something he hadn't been able to get her to admit.

Her bruised ribs hurt from laughing. She wasn't over the shock that she was innocent. She'd struck Lester with the whiskey bottle, not the bat. She didn't kill him. But then who did?

Maybe the detective was playing with her, but for what purpose? What would be his angle? It didn't make sense. No, he clearly believed she'd done it. All the evidence had certainly pointed in her direction—her bat, her motive. If he was hoping for a confession, he could suck it. She was innocent.

She searched her memory, concentrated hard on who would've taken the bat from her bedroom. Her mother was the most obvious person, but what would her mother have been doing in the woods?

She shifted her weight in the seat. Her bladder was full. She'd had three beers since the last time she'd used the bathroom.

She stared at the camera, knowing the detective and his partner were watching her. She continued to glare at it, hoping to make them as uncomfortable as she was. She stayed in the same position, looking at the camera mounted on the corner wall until her neck became stiff. Finally, Detective Reed opened the door.

"Am I free to leave?" she asked and stood. "I really need to use the restroom."

"Sorry it took so long," he said and looked a little embarrassed about it, but he didn't offer an explanation. "The restrooms are right around the corner." He followed her out, watched her until she'd disappeared inside the bathroom.

When Trisha finished, she washed her hands, splashed cold water on her face. She looked at her reflection in the mirror. Sid had given her two days. She couldn't waste any more time.

꙰

Detectives Reed and Brassard dropped Trisha off at her mother's house.

"Don't leave town," Detective Reed said and drove away.

Trisha noticed Carlyn's car was parked across the street in front of Evelyn's place. Then Trisha turned toward her own house, headed up the porch steps, caught her mother peeking out from behind the curtains of the living room window. She was struggling to get up from the couch when Trisha stepped through the door. The house reeked of cigarettes and one of her mother's frozen fish and chips dinners.

"Is your hip giving you trouble tonight?" Trisha asked and shed her coat before slipping her hand underneath her mother's arm to help her stand.

"Never mind that," her mother said. "I was getting worried. You weren't coming home, and you weren't coming home." She wasn't steady on her feet. She leaned on Trisha.

"How much did you have to drink?" she asked.

"Not enough," her mother said. "What happened? What did they say? Why were you gone so long?"

"Why indeed," Trisha said as they made their way to the kitchen. Her mother sat at the table. Trisha got them each a beer. She took several long swallows, scratching the itch.

"Well?" her mother asked.

"I don't know anything, Mom." She'd made a mistake by telling the detective too much. She shouldn't have told him she hadn't done it. He'd believed her, or she thought he had. Now he would look at someone else—her mother, her friends—anyone she'd had contact with. It didn't sit right with her. She had a bad feeling.

"I'll be back," she said.

"Where are you going?"

"Evelyn's."

Trisha crossed the street, walked around the snow piles, wishing she hadn't forgotten her winter coat back at her mother's. Two minutes in the harsh cold air was enough to make her shiver. The sun had set hours ago. The neighbors' Christmas lights were turned on, giving the sidewalk a soft glow. She wasn't two steps on Evelyn's porch when the front door opened and Carlyn stepped out.

"Hey," Carlyn said. "Were you looking for Dannie? She already left. We're just about done here. She's going to pick up the last few boxes tomorrow."

"I was looking for you."

"Oh?" Carlyn touched her neck where the skin peeked through the thin scarf that was meant to keep her warm. Her coat was open; the ends flapped in the breeze, revealing a white oxford shirt underneath.

There was something sensual about her, vulnerable. It was then Trisha remembered laying the softball bat on the floor in Carlyn's bedroom all those years ago. The next day, Lester had found Trisha in the woods.

"What did you do?" Trisha asked.

"Do you want to talk inside?" Carlyn asked and opened Evelyn's front door.

Trisha followed her in. She hugged herself against the cold. The heat had been turned down low. No one was living here, so it made sense. The living room had been emptied out. The dining room and kitchen tables and chairs had been donated. They had nowhere to sit.

"Who told you?" Carlyn asked. "Was it your mom?"

Trisha shook her head. *My mother knows?*

"I would've told you myself, but I don't know. I guess I didn't know how." Carlyn crossed her arms. "But what you heard is true. I looked for you right after graduation. I flew to Chicago and got on a bus. I spoke to your dad in prison."

She was taken aback, confused. "You went to see my dad?"

"Well, yeah. Our moms knew. Dannie knew. They all knew I went looking for you. Dannie even gave me money to pay for the bus trip, and you know how little money she had back then. I wanted to tell you I was sorry for the way I acted. I wanted to bring you home."

Trisha struggled with the magnitude of what Carlyn was saying. "Wait. Back up. You talked with Frank? Frank Ciccerone? My dad?"

"Yes," Carlyn said.

"In prison?" she asked.

"Yes. But he wouldn't tell me where you were—just that you'd been to see him, and he'd set you up with someone he knew on the outside. Did he? Did you work on the street?"

"Yes," Trisha said. "I mean no—not in the way you're thinking."

"I'm glad," Carlyn said.

"You came after me? You wanted to bring me home? Dannie too?"

"Why is that so hard for you to believe?" Carlyn asked. "We were best friends."

This wasn't what Trisha had meant when she'd asked Carlyn what she'd done. But Carlyn confessing she'd looked for Trisha after graduation had knocked her down harder than any fist could. She tried to swallow this new information, digest it, only to have it come back up as something singular, unfathomable, extraordinary.

CHAPTER FORTY-ONE

Parker and Geena made a return trip to Cal's store after dropping off Trisha at her mother's house. Now that they weren't sure of Trisha's guilt, they figured they'd better follow up on their other lead. They asked Cal about his relationship with Sharon.

"We were friends," Cal said. "Nothing more."

"Why didn't you mention this to us before?" Geena asked.

"I didn't think it was relevant." Cal looked at Parker while he talked, even though it had been Geena who had asked him the question. "Besides," Cal said, "I was on the road during that time. I had a couple sales appointments in New Jersey. I keep records of everything. I didn't know where you were going with all your questions the other day, so I had Eric dig everything out." He nodded to Eric. "Why don't you show them?" he said.

Eric disappeared into the back office. He returned a minute later, handed Parker an open ledger with a hotel receipt. Parker glanced at it, passed it to Geena. It was an expense report from 1986 confirming Cal had been in Edison, New Jersey, during the week of December 4.

"We'll be back if we have any more questions," Geena said and turned to go.

Parker followed her out. They got into the car. Parker drove, headed back to the station.

"Do you believe him?" Geena asked of Cal.

"Actually I do," Parker said.

❧

Parker stood in front of the only whiteboard in the small conference room at the station. A picture of Lester that was taken from the missing person file was taped to it. Sharon's and Trisha's names were written underneath the photo.

Geena came to stand next to him. "What are your thoughts?"

"Why did Sharon wait to report him missing?"

"Because she killed him, thought it through afterward, and decided it would look suspicious if she didn't at least report it."

"Maybe," he said.

Geena continued. "She could've buried him, thinking he'd never be found, so might as well report it before anyone started asking questions about where he was. It makes her look like the concerned wife."

"Sounds plausible," Parker said.

"Maybe she had to wait until the snow melted before she could bury him, and only then she decided to report him missing," Geena said.

"If all that's true, then how do we put her in the woods with him? It made more sense that Trisha was the one in the woods. It was her bat, and he was found where she was known to hang out with her friends. But I'm not convinced she did it, not after talking with her today. No one is that good of a liar."

"Maybe. Maybe not," Geena said. "We could ask her to take a polygraph."

"We could," Parker said, but he suspected if anyone could beat it, Trisha could. "What about Carlyn?" he asked. "She lied about the bat. Why don't we see what else she's lying about?"

"Why don't we bring all of them in—Sharon, Trisha, Carlyn, and even Danielle, since we didn't have an opportunity to talk with her yet—and do this old school?" Geena said.

"You mean play them against each other?"

"Exactly. See who flinches."

"Okay," he said. "It's worth a shot."

҈

Parker and Geena mapped out a plan on how they were going to proceed with interviewing the four women. It was late by the time they'd finished. Geena had gone home, mentioning something about letting her old bulldog, Rufus, out while Parker caught up on paperwork. When he finished, he watched the video of Trisha's interview one more time, checked his phone repeatedly. He was distracted by the silence around him, minus the occasional phone going off, the night shift coming in, the bits and pieces of conversation about kids, sports, weather.

It was after midnight by the time he pulled into his driveway, cut the lights, sat in total darkness. He tried to imagine what it would be like to have Becca inside the cabin waiting for him to come home. He didn't expect her to cook dinner for him or fold his laundry or do any of the other domestic chores that always seemed to fall on the woman. He'd been living alone long enough to do those things for himself. But the thought of finding her curled up on the sofa with a book, watching television, Romy, her German shepherd, greeting him at the door, tail wagging, gave him a warm feeling. Or perhaps she'd be in bed, sleeping, tired after a long day at the clinic. Parker liked the idea of slipping under the covers, wrapping his body around hers, holding her close . . . among other things.

He got out of the car. The air was cold, the river quiet. His house was dark. It would be nice to come home to a light on, at the very least.

He fished in his pockets for his keys, nearly slipped on the ice on the pavers that led to his front door, said a few choice words.

Inside, he heated a bowl of leftover beef stew, his mother's recipe. She was always emailing him new recipes from the *Food Network Magazine*. But he preferred her old recipes, the ones written in her sloppy handwriting, the pages stained from her greasy fingers, drippings from butter and oil. While he waited for the stew to warm, he pulled out his phone and typed a message to Becca. He wasn't sure when he'd get the chance to apologize to her face-to-face. He decided sending a text was better than nothing.

I'm sorry about the other night. He hit send as the microwave dinged. He ate at the table, his stomach growling from having skipped dinner. He kept his phone next to his plate, waiting, hoping she'd text him back. After cleaning up the dishes, wiping down the counter, he picked up his phone again. His text to her was marked as having been read, but she'd never replied.

CHAPTER FORTY-TWO

JUNE 1987

Trisha had never seen anything like Las Vegas before. The second her foot stepped off the bus, hit the hot pavement, she was breathless, nearly giddy with anticipation. She walked through every casino on the Strip, one after the other, taking in the flashing lights, mural-covered walls, obnoxious chandeliers, red and gold chintz. Gaudiness abounded. The buildings, slot machines and tables, the people—everything seemed supersize, larger than life. Even the seedier side—middle-aged men in business suits leering at young girls, so young they were considered jailbait, showing so much skin to the point of being indecent—made her smile. This she understood. Cheap perfume and smoke filled her nose. And the noise! Buzzers and bells amid chatter and laughter. Her senses were under attack, assaulted by the sights, the sounds, the smells.

Trisha fell head over heels, swept off her feet in love. Vegas was a place where things happened, *big* things, so colossal she could taste it, the very air she breathed vibrating with it. It was nothing like Second Street in Pennsylvania. She had a feeling her luck was about to change.

But first she had to look the part. Her clothes were a mess, wrinkled and tattered, her hair in knots. Chicago had been a good idea. Seeing her father had been an even better one.

She slipped into the public bathroom in one of the casinos, wet her hair, ran her fingers through the strands, drying them under the hand dryer. Next, she ducked into the nearest clothing store. The best she could afford was the clearance rack. She found an emerald dress made of a silky fabric, spaghetti straps, size extra small. She headed to the fitting room. The lush green complemented her pale skin, her dark hair and eyes. She turned herself around, checked how she looked from every angle. The salesclerk knocked, poked his head inside the small room.

"That looks like it was tailor made for you, honey," he said.

"Yes," she agreed; it did. But it cost all the money she had left in the world after the plane ticket, the long bus ride from Chicago, her visit to her father. He'd told her that he knew a man in Vegas, that he owed this man, and she needed to find him. "You do this for me, and I promise you'll be rewarded, but you're going to have to get the reward yourself. And you're going to have to be sneaky about it. Only take a little money at a time." He'd given her a description of what this man looked like. "His eyes are blue," her father had said. "Like ice." When she'd asked what she was supposed to say to this man, assuming she'd even find him, he'd said, "Tell him I sent you." She'd left the prison determined to do what her father had asked. And why not? She had nothing to lose, nowhere else to go, no one left to turn to.

She looked at the sales guy. "I'll take it," she said about the dress.

"What about shoes?" he asked. "We have the perfect sandal for it: nude, a nice heel to lengthen those legs."

"I'm not sure." She made a show out of looking at the price tag on the dress, letting him know she couldn't afford it. Heat burned her chest, warmed the skin on her neck.

"We take credit cards," he said.

She looked at the floor, furrowed her brow. She hadn't thought to steal her mother's credit card, but it wouldn't have worked out anyway. She was pretty sure the credit card would leave a paper trail, and she didn't want to be found—not that her mother or her friends cared enough to try.

"I'll put them aside," the clerk said about the sandals. "Give you some time to think about it."

She paid for the dress in cash, walked out wearing it, her old clothes in the bag. Once the salesclerk could no longer see her, she slipped her tennis sneakers off, tossed them into the bag too. She was going to have to do this barefoot, whatever "this" was. She lifted her chin.

§

Trisha wandered around the casino and soon learned the slot machines were for the low-budget crowd, and some of the poker tables were too. She was looking for the high rollers, the VIP rooms, where the real money was thrown around. As long as no one looked down at her feet, she was certain she could pull off pretending to be with the upper echelon, the rich crowd. It was all about attitude and appearance. Walk confidently, eyes alert, flirtatious. Several men had approached her in the last two hours looking for an hour of her time. She'd convinced herself it wouldn't come to that.

She circled what she believed was a high-end roulette table. One man in particular had quite a few chips stacked in front of him. She squeezed her way in between two blondes who weren't much older than she was to get a better look. The girls reeked of insecurity and desperation. They were trying too hard, with their teased hair and low-cut, flamboyant dresses.

Trisha's dark locks were straight, sleek, and a little greasy from traveling, but her slinky, understated dress separated her from the pack. She turned it into a positive thing, but she lost all her tact when the word *wow* slipped from her mouth as she gawked at the stacks of towering chips, tried to calculate their worth in her head.

The man with the money glanced in her direction. He was older, pushing forty, if the gray hair at his temples and the small lines by his eyes were any indication. He fit the description of the man her father had given her. She was feeling lucky.

"How much are you up?" she asked him.

He looked her over. "I'm down sixty thousand today. But I'm up seven hundred thousand for the week."

She nodded, tried hard not to be impressed, as if chatting with rich older men was an everyday occurrence in her sad little life.

He tossed her a chip. She snatched it out of the air, turned it over in her palm. *Twenty thousand dollars.* She sensed the two blondes closing in on her, threatened by her presence. Trisha might be young, but she wasn't stupid. She was being tested by this man. If she said the wrong thing, the blondes would swoop in, push her out. But if she guessed right, she'd claim the prize. Play it cool and act like this happened to her all the time.

She gazed at the man at the table. Was he the one she was looking for? "No, thanks," she said and put the chip down. Her stomach dropped when she turned to walk away, imagining what she could buy with that kind of money.

He reached out, touched her arm. "Where are you going?" he asked.

She turned back around.

"Stay." He said the one word that was enough to keep her forever. Someone wanted her around. She'd forgotten what that had felt like.

"What's your name?" he asked, pinning his ice-blue eyes on her.

"Trisha," she said and shivered, mistaking his cold gaze for excitement.

"Do you have a last name?"

"Just Trisha."

"Well, Just Trisha. Stick around."

The two blondes faded into the background. Trisha took her place by his side. He started winning and winning and winning. Many drinks later, deep into the night, she found herself in his suite standing next to a king-size bed.

He came up behind her, pushed her hair to the side, murmured into her ear, "My very own Lady Luck in a green dress."

She looked up at the mirror on the ceiling, her head dizzy, thinking she'd made it. Thanks to her father, she'd reached paradise.

"Where are your shoes?" he asked, noticing her bare feet, the bottoms black from the casino floor. He stepped away from her, picked up the bag with her old clothes and sneakers, and looked inside. "What's this?"

She shrugged. What did it matter? She was here, wasn't she? He wouldn't send her away. She couldn't explain how she knew, but she knew.

"Don't tell me you're a runaway?" He seemed amused.

"I'm eighteen," she said. "My father is Frank Ciccerone. He sent me."

He laughed. She didn't understand why. Maybe he was laughing at some private joke between him and her father.

"He pays off his debt by giving me his daughter." He laughed some more, then tossed the bag with her clothes in the trash. "We'll get you new ones tomorrow," he said and scooped her up, threw her onto the bed. She was surprised by the forcefulness of it, the way he tore at her dress, his urgency to get to her, to touch her skin, as though he couldn't stand to have even the slightest material between them. He inhaled her scent under her arms, between her legs. It wasn't until he was on top of her, pushing himself inside of her, that he said he was the man she'd been searching for.

Sid Whitehouse.

She stared at herself in the ceiling mirror, watched him move on top of her. His hands were in her hair, pulling her head to the side as he pounded away between her legs. He slapped her across the face, flipped her over, pushed her head into the pillow. She couldn't breathe. Next came the punch to the ribs, the spreading of her cheeks, and the hammering from behind. She was shocked, felt betrayed. Even her own father believed she wasn't worthy of love, believed she deserved this. It must be so. He was her last hope. She lay there, took it willingly. After a while, she found freedom in the pain, a release from what was rotten inside of her.

Later through the years, it would feel as though it were happening to someone else, as though she were a spectator in what Sid had convinced himself, convinced *her*, was nothing more than a business arrangement.

She became his Lady Luck, his four-leaf clover in the shape of a green dress, a charm he owned, possessed, a thing to be abused.

CHAPTER FORTY-THREE

Parker brought Sharon Haines a cup of coffee. She'd sat in the interview room for the last ten minutes, ever since he'd called and asked that she come in to see him. Her short gray hair was stuck to her head with grease. She leaned to one side, unable to sit up straight. Parker thought it had something to do with a bad hip. She'd limped into the station. He'd forgotten she was in her seventies and how old this case was.

"Black okay?" he asked and set the cup in front of her.

"Perfect," she said. She had a smoker's voice, rough and scratchy.

Parker smelled the sourness of her skin. He leaned back. "Thanks for coming in this morning," he said. "I have some additional questions about your husband." He let her know he considered this a formal interview and read her her rights, explained she was being recorded.

"Uh huh," she said and sipped the coffee.

He slid the photo of the woods and the Kilroy tree in front of her. "Does this look familiar?" he asked.

She picked it up, looked it over. He noted it was more than Trisha had done when he'd shown it to her.

"No," she said and set it back down on the table. "It doesn't look familiar to me. I told you, I'm not much of an outdoors type of person."

"Right, the bears," he said, recalling their previous conversation when he'd first met her. "Could you take another look? Does this look familiar? Have you ever seen this before?" He pointed to the carving in the oak tree.

"No, I can't say I have."

He nodded, put the photo aside. He pulled out the picture of the softball bat. "What about this?" he asked.

She hesitated. "It's a baseball bat," she said. "Are you going to show me a picture of a cat next and ask me if I know what that is too?"

He smiled. "No," he said. "Does this bat look familiar to you? Have you ever seen it before?"

She picked up the photo, studied it. "I might have. I can't say for sure. I've never had any use for sports." She put it down, looked around the small room.

"What about this?" He pointed to the engraving. "Does that mean anything to you?"

She looked at the photo again. "No," she said.

"Okay, well, Mrs. Haines, the letters stand for the friendship club your daughter was in when she was a kid."

"Is that so?"

"Yes. And your daughter confirmed the bat belonged to her."

"Uh huh," she said again and looked around the room, fidgeting in the chair.

"Would you like a cigarette?" he asked, searched his jacket pockets for the pink lighter and pack of smokes.

"Thanks, but I got my own," she said and pulled her own pack from her coat pocket.

"Let me find you an ashtray. I'll be right back." He left in search of an ashtray. He wanted to get a look at the lighter she used. He couldn't find anything and ended up filling a cup with water. He leaned over Geena's shoulder. "What's she doing in there?"

"Nothing. I was hoping she'd take another look at the photos, but she hasn't even glanced at them since you left."

"Do you think she's lying?"

"Definitely," Geena said.

Parker returned to room one, where Sharon sat waiting with a cigarette in her hand. He put the cup of water in front of her. "This is the best I could come up with."

"Thank you," she said and pulled a pink lighter from her pocket and lit up.

"Pink, huh?" Parker asked.

"What, this?" She held up the lighter, then shoved it back inside her pocket. "I've been using a pink lighter since before you were born."

"Is that right?"

"Yeah, they're cute. I kind of have a thing for them. Some women like knickknacks and figurines. I like little pink lighters. It probably sounds silly, but there it is."

"It's not silly at all. We all have certain things we gravitate toward."

"Yeah, I suppose we do. What do you gravitate toward?"

"Fishing," he said. "Let's go over again the last time you saw your husband."

She blew smoke into the air. "I saw him the morning before he was supposed to go to work. You said it was early December or something. I don't remember the exact date. It's been too damn long, and I'm too damn old."

"You worked at a bar called Foxy's?"

"Yeah, that's right," she said.

"And Lester was supposed to be at Cal's Carpets and Flooring working in the warehouse. You slept much of the day because you worked the night shift the night before. And then you went back to work at Foxy's that night?"

"That's right. I was working most nights. Lester wasn't always showing up at the carpet place, and we needed the money."

"Did that make you mad that he was blowing off work, and you had to pull extra shifts at the bar?"

She tapped the ashes from the cigarette into the cup.

"Mrs. Haines, did it make you mad?"

"I don't remember," she said.

"There was a bartender back then who confirmed you were working both shifts." He pulled the statement from the file in 1986.

"I guess," she said.

"It says here your coworker, Nancy, said you worked with her behind the bar."

"She's dead, you know."

"Who is? Nancy?"

"She died a couple of years ago. Cancer, I think." She finished the cigarette and dropped it in the water. "You hear stuff in small towns."

"On the day of December fourth, you didn't see anyone at all until your shift that night?"

"I was sleeping."

"Let's go back to the bat." He slid the photo in front of her again. "Is it starting to look familiar?"

"You tell me. You seem to remember more than I do."

His phone went off. Geena texted one word: Trisha. "Wait here," he said and walked out of the room, purposely leaving the door wide open.

༂༚

Parker thanked the trooper who had picked up Trisha and brought her to the station for him. Then he went out to the reception area, where Trisha stood waiting. Her winter coat was draped over her arm. Her sweater hung on her small frame. She wore the same fur-lined boots, but it was the way she carried herself that didn't match the image of the typical Slate Belt resident. She couldn't hide the scent of money on her, regardless of what she wore.

She was unmoving, as she'd been every other time she'd been in his presence. But there was something more going on behind her still body and the mask on her face, something in her eyes he recognized in other victims of abuse. He'd seen it enough times on the job: the battered woman who couldn't quite meet his eyes, or, if she had, the pain and broken will that had poured out of them. He'd suspected as much when he'd interviewed her just yesterday. Trisha was not only hiding the alleged abuse by Lester in her past but also things in her present life. He was now certain her marriage was more of the same.

He caught himself staring and diverted his eyes. "Thanks for coming in again." He escorted her past interview room one on their way to room two, making sure both Sharon and her daughter got a good look at each other.

So far the plan he'd put together with Geena late last night was working.

CHAPTER FORTY-FOUR

For the second time in less than twenty-four hours, Trisha was sitting on the hard plastic chair across from Detective Reed. She held her coat in her lap and her spine straight. He didn't speak for a long minute, holding a file in his hands, his finger rubbing the frayed corner. She suspected he was waiting for a reaction from her at seeing her mother in the room next door. Her mother had left the house early. Trisha had been woken by the phone, and then her mother had rattled around in the bathroom before Trisha had heard the front door open and close. Her mother had been gone about an hour before the phone rang a second time, this time summoning Trisha. They'd sent a patrol car to pick her up.

She sat unmoving, eyeing the detective. He was up to something. He had a plan.

A small part of her respected him for it. She sensed confidence in him despite his young age. To his credit, he hadn't tried to sway her with his good looks. He hadn't resorted to charm or flirtatious banter. Lesser cops would have. She'd known plenty in the past who'd look the other way if offered a free blow job. But not Detective Reed. He was a guy who firmly believed there was a right and wrong way of doing things. He'd end up on the right side, no matter the circumstance. In some ways, he reminded her of Scott, although she hadn't decided whether this was a good or bad thing.

Time would tell.

"We had a nice long chat with your mom," the detective said after reminding her of her rights again and that the interview was being recorded. A trace of stubble covered his chin. His clothes were rumpled, as though he'd slept in them. Shadows lurked on his handsome face, the kind that clung to the skin from lack of sleep. She wondered what had kept him up at night, considered asking him but then thought better of it.

He continued. "Why don't you tell me what happened on that trail?"

"I already told you everything I know," she said.

"No, I don't think you did." He leaned forward. "Your mom told me a few things that you left out the last time we spoke."

"I doubt that."

"You doubt your mom talked to me?"

"I think you're playing games, Detective."

His body language changed. He held the file more firmly in his hands. His face showed frustration. "It was your softball bat, your hangout by the trail. You have no alibi for where you were that day. Give me one good reason why I shouldn't arrest you right now."

"I didn't do it."

"So you said."

She didn't respond.

"If you didn't kill him, then who did?" he asked.

Trisha hadn't asked Carlyn if she'd killed Lester. It had been too much to process at the time. Trisha's head had been a mess, her heart turned inside out. Her whole life she'd thought things were one way, only to find out they were another. She'd been wrong about everything. She'd clung to the idea for so long that her friends had abandoned her, that it had been her hands that had taken her stepfather's life.

But Carlyn had gone looking for her, had wanted to bring her home. Dannie might've gone, too, if she hadn't been strapped from taking care of her mother.

If Carlyn was the one who had killed Lester with the bat, then she'd done it for Trisha. It was time Trisha returned the favor.

"If you didn't do it, then who did?" the detective asked again.

Trisha picked at the underside of her wrist that she'd hidden underneath her coat. Her breathing slowed, and, like dominos falling in a choreographed dance, she shut down. Her mind became a blank slate as her thoughts receded, drifted away. She'd practiced this meditative state of nothingness to perfection. She could summon it at will. It was a place she'd turned to time and again where nothing could touch her: not the fists, not the ropes around her ankles and wrists, not the beating between her thighs. It was a place where words lacked sharpness, their syllables too blunt to cut. Even the pain in her ribs, the bruises on her flesh, became nothing more than a distant ache.

The detective kept talking.

"You need to talk to me, Trisha, if you want my help. If you don't tell me what happened, then there's nothing I can do for you. Do you understand?"

His phone went off. He ignored it and continued. "I think you were a scared kid who got caught up in something that wasn't your fault. He never should've hurt you. You're not to blame for the things he did."

His phone went off again. "Were you protecting yourself? Is that why you stole the bat from gym class?"

He glanced at his phone. Trisha listened to the bustle of activity outside the small room, the shuffling of papers, electronics beeping, phones ringing. White noise.

"Did you go to the trail that day hoping he'd show up? Did you want to get back at him for what he did to you?" He paused. "No one would blame you if you did. I think a judge would understand, might go easy on you."

His phone beeped for a third time. "*I* wouldn't blame you," he said.

Trisha stared at a spot over his shoulder, her mind a black hole where sounds echoed in the dark.

Detective Reed pushed his chair back, the metal legs scraping against the tile floor. He got up and walked out of the room, leaving the door wide open.

CHAPTER FORTY-FIVE

Parker looked over Geena's shoulder at the screen, watched both Sharon and her daughter on the CCTV. Sharon smoked another cigarette, readjusted her hips on the chair. Trisha sat unmoving, her eyes staring at a spot on the wall.

"What do you think?" Parker asked.

"I don't know." Geena tilted her head toward Parker. "She's hard to read." She pointed to Trisha. "Is she on something? Some kind of medication?"

"I don't think so. I never thought to ask." He made a mental note to bring it up. Somehow, he didn't think that was the reason for her strange behavior. It seemed more like a defense mechanism or some kind of self-preservation tactic. He'd heard about victims of abuse going into what was referred to as a freeze state, or a form of disassociation. This freeze response was thought to be the biggest factor in how some victims survived trauma. Had Trisha trained her body to shut down and her mind to black out when she felt threatened? "What about Sharon?" he asked.

"She's lying," Geena said. "She knows something."

Parker nodded. "Let's keep going."

🙰

Parker returned to the reception area. Carlyn was sitting on the bench, waiting. She stood when she saw him. She wore workout clothes and sneakers. Her hair was pulled into a slick ponytail.

"Thanks for coming in again," he said.

"I don't have much time," she said. "I'm seeing clients later this morning." She clutched her car keys in her hand.

"It shouldn't take too long." He escorted her past interview rooms one and two on their way to room three, making sure Sharon, Trisha, and Carlyn all got a good look at each other.

"Have a seat." Parker motioned to the chair on the other side of the small table. He sat in the chair opposite her. Room three had the same setup as the other two interview rooms: the same plastic chairs, gray tables, beige walls.

Carlyn glanced at the camera mounted in the corner, up high and close to the ceiling.

"This interview is being recorded," Parker said. He asked if she was okay with it, advised she was free to go at any time. "Are we good?"

"I guess so."

"Have you ever heard of the term *freeze state*?" he asked.

"Yes, it's when a person experiences some sort of trauma, and they go into what they call a freeze state as a way of coping or surviving whatever is happening to them. They disassociate from the event; the body protects itself, and the person checks out, so to speak. It can occur when fight or flight is not an option."

"Is it possible for a person to consciously put themselves into this state?"

"I believe it's a reflexive action: a survival instinct that occurs in extreme circumstances." She paused. "But I suppose anything is possible," she said. "This isn't my area of expertise. I work with children with behavioral problems. Sure, some of my clients have mild disassociation, like constant daydreaming, but freeze state is quite different.

The person often feels trapped, with no way out. They perceive they are in a serious life-threatening situation, either physically or emotionally. You hear it occurring most often with victims of abuse."

"Domestic abuse?"

"Well, yes, I would think it's possible that some victims, no matter the type of abuse, may experience a form of freeze state as a way to cope." She leaned forward. "Who are we talking about here?"

"Why don't you tell me?"

Carlyn sat back, turned her head to the side, not looking at him when she spoke. "If this is about Lester, I already told you I think he was abusive. I already told you I never witnessed it personally. And yeah, I think the whole street knew what was going on inside their house. Everyone knew, but no one did anything to stop it."

"Well, I have on record that someone called the police on several different occasions."

"Yeah, you said that the last time I was here."

"You told me you saw bruises on Sharon Haines. What about Trisha?" Parker asked. "Did Lester abuse her too?"

"Trisha never came right out and said it, but sometimes I'd see bruises on her arms, too, and occasionally on her legs."

"Did you ever ask how she got the bruises?"

"No. Again, it was just something I knew. I didn't have to ask. Besides, she wouldn't have answered me. I think she was ashamed."

"Was Lester sexually abusing her?"

"Is this why you called me down here? To find out what Lester was or wasn't doing to Trisha three decades ago?" Carlyn asked. "I don't understand what this has to do with anything now."

"I'm trying to establish a motive as to why Trisha would've wanted him dead."

"I can't give you a professional opinion, if that's what you're asking for. But if you want my personal opinion as her friend, then yeah, I think he sexually abused her." She glared at Parker. "And for that, who could blame her for wanting him dead?"

He couldn't disagree. Or wouldn't. The more he learned about Lester, the more Parker loathed him. But personal feelings aside, Parker had a job to do, and that was to find out who had killed him. He pulled a report from the file. "Where were you the day Lester disappeared?" He recited the exact date he was last seen: December 4.

"I told you I was in school. You can check their records."

"I already did," he said. "What about after school; where did you go?"

"Probably the library. I did my homework there most days. I was trying to keep my grades up."

"Can anyone confirm you were there? Did you see anyone? Check out any books?"

"We covered this. I don't remember."

"Okay," he said. "You're right; we did. What did you do after the library?"

"I went home."

"Were you alone?" he asked.

"No, Trisha came over. She spent the night."

"She slept over?"

"Yes, I told you this before, that she slept over."

"Okay, so on the night she slept over, was anyone else with you, or was it just the two of you?"

"It was just us," she said in a low voice. "No, that's not right. Dannie was with us. She was there too. In fact, they both slept over a couple nights that week."

"Was your mother home during that time?"

"No, I already told you: she would've been working the night shift at the hospital. We would've been alone. And Sharon would've been working at the bar," she said. "Our mothers worked nights back then. I have no idea where Lester was."

He dropped the image of the softball bat on top of the table. "You sure you don't recognize this?" He pulled out the enlarged image of the engraving. "How about now? Look familiar?"

She didn't say anything.

"I know it's the bat Trisha stole from the high school gym," Parker said. "I know what *S. S.* stands for. Remember Scott Best? He's a police officer now. I believe you were friends back in high school. He's been a big help in clearing some of this up for me."

Carlyn still didn't say anything. She looked uncomfortable.

"Do you want to tell me what you know about it?"

"Sounds like you already know everything."

"Come on, Carlyn, level with me. Did Trisha hit Lester with the bat?"

She sat back in the chair, arms folded, and she almost looked smug when she said, "No, she didn't."

❧

Parker was back with Geena, staring at the screen and the images of the three women. Sharon was on her third cigarette. She was fidgeting again, adjusting her position in the chair. Parker regretted letting her smoke. He was going to smell like cigarettes the rest of the day.

"Did Trisha have any reaction at seeing Carlyn walk past?" Parker asked. He was worried that Trisha hadn't been paying attention and that she'd been too zoned out to take notice.

"She watched her walk by, but otherwise she hasn't moved." Geena motioned to the corner of the screen, where Carlyn was on camera. "She looked pretty certain that Trisha didn't swing that bat."

"I thought so too," Parker said. "We're missing something."

"Do you see what I see?" Geena asked, pointing at the screen again.

Carlyn had pulled a pink lighter from her pocket, and she was turning it over in her hand.

"How many pink lighters can there possibly be?" Parker asked.

"Let's get the fourth one in here," Geena said. "And continue to bounce between them. Something is bound to shake out."

⁂

For the fourth time that morning, Parker entered the reception area. Danielle was seated in the far corner of the bench, clutching her purse in her lap.

"Danielle Torino," Parker said.

"Yes," she said and stood, keeping her purse close to her chest. She was short, her face full, her body round underneath a long winter coat.

"I'm Detective Reed," he said. "Thanks for coming in. Would you follow me, please?" He escorted her to interview room four. She looked scared, and he was glad they'd saved her for last, putting her in the room where there was a little more comfort, the one with the artificial plant and box of tissues.

He took the long way around, making sure to showcase her in front of the other three interview rooms, where the doors had been left wide open, and the others could see them.

Parker glanced over his shoulder repeatedly. Dannie looked inside each room as they passed by. At one point, she looked directly at Parker. She gave him the impression she had no idea what was going on. That might be. He was going to find out.

"I appreciate you taking the time to come down to the station," he said once they were seated. "I'm sorry to hear about your mother."

"Thank you," she said, keeping her coat on, her purse in her lap, her fingers gripping the strap. "What's this about, anyway?"

He went through the routine again, as he'd done with the other three: secured her permission to record the interview, asked her where she was the day Lester had disappeared. She said she was in school and then spent the rest of the time taking care of her mother, eventually sleeping over at Carlyn's house. He showed her the softball bat, the engraving.

"Yes," she said. She recognized it. No, she didn't smoke. She tried it once when she was a kid but didn't like it.

Parker was about to ask if she thought Trisha had hit Lester with the bat when Geena texted him. We've got activity in room one.

"Excuse me," Parker said and exited the room, but this time he shut the door. He peered over Geena's shoulder again. "What do we have?"

"Sharon," Geena said. "She's been up and pacing. She dropped her cigarette twice. She's definitely anxious about something."

"Keep an eye on her," Parker said. "I'm going back to talk with Danielle."

༚

"Detective Reed." Sharon stuck her head out the open door as Parker walked past on his way back to the room where Danielle was waiting. "Can I have a word with you?" she asked.

"Sure," Parker said and went into the room with Sharon, closed the door behind him. "Have a seat," he said.

Sharon sat down. He sat across from her.

"I haven't been completely honest with you," she said. She brought the cigarette to her lips, sucked in hard, exhaled.

"I see. Are you ready to be honest with me now?"

"Yes." She nodded. "Yes, I am."

"Do you understand this conversation is being recorded?"

"Yes." She pointed toward the door. "Those girls don't have anything to do with this."

"Which girls, Sharon?"

"My kid and her friends."

"Would you state their names for the record?"

"Trisha, Carlyn, and Dannie. Jesus," she said. "Dannie just buried her mother last week—a woman who was one of my dearest friends." She took a deep breath. "They've got nothing to do with this. They just got caught up in adult matters when they were kids. That's all."

"I'm going to stop you right there." He reminded her of her rights. "Do you understand what I just said to you?" he asked.

"Yes, yes," she said. "I understand."

"Okay. Why don't you tell me what happened?"

"I got a call that Thursday morning from the high school. They told me Trisha skipped again, and if she didn't show up for the rest of the school year, she'd have to repeat senior year. My kid wasn't about to repeat a grade. It made no sense to me. If you can't get her to show up the first time around, what makes you think she's going to show up the second time?"

"Go on."

"I was upset, of course. I wanted her to know she was in trouble with them and me." She took another long drag from the cigarette, exhaled, and continued. "I figured I knew where I could find her. She was always hanging out with her friends on that trail in them damn woods. I bet they were drinking and smoking and who knows what else. Kids." She snorted.

"Did you go to the trail, Sharon?"

"Yeah, but you know I hate them woods. I was scared of them, so I grabbed her bat. You know, to fend off those bears and whatnot." She swallowed.

"What did you find when you got to the woods?"

She took another drag of the cigarette. "Trisha wasn't there," she said.

"Who was?"

"Lester." She stared off to the side. "We had a fight the night before, when I got home from the bar. It was a bad one."

"You and Lester?"

"Yeah. There were bruises on my neck. I was going to have to wear a turtleneck to the bar that night. I didn't get many tips when I wore turtlenecks, if you know where I'm going."

"I do. What happened next?"

"I was surprised to find him there. I mean, what's he doing hanging around the place my kid goes with her friends? Does that make any sense to you?" Her voice broke. "He was supposed to be at work, anyway. And that's what I told him. He didn't like that. He'd been drinking. He came after me."

"What do you mean he came after you?"

"He came at me. I didn't know if he'd choke me for good that time or not. I thought he was going to kill me, you know? But I had the bat." She rubbed her brow. "I had the bat, and I hit him with it."

"What happened next after you hit him with the bat?"

"I was afraid of what he'd do to me. I never hit him before," she said. "So I ran."

"And you reported him missing two weeks later. Why?"

"I didn't know he was . . . you know. I didn't know."

"You didn't think it was strange that he didn't come home after you hit him in the head with the bat?"

"I thought he was punishing me by making me worry. Or maybe he was off on a bender. I didn't know." The ash from her cigarette fell onto the table. "I didn't know what he was doing to my little girl. I want you to understand. *I didn't know.*"

"What was he doing to her?"

"Don't make me say it."

"Was he abusing your daughter, Sharon? Is that what he was doing?"

"Yeah," she said. "Damn you." She rubbed her eyes. "Yeah, he was."

"Why didn't you tell the cops all this back then?"

"Why do you think?"

"I don't know. Why don't you tell me?"

"Because I didn't think they'd believe me. I didn't think they'd believe I'd hit him to stop him from killing me."

"Okay. So why bother reporting him missing at all? I mean, what was the point? Or were you covering your tracks because you knew he'd never be found?" He waited for her to respond. When she didn't, he leaned forward, his voice clear when he asked, "Did you report it before or after you went back up the trail to bury him?"

She brought the cigarette to her cracked lips.

"Sharon," he said. "Did you bury him before or after you reported him missing?" He paused, waited for a response. When she didn't give one, he asked, "How long did you have to wait for the snow to melt? Was it two weeks?"

She blinked several times, the smoke cloudy in front of her face. She seemed to consider what he'd asked, and then she said, "I think I'd like that lawyer now."

⁂

"Wait here," Parker said to Sharon. He returned to where Geena was sitting behind the screen. "Did you get all that?"

"I sure did," Geena said.

"Are you buying it was self-defense?"

"It could've been. She could've panicked and gone back later and buried him. But even if we didn't get that out of her, look at it this way—she had motive, access to the murder weapon; she prefers pink lighters, and one was found at the scene; but most importantly, she just confessed. We're done here. Let's wrap this up." Geena stood, stretched her neck and back. "I'll let the others know they're free to go."

"Keep Trisha in room two for me. I want to tell her myself." Maybe he was overstepping his bounds, but if he could help her in some way, he would. No one should have to live in fear of the very man they'd married.

Parker returned to room one, where Sharon waited. "I'm going to have to ask you to stand." He pulled the handcuffs out. "You're under arrest for the murder of Lester Haines."

CHAPTER FORTY-SIX

Trisha sat patiently waiting for Detective Reed to return. She continued picking the tender skin on the underside of her wrist, her hands hidden beneath the coat in her lap, concealed from the camera aimed at her. The detective was playing games, all right, marching Carlyn and then Dannie past the open door for Trisha to see. She had to muster every bit of strength she had to remain calm, unmoving, *frozen.* It was harder for her to maintain this frozen state when there were other people involved and she had no control over what they might say or do. When Trisha was the sole target she could slip away, remove herself from the situation, as though she wasn't a participant in whatever was happening. But how could slipping away protect the three people in the other rooms? Maybe what she should be worried about was whether or not they were protecting her.

She was feeding into the detective's plan, second-guessing herself, allowing him to sway her into making a decision that could be costly.

Breathe. She talked herself down.

All she had to do was breathe.

Someone walked by the small room where she was waiting, then closed the door, boxed her in. Sounds came from the other side: the shuffling of feet, people moving about. Something had happened. The air became charged, sizzled with activity. She closed her eyes, inhaled deeply. The bustle outside the door could only mean one thing.

Someone had talked.

༄

Detective Reed stepped into the small room. He sat down opposite her. His expression told her that he'd gotten what he'd wanted out of one of them. However, she sensed there was something more he wanted from her.

He motioned to the corner wall, where the camera was mounted. "The camera has been turned off," he said. "Nothing we say from this point on will be on the record."

"Whatever."

"We can talk freely if you'd like."

"I have no idea what we'd talk about."

He passed her a card: a number for victims of domestic violence to call for help. A pinkish hue traveled from his neck to his cheeks.

She enjoyed his discomfort; let him see how it felt.

He continued. "Maybe you've already spoken to someone about it, but you do know there are groups you can join, other people who have gone through what you're going through. There's help out there if you want it."

She kept her face neutral. She couldn't believe he was talking to her about joining a victims' group.

"There are people who would be happy to talk with you. I can get someone here in a few minutes. All you have to do is say the word."

"That isn't necessary." She wasn't denying it. Why should she? Her two days were almost up, and besides, she was putting together her own plan.

The detective nodded. His hands were folded on the table. He was so young, too young to be messed up in her bullshit.

"Your mother," he said. "She confessed to hitting your stepfather with the softball bat."

For a split second, Trisha was sure her jaw had dropped. She quickly recovered, removing all expression from her face while her mind raced. *That can't be.* Her mother couldn't have been the one to kill him. She hated the woods. She'd had no reason to be on the trail. Her mother hadn't fought back, *ever.* The detective had it wrong. Trisha had left the bat on the floor in Carlyn's bedroom. She may have forgotten then, but she was sure of it now. There was only one plausible explanation.

Her mother was lying.

The detective kept his eyes on her, as though he wanted confirmation he was right, and her mother was guilty. But she wasn't. Trisha wished he'd leave her alone. His pitying stare was enough to make her want to slap him. She knew what that would get her, though—a night in jail for assaulting a police officer. She'd been there, done that, kicking the shins of some cop repeatedly during one of her drunken outbursts. It wasn't until she'd swung at him that he'd added the assault charge on top of disturbing the peace. Later, Sid's lawyer had gotten the assault charge dropped.

The detective continued to stare. Maybe she should do it: one quick crack across his cheek, and mother and daughter locked up in the county jail together. Then Trisha could ask her what she thought she was doing by confessing.

"Your mother said Lester choked her the night before. She thought he was going to kill her. Does that sound right to you?"

"Yes. I remember seeing bruises. On her neck. Where his hands had wrapped around her throat." She had to be careful what she said, since she didn't know exactly what her mother had told him.

"What happened next?" he asked.

"I don't know."

"Your mother claims he came after her again the next day. She said it was self-defense. Do you think it was?"

"He used to beat her up," she said. "So yeah, I'm certain it was self-defense. Don't *you* think it was?"

"That's not up to me to decide, but I'll let the DA know."

"What happens next?" Trisha asked. A drop of blood trickled down her arm where she'd dug too deep into her skin on the underside of her wrist.

"Your mother is being processed now, and then she'll have to wait in lockup for the arraignment."

"Will she get bail?"

"She's lived here a long time. I don't think she'll be considered a flight risk. There's a good chance the judge will see it that way, too, but that's up to the court."

Trisha's eyes flickered to the door. How long had she been here? "Can I see her?"

"I'm afraid not," the detective said.

She could tell by his expression she wasn't going to get anything more out of him. "Am I free to go?" she asked.

૪૬

Trisha didn't see Carlyn or Dannie when she left the police station. A different trooper drove her back to Second Street. He didn't talk much to Trisha, but he kept glancing at her in his rearview mirror.

Once Trisha was home, she shrugged off her winter coat, then went straight to the refrigerator and pulled out a six-pack. She carried it with her to the living room, where the box of Christmas decorations lay on the floor. She plopped on the tattered couch, opened a can of beer.

The front door banged open. If Trisha was anyone else, she might've jumped. Maybe she did. She licked the droplet of blood from her wrist.

"What happened?" Linda asked. She wasn't wearing a coat. She pulled her cardigan tight across her chest. "I saw you get out of a cop's car. Where's your mother?" she asked, noticing the six-pack on the floor at Trisha's feet.

"They arrested her."

"For what?" Linda asked.

"For cracking open Lester's head with a bat." It was so unbelievable, and saying it out loud didn't make it any more real.

Linda opened her mouth, then closed it. She opened and closed it three more times without saying a word, her jaw clicking in the silence; then she dropped onto the couch next to Trisha.

"I was just as shocked as you are," Trisha said and reached down, pulled another can from the pack, and handed it to her.

Linda took the beer and gulped it. She lowered the can, turned her gaze to Trisha. "I can't believe it," she said.

There was a knock at the door. "Come in," Trisha hollered.

Carlyn stepped inside. "I thought I might find you here," she said to her mother. "I stopped at the house first. Dannie is looking for you. She has something of Evelyn's she thought you might want." She took off her coat and tossed it on the chair. She wore a black cotton dress, tights, and boots. "Do you mind telling me what's going on?" She nudged what was left of the six-pack with her toe. "They wouldn't tell me a thing when I left the police station."

"Sharon was arrested," Linda said.

Trisha locked onto Carlyn's face, met her eyes. *What?* Carlyn seemed to be asking her. Trisha pulled the sleeve of her sweater down over her wrist to stop herself from picking at it. She drank from the can instead, emptied it before reaching for another.

Carlyn didn't sit but rather stood by the chair, arms folded. Trisha held Carlyn's gaze, the two of them exchanging an entire conversation without speaking. Carlyn asking, *Why are you looking at me that way?* Trisha replying, *Don't you have something you want to confess?*

Linda patted Trisha's leg. Reflexively, Trisha moved away.

"You let me know if you hear anything about your mom," Linda said. "I'll go see what Dannie has for me." She got up, looked back and forth between them, then left them alone.

"What's going on?" Carlyn asked. "Did your mother really do it?"

Trisha almost laughed. "You should know."

"Why? How should I know?" Carlyn looked genuinely confused.

"My mother didn't do it," Trisha said. "But what I can't figure out is why she'd confess to it?" *Say it, Carlyn,* she urged silently. *Say it was you.* There was nothing more she wanted than for Carlyn to admit that she'd done it for Trisha. If she admitted it, then they could figure out what to do about Trisha's mother. The statement Trisha had given the detective about Lester choking her mother was true, but would it be enough to prove self-defense?

"I always thought you were the one who did it," Carlyn said. "Are you telling me you didn't?"

"I never hit him with the bat. The whiskey bottle, sure. But someone killed him with the bat. The detective was pretty clear about that."

"And your mom confessed to it? Why?" Carlyn asked.

"Self-defense. Why else?" *This is your chance, Carlyn, to tell the truth.*

"I'm speechless," Carlyn said and picked up her coat. "After all this time."

Carlyn wasn't acting like she felt guilty about letting Trisha's mother take the blame. "Where are you going?" Trisha asked.

"I have clients." Carlyn checked her phone. "I'm running late." She hesitated at the door, reached in her pocket, pulled out a pink lighter. "I kept this. It was yours when we were kids. I know this probably sounds silly, but it was all I had of you after you'd gone. I guess it made me feel as though there was a small part of you that was still with me." She handed it to her. "I wanted you to know," she said and left, pulling the door closed behind her.

PART THREE
THE BURIAL

CHAPTER FORTY-SEVEN

Parker sat at his desk at the station. Geena sat across from him. Other than the occasional phone ringing, it was quiet. The guys on the night shift walked in, slapped him on the back, shook Geena's hand, congratulated them on a job well done. Lieutenant Sayres called, pleased to have another case closed. The lieutenant let them know they'd arrested the guy in the Angel case. The burn victim's boyfriend, Boonie, had been formally charged earlier that day.

"Well, that's it for me," Geena said and stood, picked up her phone.

"Heading to Benny's?" Parker asked. He couldn't join her, or rather he wouldn't. He didn't trust himself not to have a drink, not after the other night. He didn't want Becca to ever have to pick him up again, drive him home because he was too drunk to drive himself. She hadn't said it, but he'd felt her disappointment in him.

"I'm going to drop by headquarters," Geena said. "I want to check up on an old case I worked with Albert. See you tomorrow." She headed out, didn't stick around long enough for Parker to ask which case it was, although he suspected it was the rape and murder of a girl last spring. It seemed to Parker that she'd let it get to her. It wasn't the first time he suspected something had gone wrong in her last case with Albert.

He finished his final report. He knew he should feel satisfied that he'd done his job, but the rush he sometimes got after making an arrest never hit his system. Instead, his stomach had fisted in a tight knot, and there was a dull throb behind his left eye.

He stared at the video of Trisha frozen on the screen. He played it again, watched it a dozen more times. He struggled with the feeling that he'd missed something.

He decided he'd send Trisha's file to the victim's unit first thing in the morning. He rubbed his eyes. He was tired, but he doubted he'd get much sleep. He turned off his computer, headed home. The streets had been salted. Another storm was coming. They were calling for another three to four inches of snow.

Parker pulled into his driveway, cut the lights. Darkness enveloped him the second he stepped out of the car. He picked his way along the walk through the slivers of moonlight. At one point, he stopped, peered off the back deck. Chunks of frozen ice moved slowly downriver, but other than the water lapping against the dock, the night was still.

ༀ

Parker was up at five a.m. He hadn't slept, tossing and turning, finally flipping through the TV channels for much of the night for something to do. He dressed in thermal underwear and slipped on jeans, tugged on his heavy winter coat. He poured hot coffee into a thermos, picked up not one but two mugs off the countertop, grabbed his fishing gear.

He dropped his line in the river and sat in the chair on the dock. His breath swirled in white wisps in front of his face. So far the snow had held off, but it was coming. He could smell it in the air. For the first time in ages, it wasn't about fishing. It felt like a sham: waiting for someone who might never show up.

His head was cold. He'd forgotten his knit hat in the cabin. He'd stay out here as long as he could stand it. It wasn't until he heard footsteps coming down the stairs to the dock that he felt the first inkling of warmth.

Becca sat on the chair next to him. She shoved her hands between her thighs. "This is nuts," she said.

He smiled, agreed.

"I can't stay long," she said. "I have an early surgery scheduled with a Great Dane who has an appetite for socks."

He nodded. Sometimes he was shocked when he thought about how Becca spent her days, how she could cut into people's pets. She did it out of love for animals, of course. But there had to be something more behind the ability to take a knife to the flesh of another living thing: something in her personality, her genetic makeup that allowed her to take such actions. He filled a mug full of hot coffee and handed it to her, glanced at her small hands, her long fingers, imagined them holding a scalpel.

"I'm sorry about the other night," he said. "It's been a long time since I've done anything like that."

"It's okay." She gazed at the river. "What made you start drinking, anyway?"

"It doesn't matter. It won't happen again."

She didn't say anything for a long time, and Parker hoped she'd let it go.

"Does it have something to do with those bones they found by the trail? I read about it in the paper."

"It was my case," he said. "I made an arrest yesterday." His drinking hadn't been about Lester or the women involved. He'd drunk to forget his last case, and the man who'd blown his brains out in front of him. But he wouldn't tell her any of this. It was his burden to carry.

He sipped from the mug.

She turned toward him. He got the feeling she was expecting something from him.

"Would you go to dinner with me tonight?" he asked.

"You mean like a date?"

"Yes, that's exactly what I mean."

"Don't you think we're past that?"

"No, I don't think we're past that at all. If I recall, I've never taken you out before. Not properly." He'd driven her around in the old pickup truck he'd owned in high school more times than he could count. Every memory he had of his teen years, she'd been by his side. But he'd never dated her. Maybe that was what they needed to get their relationship going. "What do you say? Should I pick you up at seven?"

"Okay," she said, smiling back at him.

A comfortable silence settled between them, a companionable quiet they'd often shared when they were kids. He checked the line in the river, then laid the fishing pole on the dock.

After some time had passed, Becca got up to leave. "Whatever is going on with you, don't shut me out, okay?" she said and touched his shoulder before turning to go.

CHAPTER FORTY-EIGHT

Twenty-four hours after Trisha's mother was arrested, Trisha sat in the back of the courtroom waiting for her mother to appear for her preliminary arraignment. Trisha hadn't been able to talk with her since Detective Reed had locked her up. Her mother's one and only phone call had been to Linda. Trisha felt slighted, but given her absence in her mother's life all these years, she supposed Linda was the one her mother had come to rely on.

Trisha watched a parade of prisoners being shuffled in and out of a side door by an armed guard. The charges ranged from petty theft to armed robbery. It was late morning. Trisha's mother was the only prisoner who'd been charged with murder. Finally, her mother appeared from behind the closed door, stood before the judge, a court-appointed attorney coming to stand by her side.

After some discussion, much of which Trisha didn't understand, bail was denied.

The system couldn't help her mother all those years ago. Trisha should've known it wouldn't help her now. "Mom," she called, rushed to the front of the room, leaned over the railing that was meant to keep spectators separated from prisoners and officers of the court.

"It's okay," Sharon said. "Don't worry about me. You just take care of yourself."

I will, Mom. She waited to leave until her mother had disappeared behind the door. Then she turned, walked out of the courthouse, pulled her hood up to fend off the cold, shoved her hands into her pockets.

"Trisha." Detective Reed strode after her.

She stopped walking, allowed him to catch up. They stood on the steps. He was clean shaven. The dark circles under his eyes made it look as though he hadn't slept. "What can I do for you?" she asked.

"I'm sorry to bother you with this, but there's the matter of your stepfather's remains. They're expected to be released today to his next of kin. And that happens to be you."

"I'm not a blood relative."

"No, but I'm afraid you're all that's left."

"You must be joking."

He shook his head.

"Keep them. I don't want them. I don't want any part of him."

"The state can retain them, if you're not willing to claim them."

"I'm not."

He nodded.

She turned to go.

"One more thing," he said.

She stopped.

"Will you be staying in town if this goes to trial?" he asked.

"My husband is coming for me today," she said. "I'm flying back to Vegas with him tonight." After Trisha had returned from the police station yesterday, she'd thought more about what she was going to do when Sid came for her. She'd finalized her plan, but she wasn't going to tell the detective that.

"Are you sure that's a good idea?" he asked.

She looked at him curiously. "May I ask you something?"

"Go ahead," he said.

"The injury to Lester's head. Was it on the left or the right side?"

"The left. Why?"

"No reason." She touched the pink lighter tucked deep inside her pocket. She knew Carlyn was left handed. If she'd swung the bat, the injury would've been on the right side of Lester's head. Carlyn couldn't have been the one to kill him, which meant that maybe Trisha's mother was telling the truth after all. Maybe she really was guilty. Maybe she'd found the bat at Linda's house. Maybe she had finally found the courage to fight back.

Maybe Trisha was more like her mother than she believed.

࿋

Trisha held the gun in her hand, her fingers wrapped neatly around the grip, as though it had been custom made for her. Sid would appreciate the exactness, the precise fit in her hand. He loathed anything that was sloppy, careless, less than perfect.

She sat on the mattress on the floor in her old bedroom, her suitcase by her feet. Her clothes were packed, or at least her Vegas clothes were. She'd left the cheap sweaters and winter coat she'd purchased hanging in the closet. The boots with the fur lining were downstairs, kicked off inside the door when she'd returned from the courthouse.

Her head ached. Her tongue was coated with the thick aftertaste of piss-water beer. But her hair was washed, styled sleek and straight. She scratched at her neck where the collar of the green cashmere sweater rubbed against her skin. She was wearing designer jeans, the brand she no longer remembered. And her shoes, red $700 stilettos, a gift from Sid not two months ago. She was festive, dressed for the holiday, Christmas right around the corner; but more importantly, Sid loved her in green.

He wouldn't suspect a thing.

Her plan was coming together, but so much of it depended on him.

She tucked the gun into the waistband of her jeans and wheeled the suitcase into the hall, carried it down the stairs. The bruise by her ribs was fading, but it still hurt. She set the suitcase near the tattered couch, stuffed the gun under the cushion.

She'd have to contain him to the living room. She couldn't stray too far from the couch. Her plan hinged on this one detail. She walked in a full circle. What if she offered him a drink, had it set up right here on the end table, the one with scars on the wood, burns from cigarettes, rings from beer cans? She'd bought vodka on the way home from the courthouse, thinking she'd save it for later, once it was all over, but if her plan didn't work, there would be no later. It was now or never. She found a bucket and filled it with ice, placed the bottle inside. She grabbed two orange-juice glasses—they would have to do—and set everything on the end table.

She picked at her wrist, noticed her fingernails were chipped, ragged. She didn't have time for a manicure. He would notice—of course he would notice—and this little imperfection in her appearance might set him off. If she was going to do this, if she could live with herself afterward, she had to make sure she didn't do anything to purposefully provoke him. She searched the kitchen drawers for an emery board, found one in a junk drawer, filed her nails, soaked them in dishwashing liquid until they were soft, smooth. They would pass.

She returned to the living room, poured herself a drink: two inches of vodka on the rocks.

All that was left to do now was wait.

ॐ

Trisha sat on the couch, played with the pink lighter. She had a feeling of déjà vu. She'd once put a flame close to the living room curtains while sitting on this same couch: a kid with no hope of a future, an aching, desperate desire to burn the house down, with her in it. The desolate feelings had come and gone through the years. If Trisha had learned one thing about herself, it was that she was a survivor.

Her skin itched. Her eye twitched. Another drink was what it would take to calm her nerves. But it would be stupid to get drunk, not when she was this close.

She continued playing with the lighter, but of course it was out of fluid; the flame had long been extinguished. Hard to believe Carlyn had hung on to it all this time.

Trisha went outside, sat on the porch chair, watched the snow falling. Her feet were cold within minutes, her toes cramped, shoved into the tiny points of the shoes. She missed the warmth of the fur-lined boots. It was funny how she'd gotten used to a simple comfort so quickly. She wouldn't have allowed herself the luxury a week ago.

Linda stepped outside, nodded to Trisha on the porch, joined her. The street was quiet. Their neighbors were either working, or the weather had kept them inside. Across the street Carlyn hammered a **FOR SALE** sign into the small patch of yard in front of Evelyn's house. The snow came down in big fat flakes.

"She came out when she was in college," Linda said. "I dropped in on her one day unannounced and caught her with a girl in her dorm room."

"Were you surprised?"

"Not really. I guess I always suspected. She told Dannie soon after that. I think Dannie always suspected it too." She paused. "She had a couple of girlfriends over the years—nothing serious. When did she tell you?"

"I've always known."

Linda nodded. They were quiet after that, watched Carlyn put the hammer she'd used for the sign into the trunk of her car.

"My mom didn't make bail," Trisha said.

"I heard. She called me earlier—used one of her phone calls."

This time Trisha nodded. "I've got money in a safe-deposit box," she said, handed Linda a card with the bank's name, the password. "If anything happens to me, I want you to take the money and get my mom a good lawyer."

"What could happen to you?" Linda asked.

"Just promise me," Trisha said.

Linda stared at her. Then she finally said, "Okay." She seemed to turn inward, lost in her own thoughts. After a while she said, "Your mom didn't feel she had a right to go looking for you after you left. I think she believed she'd failed you and you were better off without her."

Trisha didn't know what to say, but somewhere over the last few days in a place deep inside, she'd forgiven her mother. She'd stopped blaming her for being blind to the things Lester had done.

Linda continued. "She told me once that the only reason she'd married Lester and moved here with him was to get you away from your father."

"You mean Frank?" Trisha asked. "Her plan didn't work."

"No," Linda said. "I guess it didn't."

"He died, you know. Three months ago. In prison," Trisha said. "Complications from the flu or pneumonia or something. Did you know I cried? I actually cried when I'd heard."

"Well, I'm sorry," Linda said. "But you know, you don't have to have the same blood to be family. Sometimes friends are your family. And if you haven't figured it out yet, we're your family, Trisha."

Carlyn crossed the street, joined them on the porch, pulled her jacket closed at the collar. The gray clouds huddled close. Christmas lights flickered; strings of blinking bulbs in windows turned on up and down the street.

Linda got up, plugged in the lights Trisha had hung on the posts.

Dannie emerged from her mother's house, paused to lock the door before making her way over. The four of them stared at Evelyn's dark, empty home.

"I can't imagine anyone else living there," Dannie said and leaned against the porch railing.

Linda reached out, squeezed Dannie's hand.

No one spoke. They didn't have to. Linda was right. They were family. Trisha had been foolish to think otherwise. She couldn't replace the years she'd lost since she'd left, but their being together now was proof that some bonds couldn't be broken.

They sat in silence, watched the snow cover the slate roofs, the sidewalks, the street. Trisha was aware of time slipping away, the pressure closing in.

Carlyn touched Trisha's sleeve, rubbing the soft fabric between her fingers. "What about you?" she asked. "What's next for you?"

"I wait," Trisha said.

"You think he's coming for you," Carlyn said. She must've put it together: the change in Trisha's clothes, the lack of a drink in her hand. Carlyn was always quick to catch on.

"Yes," Trisha said. "He's coming for me."

Dannie remained quiet, making the sign of the cross, whispering her silent prayers.

"You can stay here with us," Linda said. "You don't have to go with him."

"I've got things worked out."

"You've got what things worked out? What are you planning to do?" Carlyn asked.

"It's probably best you don't know."

A black sedan pulled onto Second Street.

"You better go," Trisha said. She was calmer than she'd expected. "All of you. Go."

"I don't understand," Dannie said. "What's going on?"

The car pulled into a parking space in front of the house. The first thing Trisha noticed was that his henchman, Heinrik, wasn't with him. Other than the driver, Sid was alone. He must've dropped Heinrik off at the airport first.

"Go," Trisha said again. "You don't want to have anything to do with this. This is something I have to handle on my own."

Carlyn took Dannie by the arm. "Whatever you're planning, Trisha, don't do it. Whatever he's done, he's not worth it," Carlyn said and dragged Dannie across the street to where their cars were parked.

Sid stepped out of the back of the black sedan, stood on the sidewalk. He was wearing a long wool coat, charcoal gray, to match the silver of his hair. Snow covered the tops of his shoulders. His scarf whipped in the wind.

Linda clutched Trisha's arm. She leaned in close, whispered, "You make sure it's self-defense. Do you hear me?" she asked. "Make sure it's self-defense." She let go of Trisha's arm and hurried away. She kept her head down, avoided looking at Sid, disappeared inside her house.

Trisha stood. It was time she became her own Lady Luck, turned things around, shined some light her way. She walked into the house, left Sid standing outside in the cold.

He'd take it as an invitation to join her.

She'd taken the first step.

There was no turning back now.

CHAPTER FORTY-NINE

Parker went back to the station after leaving the courthouse. Something about his conversation with Trisha had left him with an uneasy feeling.

He logged on to his computer, checked the airlines. A private jet was scheduled to fly out of the Lehigh Valley International Airport later this evening. He bet Sid Whitehouse would be on it. Would Trisha really be with him?

He didn't believe she would just up and leave her mother. Not now. From what he'd seen of them together, he'd say they were working through everything that had happened. And you didn't just take off in the middle of something as big and important as a pending murder trial. In cases like these, the family tended to hang around, hold out hope, stick together until the end.

Nothing about Trisha's leaving town added up. And why had she asked about the injury to Lester's head? It seemed an unusual thing to bring up. The evidence in the case was pretty clear. The person who had struck Lester was right handed. Was Trisha's mother? Had he missed something?

Parker sat in front of the video they'd shot the previous day of all four women in the interview rooms. He watched the clip of Sharon first. She'd smoked with her right hand. She'd signed the statement with her right hand. He breathed a little easier. He hadn't made a mistake. She was definitely right handed.

What had been Trisha's point? Then he remembered Carlyn clutching the car keys in her hand, tried to remember if it was the left or right hand. He fast-forwarded the tape. And there she was, playing with the lighter in her left hand. He had no idea where he was going with this. Maybe Trisha just had to be sure it was her mother who had done it. But she wouldn't have confessed otherwise. People didn't confess to crimes they didn't commit.

And then there was Sharon's face at the arraignment, one of resignation. Although Parker hadn't needed to be there, he'd wanted to be. It was a sad affair: Sharon standing alone next to a court-appointed attorney, one Parker had recognized but hadn't known personally. Trisha had been the only one to show up to support her mother.

He checked the time on his phone. Trisha's flight wouldn't be leaving for another few hours. It was possible she'd already left, en route to the airport or close to it.

He grabbed his car keys, told Geena he'd be back. He had a quick errand to run.

"What about this paperwork?" she asked.

"Feel free to finish it," he called over his shoulder.

"Jerk," she called back, making him smile. Then she got up and followed him out.

"Where are we going?" she asked once they were in the car.

"I want to check up on Trisha," he said.

"Because of her husband?" Geena asked, and Parker nodded.

The snow was coming down at a good clip. What had started out as big flurries were now small, furious flakes. Parker turned the windshield wipers on. It was hard to see the stretch of road in front of them, slowing their progress: an impediment against an unexplained sense of urgency.

CHAPTER FIFTY

Trisha stood by the side of the couch, her leg pressed against the torn cushion. The front door flew open, and Sid stepped inside. He glimpsed the suitcase near her feet. The corners of his lips twitched. He gazed at the rest of the tired house with its shabby furniture, the end table with the drinks.

"Do you like slumming it?" he asked. "You must. I mean, why else would you stay here when you could've stayed with me at the casino?"

She chose not to say anything. Nothing she said would change where this was going.

"Maybe you want to show me around." He motioned to the back of the house. "Since you like it here so much."

"You've already seen it," she said and willed herself to keep her eyes on his face.

"Yes, I guess I have," he said and cracked a smile. "The little present I left on your bed—the poker chips."

"Would you like a drink?" She forced her legs to take her across the room, away from the couch cushion. She picked up the glass, dropped ice into it. Her hands trembled.

"No, I wouldn't like a drink," he snapped.

She set the glass down and picked at her wrist as he paced the room, fingered the lampshade, ran his hand over the top of the armchair. He wiped his palms as though he'd touched something vile.

"I see you've packed," he said, glancing at the suitcase again.

"Yes," she said.

"And your mother? Where is she?"

"Jail."

He raised his eyebrows at that. "Well, I'm sorry. That must be very upsetting for you." He made another lap around the small room and stopped. "We have a little time before our plane leaves," he said and took off his coat, dropped it onto the chair. Then he unwound the scarf from around his neck, tossed it on top. He was dressed impeccably, his suit tailored, a subtle pinstripe in the pants and jacket. He shrugged the jacket off, laid it on top of the scarf. He loosened his tie, tugged his collar open. "How would you like to do this?"

She shook her head before she could stop herself. No. She wanted to scream, *No!*

"You never make it easy on yourself, do you?" He stepped closer to her, close enough that she could smell his cologne and the gel in his slicked hair.

He took a deep breath through his nose, inhaled her scent like an animal. "But that's what makes you so damn exciting," he said. She tried to run to the couch, but his hand shot out and grabbed her by the hair. He was fast for an aging man, agile like a gray fox. He smashed her face against the wall. Blood dripped from her nostril into her mouth.

"You didn't think I'd let you come back without paying for what you did to me, did you? You think you can leave me?" he whispered into her ear, pulled her hair so her head snapped back. Then he rammed her head against the wall again, pinned her up against the plaster with his body. "You think you can walk out on me?" He pressed up against her, his nose in her hair, on the back of her neck, breathing her in.

Blood rushed to her head, buzzed in her ears, seeped from her nose to her lips, ran down her chin. She felt herself slipping away, leaving her body to a place he couldn't reach her, to a place where she could leave him behind. *No.* She had to fight to stay here, to be present for every ache and pain and degradation. She had to remember her plan. She had a plan.

His hand reached under her sweater. She elbowed him hard in the gut, used the wall to propel her body backward, pushing him off her. She lunged toward the couch, her arm outstretched for the torn cushion, toppling the suitcase. He grabbed her waist, wrestled her to the floor. Her cheek pressed against the stained carpet, the fibers reeking of mold and dirt and cigarettes. He kept his knee lodged between her shoulder blades, his hand on the back of her head. She kicked, but otherwise she couldn't move. Tears blurred her eyes.

"Not like this," she said. Hair and dust and blood stuck to her tongue. She tried to flip over. He punched her ribs. For a second everything went black. When the haze cleared, she said again, "Not like this," searching for a way out, finding one.

"What?" He pulled her up, slammed her against the wall again, pressed his body against hers. She was barefoot. When had she lost her shoes?

"Binds," she managed, her disgust backing up in her windpipe.

He moved away from her, giving her an inch to breathe. He laughed. The sick motherfucker laughed.

"You dirty girl," he said, not bothering to hide his excitement as he grabbed her by the hair, yanked her away from the wall, and threw her to the floor. "Get them."

She pulled herself up to her hands and knees, not trusting her legs to stand. She licked the blood from her lips, the taste sharp on her tongue. Pieces of plaster fell from her hair from where her head had put a hole in the wall. Her nose was no longer centered but pushed to the side of her face. She opened the suitcase. His foot slammed against her rib cage. She grunted. More blood spilled from her mouth.

"Don't try anything stupid," he said and rolled up his shirtsleeves. He was just getting started.

She pulled out clothes, toiletries, placed them on the floor, but she was too slow for him.

"Move," he hollered, pushed her out of the way to search the suitcase himself.

She crawled to the couch, reached underneath the tattered cushion, the one with the foam oozing out, found the grip of the gun.

She pulled herself up, aimed the barrel at his head.

He looked at her. Surprise registered on his face. Fear colored his eyes.

"Get up," she said.

He stood. "What do you plan to do with that?" he asked.

He had to step toward her, to come after her. There could be no mistake once she pulled the trigger that he was going to kill her.

Her hand shook. But she wouldn't miss her target, not at close range. "I'm not coming with you. I'm never going anywhere with you again."

He was panting, glaring, his rage building.

"You can walk out that door now," she said. Blood and spit dripped from her mouth. "And never come back."

He stared at her as though he was trying to decide if she was serious. Then he shook his head and smiled, a cold, heartless smile. "You know I can't do that." He lunged at her. He was quick. She wasn't expecting it. She didn't have time to react. His hands wrapped around her throat.

She tried to breathe, but it was as though her windpipe had collapsed. He squeezed harder, his fingers digging into her neck.

Her eyelids fluttered. She was losing consciousness. She pointed the gun at what she hoped was his head.

CHAPTER FIFTY-ONE

Parker pulled onto Second Street, parked two cars behind a black sedan. "Must be the car service," he said. "Her husband either sent it for her, or he's in there with her."

"Yup. What's the plan?" Geena asked.

"I don't know," he said. "I hadn't thought that part through."

"We have to think of something. We can't just say we stopped by to meet her husband—" She broke off at a popping noise that sounded like it had come from inside the house. "That was a gunshot."

Parker threw open the driver's side door. Geena was already out of the car, racing down the sidewalk. He caught up to her, sliding on the slick, snowy surface, gun drawn. The driver of the black sedan stepped out of the car.

"Stay back," Parker shouted to the driver. Then he leaped onto the porch, stopped by the front door across from Geena. He listened. He didn't hear any noise coming from inside the house. He peered between the curtains of the living room window. The sound of his own blood pumping through his veins filled his ears. Two bodies lay on the floor.

"Two down," Parker said. "I don't see any movement."

Linda Walsh was walking toward them.

"You need to go back inside your house," Geena said. "Now."

Linda nodded, retreated down the snow-covered sidewalk, stopped as far as her porch.

"Trisha," Parker hollered. "It's Detective Reed." He waited for a response, but none came. He pushed open the door, gun raised. He took one step into the room, smelled the sharp tanginess of blood. The scent of death settled in his mouth and in the back of his throat. Geena came to stand next to him.

Sid Whitehouse lay in the middle of the living room floor, blood pooling around his head. Parker didn't have to check to know that Sid was dead. Trisha was crumpled on the floor near his feet. She wasn't moving. She could be alive. Parker couldn't get a good look at her injuries from where he stood. A small gun was in her hand. A suitcase was shoved against the couch, the contents spilled out. A torn couch cushion had been overturned.

Trisha moaned.

He aimed his gun at her. "Drop your weapon," he said.

She didn't move.

Parker stepped around Trisha, tried his best to avoid the blood and contaminating the scene. He kicked the gun from her hand. The second he did it, he could hear Sayres's voice screaming inside his head, *Whatever you do, don't touch the gun!* It was hard enough to lift fingerprints, DNA, from the metal, and then Parker had gone ahead and knocked it clear across the floor. Trisha didn't move. He bent over her, got a better look at her. Her face was smeared with blood. Her nose was off center, her skin the color of ash. He squatted next to her, found her pulse. It was weak.

"Hang on, Trisha," he said. "Help is coming." He looked up at Geena. She was on her phone, calling it in, requesting an ambulance. Linda stood in the doorway.

"Get out," he said to Linda.

"I'm a retired registered nurse. Can I help?"

"No," he said and stood, took her by the arm, and led her outside.

Linda pulled her arm away. "That's my best friend's daughter in there, and if there's anything I can do to help her, I'm going to."

"I'm afraid I can't let you inside." Not with a gun lying on the floor.

"Is she alive?" she asked. "Just tell me if she's alive."

"Ma'am, I'm going to have to ask that you take a seat." He directed her to the curb.

Sirens cut through the air, getting louder and louder the closer they got to Second Street. Within minutes a team of cruisers had pulled up, lights flashing. A couple of local police officers blocked off the street, stopping traffic from coming through. They held off the neighbors who had stepped outside to see what was going on.

Parker hadn't moved from the porch. Geena was inside. He should go back in, help her process the scene. Officer Best approached him.

"What happened?" Scott asked. "Is it Trisha? Is she okay?"

"She's alive," Parker said. "An ambulance is on the way. That's all I can say at this time."

⁂

Parker stood on the porch a little longer, pulled himself together as he watched the snow pile onto the cars, the street, the walkway. He took a few more seconds to gather himself, wiped the sweat from his palms. He had to go back in the house. His partner was in there. He told himself he just wouldn't look at the pieces of brain and bone fragments on the floor from Sid's skull. Then he took a deep breath and went inside. Geena squatted next to Trisha.

"Can you hear me, Trisha?" Geena asked. Trisha didn't respond.

The ambulance arrived. The EMTs worked on Trisha, stabilized her, lifted her onto the stretcher, carried her out. Linda Walsh got into her car and followed the ambulance.

It wasn't until after Trisha had gone that the forensic unit took over the living room. Parker had been avoiding looking at Sid's body the entire time until Nathan, the county coroner, called him over.

"Single gunshot wound to the head, close range," Nathan said and pointed to an area on the skin near the temple. "You can tell it was close range by the burn marks from the gunpowder."

All Parker could do at this point was nod. He didn't trust himself to speak, not with so much saliva collecting on the back of his tongue. When he'd gotten what he needed from Nathan, he found his voice, thanked him, and stepped outside. He'd get the rest from the autopsy report. He leaned against the side of the house, shoved his hands into his pockets to keep them from getting cold. Geena was writing down information on Sid Whitehouse from the driver of the black sedan. A crowd had gathered—neighbors, law enforcement, emergency personnel—all cluttering the street.

When Geena finished with the driver, she leaned against the side of the house next to Parker. Snow caught in her hair and eyelashes.

"You okay?" she asked. "That's about as fresh as a body gets."

"I'm fine," he said: not an outright lie but not the truth either. For the first time since he'd been promoted to homicide, he wondered if he could cut it. "Why did you become a detective?" he asked.

"The short version. One day I was writing speeding tickets; the next day I was being promoted. It seems I have a unique skill that someone in command deemed useful."

"What's the skill?" he asked.

"I have an eidetic memory, or some call it a photographic memory. I study a scene, a face, information in a file, and it becomes snapshots in my head. I'm a useful pet to have around if you need to recall something pretty quickly."

He remembered the way she'd examined the crime scene when they were in the mountains, how she'd only ever read the missing person file once and never checked her notes after interviewing witnesses. "What's the long version?"

She shrugged. "What about you? Why homicide?"

"I wanted to get the bad guys off the streets."

"Deep," she said, nudged him in the arm. "What's your take on this?" she asked, motioning to Trisha's house, the same house they leaned on.

"There's no doubt she's the shooter," Parker said. "But by the looks of her, I'm not sure she had a choice." He didn't feel good about being right that Trisha's husband had abused her. There was nothing good or right about it.

"Appears to be a case of self-defense," Geena said. Then she added, "Like mother, like daughter."

❦

The snow had stopped but not before dumping another four inches on the town. The roadways were slippery, even though the plows had done their best to clear them. It was evening. Dusk had long gone, taking the gray haze of winter with it, knocking out any chance of remaining daylight.

Parker pulled into the driveway of Becca's late father's house. The floodlights were on. She was outside shoveling the walkway that led to the front door. She stopped shoveling when Parker got out of the car. He walked up to her, wanted to wrap his arms around her. Romy jumped around his feet. Becca gazed up at him. He never wanted to stop looking into those careful gray eyes.

"Bad day?" she asked.

"Yeah," he said.

She nodded.

He got another shovel from the garage. He rejoined her in front of the house. They finished clearing the walkway in silence, then went inside, sat across from each other at the kitchen table, mugs of hot chocolate in front of them. Romy lay on the floor at their feet.

"My dad never talked about the job," Becca said. Her father had been the chief of police of Portland before he'd passed.

"Becca."

She held up her hand. "Please, let me finish," she said. "He never talked about any of it: the things he'd seen, how it affected him, made him feel. I used to think that if he would've just opened up about it with my mom, things would've been better between them. He wouldn't have done some of the things that he did. They wouldn't have divorced. They would've stayed married."

"We're not your parents," he said.

"I know that," she said. "But it doesn't mean we don't have the same problems."

He took a moment to think about what she said, couldn't come up with anything to prove she was wrong. Then he opened his mouth to tell her about the bad dreams he was having, how he couldn't sleep, but the words wouldn't come, fell away before they ever reached his lips.

"I know you, Parker. I know you better than you know yourself sometimes." Her lips turned up at the corners for a brief moment before falling to a straight line.

He was tired suddenly. He had a pile of paperwork waiting for him at the station: evidence to sift through on Sid Whitehouse's death. He didn't want to talk about his job and the problems that had somehow sprung up between them like weeds. They would have to talk about it eventually if they were ever going to get past it. But right now, all he wanted was to be with her, feel her next to him, hold her close.

"I'm sorry I had to cancel our dinner date tonight," he said.

"It's okay," she said and crossed her arms. It didn't look to Parker like it was okay at all.

"Do you just want me to go?" he asked.

"No." She reached across the table, squeezed his hand. "I want you to stay."

CHAPTER FIFTY-TWO

Trisha opened her right eye. The left eye was swollen shut. She reached up to touch her throbbing head. Wires hung from her arm where the IV was dripping medicine into her vein. *Pain medicine,* she hoped. Her chest ached with every breath. Tubes were shoved up her nose.

Linda appeared by her side. "The doctor will be in to talk with you soon." She gently squeezed Trisha's hand. Carlyn and Dannie emerged, flanking Linda.

"How bad is it?" Trisha asked.

"You have a concussion," Linda said.

"That explains my pounding head. What about my ribs?" She winced. Talking wasn't easy. It made her side so much more painful.

"You have two fractured ribs. A punctured lung."

"Ah, well, that explains why it hurts to breathe." Her mouth was dry. Her throat hoarse. She tried to swallow, but she didn't have any spit.

"You were lucky," Linda said.

"Lucky." Trisha smiled, but even smiling hurt.

"It could've been worse," Linda said.

Trisha reached up, touched the tubes going into her nostrils, wondered if her nose was still pushed onto her cheek.

"It's back in the center of your face where it belongs," Carlyn said, touched Trisha's brow.

Trisha tried to assess where the pain was radiating from the most. Was it her head? Her ribs? Her throat? Maybe it was her heart. "Is he dead?" she asked.

"Yes," Carlyn said.

Dannie leaned over the bed rail, her expression full of concern, worry. A rosary dangled from her fingers.

Trisha turned her head away; the slightest movement felt like a jackhammer was pounding against her brain. But she couldn't look at her friends, Carlyn's mother. She'd spent her entire adult life with Sid, and that small *sick* part of her grieved, and yet a bigger part of her felt relieved. He could never hurt her again.

The door to the hospital room swung open. Detective Reed stepped inside.

Linda patted Trisha's hand. "We'll be right outside if you need us." Carlyn and Linda both nodded at the detective on their way out.

Dannie lingered. "I need to get home to my girls," she said to Trisha. "But I'll check in on you later, okay?"

Once her friends had gone and Trisha was alone, Detective Reed approached, stood alongside the bed. He put his hands in his pants pockets.

"Does my mother know?" she asked.

"If she doesn't know yet, I'm sure she'll hear about it soon. Prisons are a good source of information if you know who to talk to. But if you'd like, I can relay a message to her."

"Tell her I'm okay."

"That's all you want to say, that you're okay?"

"That's it." It was best neither she nor her mother said too much from here on out, given their current situations. "Thank you," she said, realizing he had offered to do her a favor.

"You're welcome." He was talking in a kind voice, the one he probably used with friends and family when he wasn't being a cop. "I put a guard outside your door." His tone changed, back to business. "It will be up to the DA whether or not he wants to press charges. My partner is with him now."

"I understand," she said.

"What happened between you and your husband?" he asked.

"Shouldn't you read me my rights before you start asking me questions, Detective?"

"Tell me what happened," he said.

"I think it's pretty obvious what happened." She scratched her wrist. It was time for a drink. Funny how her body could be broken, but still she craved the one thing that could potentially kill her.

"Maybe it is obvious; maybe it isn't," he said. "I'd like to hear it from you."

"He choked me." Her fingers touched the skin on her neck. It was sore. "He was going to kill me."

The detective gently took her hand and moved it away from her throat. "You have bruises," he said.

The air in the room thickened, or did it just seem that way? She struggled to inhale. She coughed, which felt like an explosion inside her chest. A nurse breezed in; the detective stepped back. The nurse, Kelly, her name written on the whiteboard hanging on the opposite wall, gave the detective a dirty look. She smiled at Trisha, a conspiratorial wink.

Let the detective play his games, Trisha thought. What woman would convict her for killing her husband after what he'd done to her? The detective didn't know the half of it. Or maybe he did. Maybe he understood why Trisha had done it. Maybe he'd seen it before.

Kelly checked the machine next to the bed, the one that had beeped and buzzed nonstop since Trisha had opened her one good eye. "Here." She handed Trisha a kind of remote. "If you need anything, you press this button." She glanced at the detective. "The doctor should be in shortly. He's making rounds now."

Once Kelly left the room, Detective Reed placed his forearms on the bed rail, bent toward Trisha. He lowered his voice. "I have one more question for you."

The pain in her head, chest, intensified.

"Why did you pack?" he asked. "Were you really planning on going back to Vegas with him?"

She knew this question would be coming. He was trying to establish motive, her frame of mind, whether or not it was premeditated. "I guess I was hoping he would change. Isn't that what all battered wives wish for, that their husbands will keep their promise and never hit them again?"

"If that's true, then why did you buy the gun?"

"In case he didn't keep his promise."

He seemed to consider her explanation, as though he were trying to decide whether he believed her. "Okay," he said finally.

He left after that, and she was alone. And in spite of the pain in her head, the pressure in her chest, the tubes up her nose and running from her arm, she felt weightless, light, but most of all, she felt free.

CHAPTER FIFTY-THREE

DECEMBER 4, 1986

When Dannie came home after school, she found her mother lying on the couch, as usual. A soap opera blared from the TV. One glance and Dannie knew it was *General Hospital,* her mother's favorite daytime drama. Although she often complained that it wasn't the same since Luke and Laura had left the show.

Whatever. Dannie turned off the TV.

"Hey," her mother said.

"Get up," Dannie said. She was sick of it—disgusted by her mother's lack of, well, mothering. "Get a job!" she hollered.

Her mother stared at her, tried to pull herself up, but she was too fat to do it herself. Dannie dropped her books, sighing heavily, and reached underneath the rolls of her mother's arms, pulled her up.

"Did you have a bad day at school?" her mother asked.

"No," she said. It wasn't a bad day that had set her on edge. Lately, her friends had been shutting her out. Carlyn would steal glances at Trisha. Trisha would wink back, as though they were in on some private joke that no one else was meant to know about. But why couldn't Dannie be in on it too? Why were they excluding her? And where was Trisha today, anyway? Why had she skipped school? Dannie knew darn well Trisha had slept at Carlyn's last night. They hadn't included her in their little slumber party either.

Dannie grabbed a pound of ground beef from the refrigerator. She made Hamburger Helper for the third night in a row. She didn't have to look at the instructions on the package. She could cook it in her sleep. When it was done, she carried a big plate of it on a tray, set it across her mother's stomach.

"I'm going out," she said and left before her mother could ask her where she was going.

She marched across the street, hurried past Trisha's house on her way to Carlyn's. Dannie had stopped knocking on Trisha's door weeks ago, too scared Lester would answer. Instead, she knocked on Carlyn's front door before walking in. "Hello?" she called.

The inside of the house was quiet. Mrs. Walsh must either be sleeping or at work. Dannie tiptoed up the stairs, stopped outside Carlyn's bedroom. Her friends weren't there. Her shoulders slumped. Where had they gone? Why hadn't she been invited again?

On the floor next to Carlyn's bed, Dannie spied Trisha's softball bat: the one she'd stolen from gym class and kept in her bedroom for reasons she hadn't come out and said, but everyone knew why anyway.

But what was the bat doing here?

Dannie picked it up, noticed the engraving, ran her fingers over the *S. S.* and the heart. Trisha must've brought it with her when she'd slept over last night. It was the only thing that made sense. The truth of it stung. *Include me,* Dannie begged silently. It felt like an obvious betrayal of their promised friendship. And Dannie needed her friends. She hadn't been herself ever since Lester had touched her on the side of her house.

The longer she stood in Carlyn's bedroom holding the bat, the more her anger flared.

She stormed from Carlyn's room, the bat gripped in her hand by her side. She'd find them and show them the engraving with the heart, remind them that there were three of them in this club. They were supposed to all be in it together. Always. Underneath her anger that they'd had a sleepover without her ran a deeper resentment, one that had to do with her father leaving, the care she'd had to give her mother in his absence. And then what Lester had done to her, and having to live with the fear of bumping into him again. The strain was getting to her. She wanted to find her friends, be a kid with them, if only for a little while.

Where could they be?

There was only one place she could think of, and she made her way to the mountain trail. It was likely they'd be hanging out near the Kilroy tree. It was their favorite place, even in winter. They weren't expecting more snow until later that night.

She trudged up the trail, bat at her side. Every step brought a sharp pain in her knees, her chest. She was out of shape. *The fat friend*, the boys at school called her whenever they'd talk about the three of them. She looked at her feet, the couple of inches of snow on the ground, and pushed forward. She'd been pulled tight the last few weeks: a rubber band that had been stretched too far. She didn't look up until she reached the Kilroy tree.

She had a peculiar feeling: an instinct she wasn't alone. The chill at the back of her neck had nothing to do with the weather. She looked around, and that's when Lester stepped out from behind another tree not far from where she was standing. *Oh, God, no!* She didn't know what to do. She was too frightened to move. Blood dripped by his temple. He reached up and wiped it away, smearing it onto the back of his hand. "She'll pay for that," he said.

Dannie had no idea who he was talking about. He walked toward her. Something about him wasn't right. It was his eyes; one of his pupils was dilated more than the other.

"Stop," she said or thought she said. She heard the word inside her head but didn't know if it ever reached her lips.

He kept coming toward her.

She might've warned him not to touch her, not to hurt her. It was as though someone else were talking as she watched from the sidelines, unmoving, unblinking, a kind of out-of-body experience.

Her limbs hummed with fear. *Stay back! Don't come any closer!*

She didn't hear Scott come up behind her, didn't feel him take the bat from her hand. What was he doing here? He was supposed to be at indoor baseball practice. He must've been looking for Trisha too. Scott was saying something to Lester. He was angry, warning Lester not to step any closer.

"I'll do it," Scott said. "I swear I'll do it."

The swinging bat was a blur, something Dannie saw out of the corner of her eye. It happened so fast. She didn't recall Lester falling to the ground. And yet, the sound of his body hitting the frozen ground reverberated in her ears, in her head.

Scott stared at her. The bat fell from his hands.

And then he was gone, running down the trail.

Wait, she tried calling, but she couldn't speak. Her voice failed her, as it had so many times before. Now she was alone, listening to the sound of silence, the kind of quiet you heard when you were in the cold woods, the only one breathing.

༚

Forty-eight hours later, Dannie sat curled in a ball on the far end of the couch, her mother propped up at the other end. Mrs. Haines sat in the chair across from them, wiping her eyes and nose with a tissue. Mrs. Walsh paced the living room.

Outside, Second Street bustled with activity, kids playing, sledding. The neighbors were up early, clearing the sidewalks of the snow that had fallen overnight. Carlyn and Trisha were still sleeping in their bedrooms the last time Mrs. Walsh and Mrs. Haines had checked.

Dannie rocked quietly, made herself as small as possible. The tears kept coming, no matter how many times she'd tried to get them to stop. She shouldn't have gone back to the trail with Carlyn and Trisha. Although, to be fair, she'd stayed at the bottom of the mountain, too frightened to see what she and Scott had done.

Her friends had found Lester buried in the snow.

Dead.

Trisha had thought she'd killed him, and Dannie hadn't corrected her. Instead, Dannie had gone home and prayed and prayed and prayed. *Forgive me, Father; forgive me, Father; forgive me, Father, for I have sinned.* But no amount of praying could undo what had happened on the mountain. She had run down the trail after Scott, leaving Lester lying on the ground, and hadn't told anyone. Scott had protected her. She was scared. She didn't know how to carry such a burden, and praying to God wasn't helping. So early this morning, before the sun had come up, she'd confessed to her mother.

"No, no, no!" her mother had shouted. "No, Danielle, not you!" She'd held Dannie, her heavy arms draped around Dannie's shoulders. Dannie had cried into the creases of her mother's neck. When she'd cried herself out, her mother had said, "Wait here." She'd pulled herself up from the couch and left the house for the first time in three years. She'd lumbered to Mrs. Walsh's place, told her what Dannie and Scott had done. Then Dannie's mom and Mrs. Walsh had confronted Mrs. Haines.

Now they were sitting in Dannie's living room, waiting for Scott. Mrs. Walsh had asked Dannie to call him and have him meet them here.

Mrs. Haines wiped her eyes, looked at Dannie. "You're sure he was doing those things to my girl? You're sure he was . . . he was *touching* her?"

"Yes, ma'am."

"And now he's dead."

"Yes, ma'am. I was scared he was going to do to me what he'd done to Trisha. He tried once before, when he was supposed to fix the downspout."

"Oh, Danielle," her mother said. "Why didn't you tell me?"

Dannie looked down, ashamed even now. She'd always believed it had somehow been her fault for attracting his attention, for having large breasts.

There was a knock at the door; then Scott stepped inside. He stood in the doorway, shoved his hands in his pockets, his shoulders rounded.

"Good," Mrs. Walsh said to him. "You're here."

"Come," Dannie's mother said and reached her hand out to him. He took it, and she directed him to sit on the couch next to her. "Thank you for protecting my baby," she said. She looked at Mrs. Haines. "They're just kids. And that man, that husband of yours, he's, he's . . ." She tugged the collar of her robe. "They don't deserve to go to jail for protecting themselves against the likes of him."

Mrs. Walsh stopped pacing. "No one is going to jail. We're going to fix this."

"I saw a poster was knocked off her wall," Mrs. Haines said.

They all looked at her.

She continued. "There was a hole in the wall, pieces of plaster on the floor. I saw it in her bedroom yesterday after she'd gone. I didn't see her again to ask her about it before I left for work. But I knew. Deep down in that place you don't want to acknowledge, I knew, and I still didn't want to believe it," Mrs. Haines said. "He hurt my kid."

Mrs. Walsh stopped in front of Mrs. Haines, placed her hands on the woman's shoulders. "He can't hurt Trisha anymore," she said, kneeling on the floor in front of her. "I know this is going to sound crazy, but we can fix this. We *will* fix this."

Mrs. Haines nodded. "Okay," she said. "But how?"

"No one's going to find him on the mountain now. There's too much snow. There's too much snow for us to hike up it. We're going to have to wait for most of it to melt, but that buys us some time." She paused. "In the meantime, Sharon, you're going to let everybody think he skipped out on you. You'll be upset, of course, but you're going to pretend you expect him back. After all, he would be crazy to leave you, right? And then later, after we take care of him, that's when you're going to report him missing. You'll report him missing because you can't accept that he left you. The cops will ask around; they'll hear the story from the neighbors that Lester skipped out. Husbands take off all the time. They'll buy it. It will work. No one will find him. No one will know what really happened to him. No one but us."

Mrs. Walsh looked to Dannie. Dannie nodded. She'd never tell. All eyes turned to Scott.

"You . . . you need to know something," he said. "I-I knew when I swung the bat it would kill him. And, and I swung it anyway." His face looked stricken, as though he couldn't believe what he'd admitted about himself.

"No one here is judging you," Mrs. Walsh said. "You did what you had to do. You protected Dannie. Now, we're going to protect you."

He might've nodded; Dannie wasn't sure. He looked so small, like a little boy who had lost his way.

"No one will ever know but us, Scott," Mrs. Walsh said again. "No one *but us*."

"But, but what about Trisha?" he asked.

"And Carlyn?" Dannie added.

"No," Mrs. Walsh said. "We leave them out of it. It's for their own good. We do this, we become accessories to a crime. And what they don't know can't hurt them."

They were quiet. Dannie thought about what Mrs. Walsh had said. It would be hard keeping the truth from her friends, but in the end, Mrs. Walsh was right. By not telling them, they would be protecting them too.

"Okay," she said. Then Scott nodded, wiped his eyes.

Dannie's mother asked, "But why should we report him missing at all? Why can't Sharon just say he left, and leave the cops out of it?"

"If someone tries to find him and can't, and Sharon doesn't make some kind of public effort to get him back, they're going to get suspicious that maybe something did happen to him, and he didn't just leave town on his own."

"I don't know," Mrs. Haines said. "I don't know if I can do that."

"You have to," Mrs. Walsh said. "We all have to play our part if it's going to work. We have to stick together. These kids will never survive in the system." She whispered the last part. "And what will become of Evelyn? What will become of all of us? We have to take a stand. We can't let him win. And he wins if these kids get sent away. They all win. Every last one of them. Who do they think they are? They think they can leave us, beat us, touch our children, and get away with it? We do this, and he doesn't get away with it."

Mrs. Walsh was talking about more than Lester. She was talking about her own husband, who had run out on her when Carlyn was five years old. And then Dannie's father had done the same a few years later. They were single moms, trying to make the best of an awful situation.

"Linda's right, Sharon," Dannie's mother said. "He's dead. Why should we continue to pay for it?"

Mrs. Haines lit a cigarette. Finally, she nodded. "You're right. I know you're both right."

"And Scott," Mrs. Walsh said. "We do this, you have to promise never to be like them. You have to promise to grow up and be a good man. That's all we ask."

"I promise," he said, sniffed.

When they were all in agreement and their plan was in place, Dannie's mother asked, "What did you mean, 'After we take care of him'? How are we going to take care of him? There's no way I can walk up that mountain."

"You won't have to," Mrs. Walsh said. "You're going to be our lookout. Sharon and I will make the trek up."

"And then what?" Mrs. Haines asked.

"And then we bury him."

EPILOGUE

Dannie pulled into the parking lot of the county jail. It had been two weeks since Sharon had been arrested, arraigned, denied bail. Dannie parked in the first spot she could find and cut the engine. She reached up, touched the cross around her neck that lay in the soft spot between her clavicles. She took a minute to collect herself, to think about everything she needed to say.

There were good men in the world.

Her husband, Vinnie, was a good man. A good father. Dannie counted her blessings every day for him. If she'd done one thing right in her lifetime, it had been marrying him. They'd met soon after she'd graduated high school, at the deli where she'd worked full time. Outside of work, her free time had been taken up caring for her mother, volunteering at church, and Vinnie had soon joined her in both. She'd been so lonely without her friends, and he'd helped her forget her troubles at home. They'd married after one year of dating, and she hadn't looked back.

And then there were bad men.

She'd known two bad men: her father, a man who had left his wife and child for no other reason than he'd been selfish. And there was Lester. He was the worst kind of man, in Dannie's mind, a man who had done terrible, unthinkable things. The way Lester had stared at her that day on the trail, looking at her in a way no man should ever look at a child. It could've easily been Dannie who had swung the bat. She had no doubt she would've struck him if Scott hadn't been there. But Scott had been there, and she'd promised to keep his secret and in turn had become an accessory to murder.

Dannie unhooked her necklace. She slipped her wedding ring off. She put both pieces of jewelry in her purse, along with her cell phone, and locked the car with everything inside but her ID. Vehicles were subject to searches in the facility parking lot. Personal property wasn't allowed inside the prison. She lifted her shoulders, her chin, and walked up the steps to the main entrance. Beyond the brick walls was a high fence with barbed wire. To say she was intimidated was an understatement, but she had resolved to do this. She kept moving. She went through a metal detector, filled out the appropriate paperwork before she was escorted to the visiting room.

Sharon was waiting, sitting on the other side of a glass partition. Her spiky gray hair was no longer spiky without the hair products she'd used at home. Her eyes were hollowed, ringed with dark circles.

Dannie sat across from her, picked up the phone, tried to keep her hands from shaking.

"How's Trisha?" Sharon asked, glancing at the guard. "I heard the DA decided not to press charges."

"She's recovering," Dannie said. "She bought a new couch for your place. She's fixing it up real nice for you."

"You tell her she doesn't have to do that. That fancy lawyer she got me is enough. More than enough."

"She wants to do it," Dannie said.

"Well," Sharon said, smiled.

"How are you?" Dannie asked, although the question seemed stupid under the circumstances.

"I'm fine," Sharon said, paused. "What are you doing here, Dannie?"

"Linda, Scott, and I—we talked." When Dannie had learned Sharon had confessed, she'd had to do something. She couldn't keep pretending, lying. Linda and Scott had met Dannie in her mother's house, like they'd done all those years ago, except they'd stood in the empty living room now that all the furniture had been removed. Scott had told them he'd had every intention of telling the detectives what he'd done when they'd questioned him. He'd said he'd gotten as close to the truth as he could, but then he'd gotten scared. He was sorry it had gotten this far. He'd faced his own demons through the years, but he'd tried to be a good man. Dannie and Linda had said they understood.

"Some criminals we make," Linda had said. "Never even thought about where that bat might've been." Dannie had considered whether they'd be in this position had they gotten rid of the bat all those years ago. But they hadn't.

In the end, they'd agreed that Dannie would visit Sharon in prison, and whatever happened next would be up to Sharon. She was the one in jail, taking the blame. They'd stand or fall by her decision.

Sharon leaned forward, whispered, "You shouldn't be here."

"Why did you do it? Why did you confess?" Dannie asked in a quiet voice.

"Because I had to," Sharon said. "It was the only thing that made any sense. Everyone knows he was beating on me. And when I tell them what he was doing to my kid . . ." She sat back, took a breath, then leaned forward again. "They'll go easy on me. I'm an old lady. They'll see me as a woman who did what she had to do to protect herself and her kid. There isn't a mother alive who wouldn't understand that."

"We can't let you sit in here for something we did." Dannie wiped her eyes. "It's not right."

"Shut it," Sharon said, glancing at the guard again. "Of course it's right."

"No, it's not. I can't." She sobbed.

"You can and you will," Sharon said and paused, waiting for Dannie to look at her. "You listen to me, and you listen good. I brought that man into our lives. And to think what he was doing to my own kid? It was my job to protect her. *My job.* And I didn't do it. I didn't. This is my penance, my price to pay. Let me pay it."

Dannie shook her head.

"You want to do something for me?" Sharon asked.

"Anything," Dannie said.

"Get out of here. Go home and take care of those two beautiful daughters of yours. Go home and do your job of being their mother. Tell Scott the same thing. Tell him to be a good father to those kids of his. And tell him to continue to be a good cop and to protect women like me. What we did, what happened, wasn't for nothing. Do you hear me? It wasn't for nothing."

Dannie nodded. "If you're sure," she said. "If you're sure that's what you want."

"That's what I want. You go on home now, tell your girls hi for me. Linda and Carlyn too. And give Trisha a hug. Tell her I'll see her soon."

"Okay," Dannie said. "I will."

Sharon hung up the phone, turned toward the guard.

Dannie hung up too. She stood on unsteady legs and walked away, down a long hallway, through security, the door locking behind her. She stepped outside and took a deep breath of cold air.

Sharon was right. She couldn't let a man like Lester keep her away from her daughters. She had to think of them. She had to be the best mother she could possibly be. She had to be the kind of friend she'd always meant to be.

Dannie would do what Sharon had asked of her.

They all would. They'd bury their secret and go on with their lives.

Dannie stopped by her car, looked across the street. Scott leaned against his car, hands in his pockets, feet crossed at the ankles. If Sharon had wanted him to confess, Dannie was supposed to cross the street, and together she and Scott would go to the police station.

Dannie opened the driver's side door, got in her car. She slipped on her wedding ring and the necklace. She touched the gold cross, prayed. Her guilt was the reason she'd had what her girls had called the "Jesus room" in her mother's house, a place where she could lay bare her sins, search for forgiveness. She'd have to find another place, a closet perhaps, where she could set up another altar, where she could ask for His forgiveness. Maybe her mother would put in a good word for her.

She wiped her eyes dry, started the engine, turned the wheel, and headed for home. There would come a day when they would be punished for what they'd done. There would come a day when they would be judged.

But that day wasn't today.

ACKNOWLEDGMENTS

I dedicate this novel to my mother, Johanna Houck, for not only teaching me the importance of having girlfriends but also the significance of maintaining those lifelong relationships. Which brings me to the novel's other dedication, my childhood friends—Tracey Evans Golden and Mindy Strouse Bailey. There's a special place in my heart for these two, because really, does anybody know you better than your childhood friends? This by no means takes away my love and dedication to all my girlfriends who have stood by me through the decades for better or worse, and I refer to them lovingly as the usual suspects—Tina Mantel, Jenene McGonigal, Kate Weeks, Karin Wagner. And Mom, I speak for all my friends when I say thanks for bailing us out. :)

When my kids were much younger, we met a family on the beach in Avalon, New Jersey. At the time I hadn't secured an agent or a publisher, but I'd told the mom of this family that I loved her first name so much that one day I would put it in a book. I'm excited to share that the day has come. Thank you, Carlyn "From the Beach" McCarthy, for sharing your name. I hope the fictional Carlyn lives up to it.

A special thanks to my agent, Carly Watters, who continues to be a constant in this ever-changing business. And a big thank-you to Megha Parekh, Sarah Shaw, Dennelle Catlett, Grace Doyle, Hai-Yen Mura, and the entire Thomas & Mercer team for allowing me to continue to do what I love. Thank you to Charlotte Herscher for understanding exactly what the story needed and for helping me make it shine.

To all the readers, bloggers, reviewers, booksellers, and librarians, thank you for your love and support. Please know that I do this for you. Although I'm shy and don't always shout my gratitude, it doesn't mean it's felt any less.

And to my local readers in Northampton County, and especially the Slate Belt, thank you for your constant support. For creative purposes, a few changes have been made regarding the geography and history of the location.

And now for the technical stuff. I spent many hours researching the field of forensic anthropology, but most of what I learned didn't make the book for one reason or another. Some examples of online articles and information I obtained about identifying trauma in a skeleton came from the Smithsonian Institution. Also, Dove Medical Press provided information in the *Research and Reports in Forensic Medical Science* journal on the investigation of cranial injuries as well as reports on the forensic investigation of skeletons. I had so much fun on an interactive website where I virtually processed a crime scene in which a skeleton had been found in the woods. If you want to give it a try and learn about some of the challenges a forensics investigator faces during a case, check out this website from the Simon Fraser University Museum of Archeology and Ethnology: www.sfu.museum/forensics/eng/.

Although I rely on the internet for a lot of my research, nothing takes the place of talking to the experts in their fields. A huge thank-you goes to Capt. Joseph Sokolofski of the Pennsylvania State Police, as well as to Sgt. Glenn Langston of the New Jersey State Police (retired), for answering all my questions. I would also like to thank Lt. Kreg Rodrigues of the Pennsylvania State Police for taking time out of his busy day to give me a tour of headquarters and for continuing to answer all my never-ending questions. Any and all errors regarding police practices and procedures are mine and mine alone.

Thank you to former prison guard Rob Brands for answering my questions about prisons and visitation. Again, any errors are my own.

Thank you to Jim Lasko for the in-depth tour of Bethlehem's casino and for explaining the etiquette of gambling. I had no idea there were so many rules and signals when sitting at the tables.

And last but never least, to Philip and our two daughters: none of this would mean anything if I didn't have you to share it with . . . always.

ABOUT THE AUTHOR

Photo © 2012 Sally Ullman Photography

Karen Katchur is an award-winning suspense novelist with a bachelor of science in criminal justice and a master's degree in education. She lives in eastern Pennsylvania with her husband and two children. You can learn more at www.karenkatchur.com.